H.G. Wells at the End of
His Tether

H.G. Wells at the End of His Tether

◆

His Social and Political Adventures

Gordon D. Feir

iUniverse, Inc.

New York Lincoln Shanghai

H.G. Wells at the End of His Tether
His Social and Political Adventures

iUniverse books may be ordered through booksellers or by contacting:

iUniverse
2021 Pine Lake Road, Suite 100
Lincoln, NE 68512
www.iuniverse.com
1-800-Authors (1-800-288-4677)

ISBN-13: 978-0-595-35019-3 (pbk)
ISBN-13: 978-0-595-67187-8 (cloth)
ISBN-13: 978-0-595-79724-0 (ebk)
ISBN-10: 0-595-35019-4 (pbk)
ISBN-10: 0-595-67187-X (cloth)
ISBN-10: 0-595-79724-5 (ebk)

Printed in the United States of America

Contents

Part VIII   *Closing The Book*

Acknowledgements

The preparation of any critical or biographical work based on an historical figure is primarily a task of reading and compilation. It's regretfully no longer possible to engage H.G. Wells in conversation, nor is it possible, with a few notable exceptions, to discuss his writing and character with anyone who knew him personally. Any student of history seeking to understand the man and the motives behind the great quantities of work he published must therefore rely on his books, pamphlets, newspaper columns, magazine articles and other bits and pieces of published material. The next most valuable resource is the biographical material published over the last seventy-five years. Wells has not prompted the mass of critical literature generated by other famous writers, but there is still a substantial list of research material available to anyone interested in his writing. Gaining access to a comprehensive library of historical publications, especially in the case of voluminous writers like H.G. Wells, requires the contribution and gracious assistance of many people and institutions. It's with the greatest of appreciation that the author wishes to acknowledge the contribution of others to the material behind this work. Indeed, without the support of a large number of people it would never be possible for the legacy of H.G. Wells to enrich the lives of a new generation of readers.

This author and his family were privileged to live in the village of Bromley in Kent during the 1970's. It was in Bromley that H.G. Wells was born one hundred years earlier, and it was here that the author's interest in Wells changed from a boyhood enthusiasm about *The War of the Worlds* to a lifetime of collecting and reading his work. The Bromley Public Library maintains an exceptional collection of H.G. Wells' books and materials. This status is due largely to the efforts of the late A.H. Watkins, former Borough Librarian. Our thanks go to him for his encouragement in joining the H.G. Wells Society and in providing guidance to some of Wells' more obscure publications.

In an effort to find long-out-of-print books by H.G. Wells the author made the acquaintance of Anthony Rota, one of London's premier booksellers. Anthony Rota is a gentleman of the old school and is forever willing to provide volumes of information and advice to accompany the printed tomes on his ample shelves. It was Anthony Rota's firm who were responsible for placement of the

Wells literary assets with the University of Chicago at Champaign-Urbana. Gene Rinkel and his staff at the Rare Book Library of the Champaign-Urbana Library deserve special thanks for providing the author with access to their library and its Wells material, particularly since this author has more credentials in plate tectonics than English literature. No less acknowledgement and credit should be given to the staff of the Cambridge University Library in England for guidance through one of the world's most amazing working libraries while the author was on a study program through the Extension Department. It requires an emotional adjustment to find that the rarest of H.G. Wells' first editions are simply shelved as modern literature with their original hand written nineteenth century library card.

The H.G. Wells Society is a small group of well lettered and generous souls who have provided encouragement on all facets of Wells investigation. John Hammond, the society's primary instigator, Christopher Rolfe, Patrick Parrinder, and John Green gave their time, advice and friendship during the author's visits to London for annual meetings and symposiums. Successful writers and prominent Society members Arthur C. Clarke, Doris Lessing, and Brian Aldiss have been generous in their encouragement and in returning correspondence. It is impossible to forget Michael Foot, the one-time leader of the UK Labour Party who could claim to know Wells personally. It was an inspiration to listen to his endless supply of historical anecdotes at the 1998 *War of the Worlds Centenary Symposium.* Thanks are also due to Eric Korn, a London bookman and reviewer of special character, with an extensive private collection of Wells material, for sharing his knowledge of books and publication history. And certainly this work would not be complete without the perennial support of the author's wife of forty plus years as she helped find, pack and move large quantities of dusty books, and waited patiently while the author disappeared into the back room of another bookshop to check out 'just one more shelf'.

The cartoon sketches or caricatures of Wells preceding each Part of this work, and the sketch on the dust wrapper, are all by the author and are intended to be abstractions of the doodles or 'picshuas' commonly drawn by Wells in his notes and correspondence.

The author has attempted to be accurate in recording historical material and quotations from Wells' books and other biographical references. Any errors or omissions that have crept into the book are entirely the responsibility of the author. Quotations and extracts have been carefully limited to meet the standards set for biographical and critical material by the administrators of the Wells literary estate. No acknowledgement would be complete without a word of thanks to

Herbert George Wells himself for producing such an extensive list of publications and for his involvement in an unending list of controversies, arguments and political issues.

Introduction

In the latter half of the nineteenth century Great Britain produced many of history's greatest writers and some of the world's finest and most enduring literary work. By most criteria this was the Golden Age of English Literature. The population had become highly literate, newspapers were the principal means of communication and books and magazines had become widely available to the general public. The publishing industry had grown rapidly into a flourishing, competitive business and publishers were anxious to find and promote new writers. In England every railway station had one or more news stands and railway reading was an industry in itself. Magazines and serial publications were designed for quick and easy reading by commuters. Newspapers carried book reviews, literary advertising, and articles by well known authors. Postal delivery of books and magazines became reliable and commonplace. The local bookseller was as important a constituent of the English community as the grocer or the ironmonger.

This was the era that produced a rich literary treasure made up of the work of George Bernard Shaw, Virginia Woolf, Rudyard Kipling, Arnold Bennett, Joseph Conrad, Oscar Wilde, Conan Doyle and dozens of others who might easily be part of any contemporary list of great writers. This was the dynamic literary environment into which Herbert George Wells was born. He perfected his craft with the advice and criticism of the best writers and editors. By the turn of the century he had published several well received novels and had established himself as one of the premier writers of what were aptly called *fantastic romances*. He also became a master of the short story. His ideas were refreshing, his technique was arresting and his personality was engaging. H.G. Wells became one of England's most sought after writers, speakers, newspaper correspondents and social critics. His career covered a wide spectrum of writings including text books, world history, novels, social tracts, prophesies, essays and short stories. He published well over one hundred books in many forms, some of which are still in print and routinely read by fans and students alike.

H.G. Wells worked hard to build his reputation as a writer and he was often showered with praise for his literary accomplishments. Much of this praise was richly deserved, but occasionally it was neither deserved nor earned. He grew up in a poor family and endured a number of false starts before he gained his stride.

His early struggles endeared him to a broad middle class readership and he often took up the cause of the downtrodden. Once he was well established financially, he participated in a number of social and political movements that were critical of Great Britain's progress in the twentieth century. He saw the beginning and end of two World Wars and became convinced that the entire world's social and political climate would have to undergo major changes if it was to survive to the end of the century. His political activism gained both friends and enemies and ensured his position on the front page of newspapers throughout Europe and North America.

Wells' notoriety continued for many years after his death and his work became subject matter for students of literature and social sciences alike. However, as his image disappeared from the front page of the newspapers, it also began to disappear from the minds of the emerging middle classes that he tried so hard to represent. To some extent Wells was an enigma. His ideas and writings continued to be of great interest to academics but his popularity among the masses as a writer was limited to his earlier works of fiction. Several of his novels were turned into films both during and after his lifetime. This endeared him to his already devoted readers but didn't help to expand the interest in his work beyond the early science fiction at which he excelled.

Today only a limited percentage of the reading public will recognize the name of H.G. Wells. In North America he has almost completely disappeared from the school curriculum. In contemporary bookstores Wells must compete with Judith Krantz and Stephen King in a publishing market that is consistently losing ground to movies and video games. Those who are familiar with his name usually credit him with *The Time Machine, The War of the Worlds, The Island of Dr. Moreau* and perhaps *The Invisible Man.* This is distressing to academics who believe that his best work has been overlooked and that he deserves a position among the great writers of the twentieth century. His advocates write endless numbers of academic papers and theses that attempt to establish Wells in what they believe is his rightful place in the annals of literature. In fact Wells has probably already reached his rightful place in history. He wrote a few brilliant and engrossing novels at the end of the nineteenth century. After the turn of the century he gained notoriety, not as a novelist, but as a controversial, self centered and arrogant journalist who contributed primarily to newspapers and periodicals. He wrote many novels in the latter part of his career, most of which have disappeared into the dustbin of history. Critics who suggest that he may not deserve a position among history's great writers are often frowned upon by devotees, especially when it's implied that the direction he took in his writing and politics made little practical sense. Further, his ideas and solutions to world problems may have been read by thousands, but they only appealed to a small group of dedicated socialists and were quickly forgotten when they were no longer front page issues.

Many facts suggest that placing Wells among the great writers of English literature is a lot more difficult than his proponents believe. This work will examine his writing after the end of the nineteenth century and illustrate that, with a few exceptions, the literary value of his writing declined steadily and his political values moved to the extreme. There is no single point at which he seems to have lost his talent as a writer, he appears to have simply put it aside because it was no longer needed to get his writing on the front page of the world's English language newspapers. Not only was talent of lesser importance in his later work but his ideas began to alienate loyal readers as his writing and politics moved further to the left wing extremes.

Thus, his lack of acknowledgement as a great writer by students and readers of the twenty-first century is not unexpected or unjustified. Perhaps Wells was not such a great writer, or perhaps his best writing doesn't really fit into an appropriate literary classification. Perhaps Wells' ideas are no longer interesting, or he may have generated more animosity than favor in his later years. When looking at the work of someone with a personality as diverse and complex as H.G. Wells it quickly becomes clear that there will never be a single easy answer to any of these questions. One thing that is clear is that he produced massive amounts of material in the form of books, periodicals, newspaper articles and speeches. It would be too much to expect any writer to maintain consistently high literary standards with this voluminous output. However, Wells literary standards were often consistently low, prompting some biographers to politely suggest that he produced 'large volumes of mundane, repetitive and poorly conceived material'.

The best way to find clues to his lack of popularity among contemporary readers is to look at a broad cross section of his writing after the nineteenth century. Unlike writers who stayed with a certain style and philosophy, Wells jumped all over the map. This work will look at examples from novels, pamphlets and newspaper articles to illustrate that much of his work was indeed poorly planned and impulsive. He was often the first to say that most of his efforts were exactly that, *efforts* or *essays*, rather than accomplishments. But his often pompous and arrogant nature suggests that after saying as much, he would return to his writing desk fully convinced of his own superiority as a writer and social scientist.

The durability of Wells' writing a century after publication has perhaps been severely hampered by the nature of his subject material. With the exception of some of his early novels and educational books most of Wells' writing was perishable from the day it was written. His newspaper articles were highly topical and not much of a contribution to literature. Most of his books after the turn of the century were intended to help promote his socialist designs for the world and many of them were repetitions of previous books with little in the way of new ideas or proposed solutions to current problems. He may have considered one or two of his books to be well developed manifestos that should become required reading for the body politic in centuries to come. But they are not required reading today, and almost certainly never will be required on anything but a graduate curriculum in history or English literature. Reading his work from a contemporary perspective makes it clear why this is the case. In the twenty-first century the reading public is unlikely to buy tracts of socialist philosophy, analyses of the progress of the Second World War, or even reprints of his so-called *discussion novels*. Their contents have little to do with today's social or political issues and his solutions to the world's most pressing problems are not only obsolete, they were not even an effective answer to the world ills when they were written. Wells had no way of knowing how perishable and short sighted some of his socialist concepts were. In today's terms he became a left wing extremist. He believed passionately in what he was doing, and like today's activists he could never be convinced that there might be another way of achieving his goals, or there might be a better solution to the problems he was trying to solve.

It's not surprising, therefore, that the great bulk of Wells' work is unknown in the twenty-first century. His commonly remembered writing includes a few of his earlier novels, and they are often grouped with contemporary science fiction. The science fiction label is probably to Wells' detriment because these early novels were correctly introduced in the nineteenth century as *fantastic romances*. They cannot, and should not be forced to compete with contemporary science fiction. The *fantastic romances* of H.G. Wells are unique in character and, perhaps with the exception of a few novels by writers like Jules Verne, or the little known science fiction of Arthur Conan Doyle, they will never be equaled. In the twenty-first century unique literary events are less and less likely to stir the minds of new readers, and indeed, new readers are less and less likely to be interested in one hundred year old adventure novels. Were it not for the interest of motion picture producers, even *The Time Machine* would likely have gone the way of the Time Traveler himself.

Wells did a fine job of alienating friends and enemies alike during his lifetime. He had numerous public spats with his publishers, other writers, politicians, and especially with businessmen and industrialists. He spent much of his life trying to promote a utopian view of the world that was as unrealistic as his novels. Wells was often as out-of-step with the world around him as his novels were. A comparison can be made between the world of Wells' utopian *Men Like Gods* and George Orwell's *1984*. They are two different views of life under a socialist oligarchy. It does not take much comparison to see that the latter is substantially closer to the reality of today. The social system in which we now live often treats uninteresting or unrealistic issues of the past as irrelevant. Many of Wells' ideas unfortunately fit into this category. As a writer and thinker Wells has thus become an artifact of history rather than a pillar of literary talent and an engaging story teller. There is no question that his work could easily exist in a world of electronic communication if the public demand would support him. The adventures and descriptive stories of Kipling and Dickens are alive and well today thanks to television, film makers and electronic publishing tools. Certainly the incredible artistry of Tolkien would be less familiar without the benefit of the contemporary film industry. Wells indeed came close, but he was off the mark and his name and reputation are fading from the minds and bookshelves of today's readers.

Wells' notorious sexual adventures and his less than admirable treatment of women were known to many of his friends but did not become common knowledge until exposed by later biographical material. Occasionally his affairs with women will appear as characterizations in his novels and in some cases long standing affairs had a measurable affect on his writing and thinking. When social indiscretions became an important factor in his writing it's important to point out the source or nature of the influence, but the specifics of his affairs are left to other publications. His extramarital dalliances are now well known to academics and are good examples of Wells' self-centered arrogance and his often two-faced approach to women's issues. He was a vocal supporter of women's rights and suffrage but he had little hesitation in tossing his intimate lady friends aside after ruining both their lives and circumstances. He produced at least two children out of wedlock and had scattered affairs that would occasionally cause him grief many years after the fact. The significance of his affairs should not be downplayed. He first began to stray at a time when Victorian mores frowned upon such activity, but this mattered little to Wells. Perhaps his attitude towards women reflected an immaturity that he never overcame. With the exception of his patient and enduring wife Jane, women were never more than second class citizens and he simply provided them with all the respect he thought they deserved.

Wells' thinking and his writing changed dramatically over his eighty year lifetime. In his autobiography he admits to a number of different phases in his life marked by sudden changes in circumstance. These changes were not always for the better. He was beset with health problems, divorce, loss of friends and colleagues, financial setbacks, political defeats and personal disappointments. Some of these events are clearly reflected in his writing, some were covertly swept under the carpet, and others were simply forgotten. A closer look at personal issues and how they affected his writing will justify dividing his life into broad career segments. Whether the writing in one segment of his career was better than, or different from, that in another segment will depend upon the reader but there is little doubt that the short period near the end of the nineteenth century produced some of his most colorful work. After that time he moved in different directions and the character of his work changed as he changed his beliefs and his domestic situation. A glance at some of his more controversial work will make it obvious that his lack of stature in English literature is as much the result of the personal and political positions he took as it is the result of deterioration in his writing. It's not difficult to find good examples to illustrate these changes,

For purposes of reviewing his work, Wells' career can be divided into four general periods. These are periods that Wells himself acknowledges in his autobiography. This work will provide many examples of changes in his writing and thinking as he matured and moved from one career segment to another. Early chapters of this work are devoted to his childhood, his education and to his writing in the nineteenth century. After the turn of the century Wells became involved in many personal, social and political campaigns that often overshadowed his writing. Later chapters look at novels and newspaper publications that illustrate the overpowering importance of political issues in Wells' work and include examples of his writing that are largely unknown to contemporary readers

Getting Started (1866 to 1894). This was the period in which Wells was born, and struggled to get out of his lower class Bromley environment. He spent these early years in grade school, a bungled apprenticeship, and several attempts at higher education. He eventually achieved a small scholarship and moved to London to study biology. Part time work teaching and writing occasional newspaper reviews and articles provided much needed income. He married his cousin Isabel. Their early life was a struggle and they were on the verge of insolvency most of the time.

His Finest Hour (1894 to 1901). After a period of struggle Wells produced several very successful short stories and novels beginning with *The Time Machine*. These generated enough money to change his social and domestic situation completely. His new found notoriety provided the recognition he needed to attract the praise of critics and the attention of publishers. In quick succession *The Island of Dr. Moreau, The Invisible Man*, and *The War of the Worlds* were produced. He married his second wife and they moved into a newly built home in Sandgate on the south coast of England.

Teaching The World (1901 to 1928). Wells work quickly moved in a new direction after the turn of the century and he began a number of campaigns to promote socialism and his concept of world government. He gained a large international following and simultaneously alienated both friends and colleagues. Like most Europeans he saw another war on the horizon and preached incessantly about the evils of nationalism, capitalism and the monarchy. He traveled throughout Europe and the USA giving lectures and mixing in elite social circles. His wife Jane died in 1928.

The Declining Years (1928 to 1946). Wells writing began to change direction again. His readership had declined and he had disagreements with many of his publishers. Personal frustration increased with his inability to change the world as it plunged into the Second World War. His publications became a rehash of earlier work. Personal wealth puts him in a position where he could devote his time and energy to any cause he wished, but his causes became less original and more impractical. Wells died on August 13th, 1946 at his London home in Hanover Terrace.

Why did Wells fade from popularity to semi-obscurity within a generation after his death? It's always easy to look at literary work in retrospect and make profound judgements about the reasons for an author's success or demise. But in fairness to Wells, even though he was considered a twentieth century prophet, and he firmly believed himself to be a successful prophet, it's necessary to look at his work from the time in which he lived and worked, not from the future he tried to predict. Wells based his novels and his political ideas on what he saw around him. His socialist philosophy was developed because of his upbringing and circumstances. His prophesies were based on things he saw happening during his lifetime. Thus, Part I of this work will outline some of the history of the period in which he did his writing. Part II addresses the development of his own brand of socialism and political activism. Parts III through VII examine some examples of his more radical and often poorly conceived writing. Finally, Part

VIII assesses the contemporary acceptance of a popular and high profile writer from the first half of the twentieth century.

It's an understatement to say that Wells possessed a complex personality. This is part of what makes him an interesting subject. And it's an injustice to suggest that he was not an influential writer of the twentieth century. He was probably more widely read in the 1930's than most other writers in the English language. It's also premature to say that he has already declined and fallen, but in spite of the devotion of his contemporary supporters, H.G. Wells is slowly fading into the mists of the nineteenth century. It's been well over one hundred years since *The Time Machine* was published. It is still a magnificent story and a landmark in the annals of fiction, but it is not a literary masterpiece. Neither are there any other literary monuments in Wells' prolific collection of publications. But without the few adventure novels he wrote at the end of the nineteenth century his name would seldom be seen or heard in the libraries of today, let alone those of the future. Indeed, Wells may have been at the end of his literary tether after his first five years of work.

PART I
Building the Fire

1

One Hundred Years of Growth and Turmoil

The one hundred year period between 1850 and 1950 was probably the most exciting and dynamic one hundred years in the history of the British Empire, if not in the world. Queen Victoria had ascended to the throne in 1837 and held the crown until 1901. In 1901 the throne was assumed by Edward the Seventh and he ruled until 1910. His son George the Fifth was crowned in 1910 after his father's death and reigned for twenty-five years. In 1935 Edward the Eighth was crowned and abdicated his throne the following year. In 1936 the reluctant George the Sixth was crowned. He reigned throughout the Second World War until 1953. The monarchy in the first half of the twentieth century was one of change and turmoil after the long and stable reign of Victoria and it was to be followed by the long and stable reign of Elizabeth II.

The British monarchy in the nineteenth and twentieth centuries had become a much different institution from that portrayed in its ancient and somewhat checkered history. Great Britain was now a constitutional monarchy and both the Royal Family and the parliamentarians took their job much more seriously than the oligarchs of the past. But the class system was still well entrenched and many resented the throne with a passion. Members of the Royal Family were prominent figures and easy objects to hate because of their high visibility. Justified or not, they were often blamed for most of the country's ills and misfortunes and got little credit for its successes. The resentment of the monarchy became much more subdued through the two wars. King George the Fifth and King George the Sixth were intensely nationalistic and devoted to their duty as monarchs. This went a long way in providing a beleaguered population with something to hold tightly in trying times. For those born in the reign of Victoria however, the inbred hatred of a monarchy, constitutional or otherwise, was a difficult burden to remove.

Universal suffrage became well established after the turn of the century and citizens gained a feeling of participation in their destiny. The concepts of equality and opportunity were beginning to form in the minds of the general population, including the women, who had been largely ignored by government and industry. There was virtually no middle class in Great Britain prior to the turn of the twentieth century. The demarcation between *upstairs* and *downstairs* was well defined and almost impossible to cross. If you were born into service, you spent your life in service. But a rapidly expanding economy, global industrialization, and international commerce began to make a difference. Its benefits included new vocations, construction jobs, and opportunities for gaining education. Entrepreneurs, shopkeepers, tradesmen, engineers and scholars who had found it difficult to climb out of poverty were now finding a way to join the growing middle classes. Vast fields of opportunity that were previously reserved only for the wealthy and titled were now at least within sight, if not within immediate reach, of thousands who desperately wanted to change their lot in life.

Shifting attitudes and growing public agitation prompted the British Parliament to pass the Education Act of 1870. This was both a parliamentary and a social landmark. It created a system of elected school boards for local administration of schools. It established a tax to pay for the system and it prescribed a uniform course of secular study for elementary education. Women were allowed to vote for school board members and could stand for election well before the issue of national suffrage had been resolved. The Act immediately provided a means for building schools in geographical areas where none existed and it opened the doors to an entire segment of the population who were illiterate. Without a fundamental education that included basic training in language and arithmetic, no youngster was able to consider any form of secondary education. Most trades and apprenticeships required basic skills that previously could only be learned in private schools, most of which were unavailable to a population that couldn't pay the tuition fees.

Within a generation the shape of the nation changed. Schools were full, secondary education was in high demand and correspondence courses were developed to reach those who could not afford boarding houses at trade schools and colleges in the cities. Most important was the effect on public literacy. Now an entire nation could read and other countries throughout Europe were adopting similar legislation. Communication at public levels created a boom in newspapers, books and magazine publications. The shift from an illiterate public to one that could read and write, send messages, total their accounts and read billboards helped promote massive advances in business and industry. All of these advantages were culminating at the end of the century. The social and political signifi-cance of this change from the nineteenth to the twentieth century far exceeds the impact of the more recent shift from the twentieth to the twenty-first century and into the second millenium.

During the last half of the nineteenth century nearly two-thirds of the world map was covered by the pink shading of the British Empire. This dynamic era saw major expansion in the industrial power of Great Britain and most of its col-onies and protectorates. Rail systems grew throughout the world and exception-ally long rail lines were created in Canada and India. The distribution of manufactured goods and foodstuffs became big business and promoted the growth of nations in geographical areas that were previously inaccessible. The British Empire had by far the biggest and most advanced steel industry in the world and produced materials for the manufacture of railroads, bridges and buildings. Steel became the global measure of industrialization, and Great Britain had the steel industry and the engineering prowess to use it. Ship building had advanced to a fine art. The Royal Navy became the largest and most efficient naval system ever created. Britannia ruled the world's seas and they embraced the use of steel in producing huge warships and passenger vessels. These industrial advances also brought natural disasters of unprecedented size like the Titanic in 1912 and the Lusitania in 1915.

The use of steel in construction produced marvels like the Firth of Forth can-tilevered rail bridge. This bridge was completed in 1890 across the Firth of Forth near Edinburgh. It's over 8200 feet long, strong, stable and still in use by British Rail after more than a century. Its place in the history books is well established by the fact that it long preceded the few other bridges that come close to its size and length. Other marvels of steel construction like the Eiffel Tower in Paris, built in 1889, and the Brooklyn Bridge in New York, built in 1883, demonstrated the impact of the steel industry and the engineering design advances that made them possible. A celebration of industrial might and engineering success in the form of a huge trade show and exposition was planned for London in 1851. The Crystal Palace was designed and built expressly for this exposition. It was a house of glass held in place by a steel framework covering over fifteen acres and it represented a startling innovation in architecture. The trade show was a resounding success and became a model for future expositions the world over.

By 1860 London had a population of approximately three million in a nation of about twenty million souls. The national rail system had expanded to over 6000 miles of busy track and the penny post made communication fast and simple for anyone who could write. Britain had become a power house of growth and commerce. Energy to drive this growth in Great Britain was provided by huge coal mines. Coal was used to power furnaces for steel production. Coal boilers generated steam for rail engines and power plants. Before the turn of the century coal gas was being extracted from coal beds and delivered by pipeline to major cities to produce heat and light. After the Luddites had been driven out of the system, textile mills abounded and sophisticated machinery was being invented to produce better products in less time and at substantially lower cost than ever before. Agricultural research was being sponsored by the government and it paid dividends in the production of fine dairy products and more meat and grain than the country could consume. The export industry thus had the resources to flourish and generate jobs, profits and more innovation.

The one hundred years between 1850 and 1950 were truly an era of invention. Photography had been developed in France by Daguerre in the 1830's and for the first time accurate records of the world and current events could become a part of history. Europe had discovered the promise of massive hydrogen dirigibles that changed the world of luxury travel and shipping long before commercial jet aircraft were even a dream. Disasters like the Hindenburg put a cap the rapid advancement of these engineering marvels and directed research toward better forms of air travel. By the time the First World War was upon Europe the automobile and the aeroplane were a part of life and were becoming useful tools in both commerce and warfare. Massive global construction projects like the Suez Canal in 1869 and the Panama Canal in 1914 were undertaken and successfully completed. These accomplishments were a substantial improvement in commercial shipping and affected the balance of naval power around the world.

The Industrial Revolution spawned a global explosion of scientific research and discovery. The work of Alfred Nobel in Sweden produced a new substance called dynamite. His personal fortune and legacy resulted in the Nobel Prize, first offered in 1901 shortly after his death. Thereafter the prizes in physics, chemistry and medicine were awarded to brilliant scientific minds, many of whom are still easily recognized today. The likes of Roentgen, Curie, Michelson, Marconi, and Rutherford were all awarded prizes before the First World War. Shortly thereafter the Swiss patent clerk Albert Einstein was awarded a Nobel prize for his work in mathematics and the Montreal physician Frederick Banting became a Nobel laureate for his discovery of insulin in 1923. In the field of literature Rudyard Kipling, W.B. Yeats and Bernard Shaw were awarded prizes for their writing in the English language. Charles Darwin published his monumental work in 1859 and Thomas Huxley was lecturing in biology and paleontology at Imperial College in London. Science was gaining a new respect that had previou restricted to the narrow halls of academia.

By 1850 most of the world's oceans had been covered by explorers. The British Admiralty had a cartographic division that produced high quality marine charts covering the seven seas. There were few corners of the maritime world that the Royal Navy was not familiar with. But there were still great chunks of terra firma that were unmapped, mountains that were unclimbed and forests unexplored. They represented a mysterious challenge to explorers from many lands. In 1871 Henry Stanley ventured into south central Africa to find the long lost Dr. David Livingston. In the Sudan Charles Gordon had built a reputation as an intrepid diplomat and military governor until he was despatched by the Mahdi in 1885 during the siege of Khartoum. In 1909 Robert Peary planted the American flag on the North Pole and prompted immediate efforts by other polar explorers to push onward to the South Pole. Roald Amundsen was successful in his quest in 1911, followed a few months later by Robert Scott.

By the turn of the century the colonial empires of Europe were at their peak and would soon face the reality of politics and economics. The Germans, Belgians, French, Dutch, Spanish and Portuguese had built huge empires in Africa, South America and South-East Asia. Trade and commerce flourished and far flung colonial holdings produced foodstuffs, minerals, timber and manufactured goods. British sea power allowed them to conquer and control the largest empire that has ever existed. The exploitation of empires throughout history has involved massive amounts of money and industrial development. The huge commitment the British made in India and Africa are no exception. The incredible rate of scientific and industrial development during the latter half of the nineteenth century could not be sustained forever. If it had continued unchecked, explorers might have been walking on the moon by 1935. It was a time that educated and encouraged men and women of genius. It was a time that created thinkers, writers, architects, and allowed the concepts of leisure and consumer goods to flourish. It was a time that could not last, and only a few could see or dared to suggest, that there might be dark storm clouds gathering over Europe.

War was a perpetual thorn in the side of British colonialism. In fact one of the reasons that colonial empires fell so quickly after the nineteenth century was not because of losses in battle, but the immense cost of war in lives and resources. The British had been through the Crimean War in 1854 to 1856, and had troops flung far and wide across the world. The Second Chinese Opium war was being fought in 1860. Skirmishes throughout Africa required the constant attention of generals and troops.

The profitable Cape Colony had to be defended during the Boer War. This was the last major conflict of the nineteenth century and perhaps one of the last conflicts fought on land with classical weapons and tactics. The smart uniforms and horse brigades of Lord Kitchener were still present on the battlefield and the honorable requirements of killing on a schedule and not torturing your enemies were still fervently practiced. However the Boers (and the Zulus) didn't seem to understand these principles. Guerilla warfare and backstabbing were becoming much more popular and resulted in the French frustration, *c'est la guerre*. The Boers were soundly defeated in 1902 by the mailed fist of British might, but not without significant cost to the Empire in coin of the realm and in political popularity. By 1914 *The War That Will End War* had begun. It was a terrifying conflict of slaughter and mechanization. The engineering wisdom and riches of all of Europe were poured into machinery and equipment designed for killing and destruction. Poisonous gas became the scourge of the battlefields, wiping out all living things in its path. It goes without saying that all of Europe had suddenly become as good at killing and destruction as it had been at building and exploring. Great Britain was simultaneously defending its colonial assets and its right of settlement overseas. The Mediterranean was one of its naval strongholds and Lawrence of Arabia was galloping across the deserts of North Africa.

The effect of the First World War on the British and on all her dominions was widespread and lasting. A lesser people might never have survived. The war ended with the Treaty of Versailles which broke the remaining bones of the massive German and Austrian empires. The Bolsheviks had begun their revolt in Russia and the Czarist Empire had been literally butchered. All of Europe struggled desperately to regain its footing and rebuild its bomb cratered home ground. The previous sanctity of imperial interests was suddenly of lesser importance. Relief from the expense of war produced a short economic boom in the 1920's, only to be replaced by more poverty and famine as the entire world slipped into the greatest economic depression in centuries.

There were few who would have been so bold as to say there would be more to come. But indeed there was more to come. The period after The Great War was one of rebuilding and rethinking. Politicians, writers and scientists saw the terror of war and regularly voiced their opinions on preventing this type of conflict for all time. But the new masonry had hardly dried before the ancient Hun reared his ugly head again. Much of Europe was in a state of denial but the Second World War soon became very real. Within twenty years the folly of the settlements made after the first Great War came home to roost. The second Great War was soon upon Europe. It is unimaginable to most in the twenty-first century how much blood was spilled and how far this conflict pushed the world back in time. Millions were killed and centuries old cities were totally leveled. By comparison, the pampered and coddled populace of today resort to a state of apoplexy and street demonstrations following the death of a few dozen troops and the loss of a few buildings during the execution of well planned precision warfare. When the second Great War was over a new power was sitting at the bargaining table. The Americans had invested heavily in the conflict and were now leading participants in the settlement and reparations. It was a new world and the glory and fireworks of the previous one hundred years would never return.

The great empire on which the sun never set was being systematically released from its colonial chains and the colonies were simultaneously losing their access to the money and political stability of the British Crown and homeland. The close of the Second World War ended the one hundred year period between 1850 and 1950. In spite of the terror of war, the conflict had produced one of the most rapid advances in science and industry that the world has ever seen. Air travel had come into its own, shipping and rail systems were extended to provide military supply lines, and all corners of the world had been thoroughly explored and mapped. Agriculture, food production, and medical science had reached new levels. Construction methods, materials and design entered a renaissance. New concepts in art and entertainment logically followed.

In 1850 the British Empire spanned the world and the British pound sterling was the currency that fueled the wheels of commerce. Few would contest Britannia's rule of the seas. However by the turn of the century Great Britain began to lose her grip on the world economy and her military might was being wasted on war. She lost control of much of her empire for the same reasons that empires have fallen throughout history. Great Britain was badly over extended and her attention was diverted to defense rather than offense. It was the defense of an entire way of life. By 1950 the political and military power had shifted to the United States and a new era had begun. Shortly thereafter the US dollar became the international unit of exchange and the reach of American military and industrial interests covered the globe. As history is bound to repeat itself, the balance of power will eventually shift again.

Here was one hundred years of change. It brought a revolution in technology and ideas; a revolution in exploration and discovery; and a revolution in warfare with new and better means of destruction. Into this revolution was born Herbert George Wells. The times shaped the man and his ideas, and his writing became a product of his times and his humble origins. What then would be the character and content of his writing as he moved through this revolutionary one hundred year epoch in history?

2

Struggles and Successes

H.G. Wells' life fits neatly into the dynamic one hundred year period of growth and turmoil between 1850 and 1950. The literature, the politics, the economics and the scientific advancements of the era molded his life and shaped his ideas. Wells was a mirror of his times. His novels reflect his upbringing and his perception of the world around him. The politics of the period encouraged the development of his socialist ideals and had a substantial effect on the friends he chose and the decisions he made.

Wells was born on Saturday, September 21, 1866, in the village of Bromley, a bustling suburb south of London. He was the fourth child of Joseph and Sarah Wells. Joseph was a shopkeeper who ran a small dry goods establishment in Bromley High Street. He was not much of a businessman and produced only a meager living for his family. The game of cricket had a much greater appeal for Joseph and he spent a great deal of his time participating in local matches. His shop carried cricket gear stacked in a disorderly fashion amid the china and glassware. When Joseph Wells was younger he had begun work as a gardener and was mentored by a kindly gentleman who provided a wide range of reading material and a basic knowledge of botany. Joseph eventually obtained a position on the estate of the Fetherstonhaugh family in Sussex. It was here that he met Sarah Neal who worked for the family as a housekeeper. Sarah was five years older than Joseph and had entered domestic service after her father died leaving the family with a mortgage and many debts. Sarah was a devout Protestant Christian and had gained a fair education for girls of her station. She was able to read and write and mange accounts at a time when education was an expensive and privileged undertaking. Joseph and Sarah were married in November of 1853 and moved to Staffordshire where Joseph had found a suitable position as head gardener at an estate near Warwick.

Joseph soon lost his position at the Staffordshire estate over some disagreement with the titled owner. After several months without work they decided to move to Bromley in Kent where Joseph had arranged to take over the High Street china shop owned by a family relative. This was risky move for the young family and eventually proved to be a bad business decision in spite of the potential opportunities. Bromley was a growing suburban village on the southern outskirts of London. Horse carts and coaches to London were frequent and inexpensive although most roads were still unpaved. A rail line through the village had been completed in 1861 and the concept of suburbs and commuting had become a real part of Victorian life.

Bromley had a population of about 5500 people around the time Joseph and Sarah moved into their accommodations beneath the china shop on the High Street. The shop never turned much trade and they lived from hand to mouth for many years. Sarah had delivered three children by the time she became pregnant with Herbert George. Her first child, Frances, born in 1855 had died before Herbert was born. This was a depressing setback for Sarah Wells and probably weighed heavily on her mind for the rest of her life. When Herbert George was born in 1866 he quickly became 'Bertie' a spoiled and precocious child who demanded her constant attention. A comment from his older brother Frank completes the image of the youngest occupant of the household. 'Woe betide, if toys his highness wanted were denied him.'[1]

At the age of seven Bertie's leg was broken in an altercation at a cricket match. This meant he was laid up for several weeks while his leg healed. He became the subject of constant attention while the rest of the family waited on him. The idle time gave him the chance to read and draw pictures to his heart's content. His mother ensured that he read the bible regularly and as soon as he was able he had to accompany her to services at the local Anglican Church. This childhood religious indoctrination was certainly a contributing factor in his later rejection of the church and his highly critical attacks on Roman Catholicism.

When Bertie reached the age of eight years, Sarah Wells found the resources to send him to Thomas Morley's Bromley Academy to further his education. This was a new type of school designed to provide a good basic education for the children of tradesmen and public servants. It was a truly Dickensian school in curriculum and character, but it provided the basic education demanded by a growing industrialized nation. The Elementary Education Act of 1870 had recently been passed as a necessary requirement to educating a newly enfranchised population who had to learn to read and write to participate in the social system. Morley's Academy was a small piece of this expanding educational system, and by all accounts Bertie learned quickly and competed for top honors among his class of about thirty pupils. This early schooling not only provided Bertie with a love for books and language, but it also provided his mother with the satisfaction that she was doing everything she could to push her son up through the English class system. Bertie attended the Morely academy until he was fourteen. Life then suddenly changed and he was forced into a new world of tribulation that would sorely test his mettle.

In 1880 Sarah Wells was offered a position at Uppark in Sussex where she had worked as a young woman prior to marrying Joseph. The position provided her with the opportunity to get out from under the drudgery of the china shop in Bromley, but what to do with Bertie? Sarah had arranged apprenticeships for her two older boys at drapers' establishments and hastily looked around for a similar situation for her youngest son. Wells later wrote in his autobiography that 'Almost as unquestioning as her belief in Our Saviour, was her belief in drapers.' Sarah desperately wanted Bertie to find something better than life beneath a china shop. The class system was still well defined in Victorian England and Sarah Wells always believed herself to be a bit higher in station than her circumstances indicated. To ensure that her boys had steady employment and the chance to succeed she insisted on the using the time honored system of apprenticeship. Young Wells thus began work as a draper's apprentice at an establishment in Windsor. Some biographers suggest that he was careless and a bit slovenly at his new found occupation and he was promptly dismissed by his employer as unsuitable for a draper's apprenticeship. By this time Sarah Wells had left her husband Joseph behind and moved, by herself, to her new position at Uppark in Sussex. She was now faced with arranging a new situation for her wayward son. After considerable worry and effort she found him a position as an assistant to a school teacher named Alfred Williams in Somerset. This undertaking lasted only a few months since authorities soon dismissed Williams as a scoundrel without proper teaching credentials. The unfortunate result was that Sarah Wells had to beg the Fetherstonhaugh family for permission to bring young Wells back into their household until she could find another position.

Young Wells spent only a few months at Uppark before his mother found an opportunity at a Chemists shop in Midhurst. However, this short hiatus with his mother at Uppark made a substantial impression on his young mind. The estate and its buildings would appear, in one form or another, in many of his future novels. Although Bertie seems to have enjoyed working at the Chemists, his mother still had a fixation with drapers and eventually found him another position in Southsea. This was a bit more pleasant situation and better food and quarters were available for the apprentices. A small collection of books was available in his dormitory and young Wells dove into the books with great delight. It was probably here that he first displayed his scientific interests and an attraction to biology in particular. The latter half of the nineteenth century was an era in which Darwin was often a topic of conversation and many arguments ensued over the blasphemy suggested by his work. This controversy did not escape young Wells and it was a subject he could read about in books and newspapers.

His dissatisfaction over the draper's trade soon rose to a head again in 1883. He was now seventeen years of age and began to look for a way to get out of his drapers indentures on his own, rather than turning to his mother for a solution. He found the answer with a teacher named Byatt, in Midhurst, who was building a small private school. He appealed to his father for some assistance, but Joseph Wells was still struggling with the china shop in Bromley and was not in a position to support himself let alone a wayward son who couldn't stick to his commitments. Byatt agreed to pay young Wells twenty pounds for the first year's service as a teaching assistant and provide the guidance necessary to get him off on a study program of his own. Wells jumped at the chance and abandoned his indentured service in Southsea at the draper's emporium. He quickly dove into a course of study that appealed to him immensely. He was soon writing exams that were producing financial stipends for both himself and his teacher. He applied to the Normal School of Science in South Kensington for a scholarship and was ecstatic when he was awarded a position with a stipend of a guinea a week for board. He later wrote to his brother Frank and declared that 'I have now become…a respectable person entitled to wear a gown…'

The scholarship program Wells had applied for was in the biological sciences and it would give him the opportunity to study under Thomas H. Huxley, one of Britains foremost biologists and paleontologists, and a formidable advocate of Charles Darwin's work. Huxley was considered a heretic by some for his beliefs and for his unbridled enthusiasm in writing and lecturing about these beliefs. Such heresy, of course, did not go unnoticed by Wells' devout mother, but by this time she could do little more than simply voice her disdain. Wells was now clearly making his own decisions. At the time the Normal School of Science was part of the London University System. Today it's known as The Imperial College and is still providing degree programs in science, in the same buildings. Wells began his course of study in September of 1884 at the age of eighteen years. It was a major milestone in his life and would affect his work and thinking throughout his career. Although Wells took only one course from Huxley, and had no personal relationship with him, he considered Huxley to be a pillar of knowledge and education. Huxley was already well on in years and died in 1889, shortly after Wells had finished his degree program.

Wells first year at the school was a major success in a life that had already been complicated by a number of failures. He worked hard and produced first class honors. He built new friendships, including a warm relationship with A.T. Simmons and Richard Gregory that would last throughout their lives. However the purpose of the Normal School was to prepare accredited science teachers and biological sciences were only part of the curriculum. In his second year Wells was faced with a different set of problems in the form of his physics classes. Wells was good at cramming and could make a success of his language studies and his biology by studying intently prior to examinations. But his physics course was plagued by poor instructors and his lack of interest. It's probably also true that he had met his academic match in the form of a physics exam. His grades for the second year were only just adequate to maintain his scholarship for completion of his Matriculation requirements. In his third year he was faced with a course in Geology which he failed at Christmas exam time. He was approaching the end of his three year course and his lack of discipline and careless interest was catching up with him. At the end of the academic year he barely passed the exams necessary to obtain his teaching certificate. He also began what was initially an innocent affair with his cousin Isabel Wells whose mother ran a boarding house in Euston Road. Wells had boarded with his aunt during the last two years of his studies and his attraction for Isabel was a distraction that he didn't need, especially when his interest in school was waning.

During his time in South Kensington Wells made many new friends and participated in student activities including the school debating society. He also helped start a small newsletter with a few of his fellow students. They called it *The Science Schools Journal* and Wells became its first editor. This journal provided the vehicle for publishing his first short stories, including *The Chronic Argonauts*, which was the seed from which *The Time Machine* eventually grew.

Wells obtained a second rate teaching position in Wales after his graduation. This employment was quickly interrupted by an illness that sent him back to Uppark where his mother still worked as a downstairs housekeeper. After a period of recuperation he ventured back to London again to search for some sort of employment. He was now 23 years old and virtually penniless. Were it not for the support of some of his friends from school at South Kensington he might not have survived. He eventually managed to obtain a teaching position in early 1889 under John V. Milne, better known as the father of the respected writer A.A. Milne. The young Milne was one of Wells' pupils for a short time. The situation appealed to Wells and it gave him the extra time and the resources to get back to his books with the goal of completing his B.Sc. in Zoology. The academic results were soon forthcoming when he passed his first set of exams with honors and won the associated cash prizes.

This was followed by an offer of employment from a man named William Briggs who had started a correspondence college and a tutorial school for students at London University. Wells accepted the offer and began work as a tutor in the correspondence department of the college. He was now earning a steady income. This made it easier for him to return to his own studies and complete the requirements for a B.Sc. degree in Zoology. Persistence paid off when he completed his examinations with first class honors. This included a jump in salary and permanent employment as an instructor at the college. A stipend of three hundred pounds per annum was enough to provide him with the resources to select better living quarters and maintain a more comfortable lifestyle.

During his work at the Correspondence College he found time to write a small two volume text book to assist students in their biological studies. This was published formally in 1893 by W.B. Clive as the *Textbook of Biology,* part of the University Correspondence College Tutorial Series. It is widely accepted as Wells' first published book. He deserves ample credit for taking the time to put together a study guide that the College considered worth publishing. It may have whetted his appetite for writing. Wells never indicated that he was proud of this first book. In fact he seemed more inclined to pan the effort. Much later, in a letter to one of his publishers outlining his work credits he labeled it 'A cram book—and pure hackwork. Illustrations grotesquely bad—facts imagined.'[2] That same year he collaborated with his friend and classmate Richard Gregory to produce another textbook entitled *Honours Physiography.* This latter textbook also appeared as a formal publication in 1893. He and Gregory received ten pounds each for their work on the book. It seems that the teaching schedule, the work, and the study schedule were too much for Wells' fragile frame. He suffered another hemorrhage and had to retire again to Uppark to recover.

While he was teaching in London he had taken up residence with his cousin Isabel Wells. Since he was now earning a meager but steady wage, this improved financial situation meant that he could start thinking about marriage. After recovery from his setback in health Isabel agreed to his marriage proposal and on October 31st, 1891 they were quietly married. They immediately moved into leased premises at 28 Haldon Road, where Wells had room to work and could continue his teaching duties with Briggs at the University Correspondence College. For a few months the domestic atmosphere and comfortable environment appealed to Wells but it was not long before he became dissatisfied with Isabel and the routine of his teaching position. Another disaster was fast approaching.

Sarah Wells lost her position at Uppark in Sussex in the Fall of 1892 and was forced to stay with young Bertie and his new wife for a few days before she could arrange to rejoin her husband Joseph. Shortly thereafter Wells' older brother Fred lost his position at a drapers shop and came to live with them while he looked for a new situation. The work load and the unsettled nature of his household became a drain on Wells' health as well as his pocketbook. In May of 1893 he suffered another chest hemorrhage and was put to bed for several days. It seemed that this might be the end of his teaching efforts. As soon as Wells was able they moved out of London where he thought he might better regain his strength.

Wells was now spending his days writing articles for newspapers and weekly magazines. He had a number of articles accepted by the *Pall Mall Gazette* which had recently been purchased by W.W. Astor. This literary market provided him with a new source of income that generated enough revenue to cover domestic expenses. It was a revolutionary period for the newspaper and magazine publication industry in London. The emerging middle class were avid readers and the potential market for publications was immense. It was an ideal time for new writers and Wells was sharp enough to sense the opportunity.

The emotional turmoil surrounding his household reached a peak when Wells decided that it was time to leave his wife of three years. He packed up his belongings and left their rented quarters to return to London. He immediately took up residence at 7 Mornington Place with Amy Catherine Robbins, one of his former biology students. Wells gives many reasons for his impetuous decision, including a description of the affair in his later novel *Tono-Bungay*. Probably the reasons don't really matter. What he had done was to begin a pattern of decisions and choices that would follow him throughout his life. The pattern often reflected impulsive actions, poor choices, and a vindictive attitude toward those who displeased him.

Luck appeared to be with the foolish couple. Wells found that he was able to earn enough from his writing to actually support himself and Catherine and to provide for the wife he had just left. The year 1894 turned out to be a banner year. He sold dozens of newspaper articles and produced the first of his short stories that were to be published later in collected editions. He also made an agreement with the publisher John Lane to prepare a collection of his *Pall Mall Gazette* stories for publication as a book. The book was entitled *Select Conversations With an Uncle*. John Lane published the work in early 1895 and printed only 650 copies, but Wells was pleased to see that he was getting some of the exposure he needed to become a recognized writer. With the exception of his efforts at writing text books and study guides with his school colleagues, this new publication was Wells' first commercial book.

In the middle of 1894 Wells and Catherine Robbins, whom he had chosen to rename 'Jane', moved out of London to Sevenoaks where they took temporary lodgings at 23 Eardley Road near the railway station. The first few weeks were difficult since his market for articles and short stories dried up quickly as a number of London papers were in the process of changing hands. However, one of his editors, W.E. Henley offered to take an expanded version of his *Time Traveler* idea for serial publication in *The New Review* and agreed to pay one hundred pounds for the work. Henley also arranged for the publisher William Heinemann to take the serialized work and publish it in book form in return for a fee of fifty pounds payable to the author. One hundred and fifty pounds was substantially more money than Wells had received for any of his previous writing. He was exuberant and knew immediately that an opportunity was staring him in the face. He began to write furiously to meet his commitment to Henley for the serial publication of the *Time Traveler*.

He and Jane left Sevenoaks and returned to their accommodations in London at the end of 1894. Here he continued writing and began to sketch out ideas for *The Wonderful Visit* and *The Island of Dr. Moreau*. In June of 1895 Heinemann published *The Time Machine* as promised and printed 10,000 copies. Dent and Company published *The Wonderful Visit* in September and a collection of short stories entitled *The Stolen Bacillus* was published in November. Wells was on a roll, and he knew it. He also knew that he had to capitalize quickly on his new found success or it would fade as soon as it had appeared. In 1895 he earned nearly eight hundred pounds from his writing. This was a substantial income in an era when five pounds per week was a more common middle class income. The extra money was easily spent. His divorce from Isabel had recently been completed and he married Amy Catherine in October of 1895. His alimony to Isabel cost him one hundred pounds a year and he was providing a sizeable stipend to assist his aging parents.

At the end of 1895 Wells and Jane moved to Woking in Surrey where he pressed on with his writing. They took a number of cycling tours of the countryside which provided him with material for *The Wheels of Chance*. His imagination was at its most productive in this environment and a century later it would be clear that his mind was producing the best ideas for novels that he would ever have. *The Invisible Man* and the *War of the Worlds* were also products of the time he spent in Woking. In fact he describes Woking in some detail as the machines of his Martian invaders advance across the countryside, destroying everything in their path. At the end of 1896 Wells was beginning to feel that his work was paying off. He was getting inquiries from publishers and magazine editors and had commitments for all the work he could produce. He quickly learned to squeeze his publishers for the maximum return and looked into hiring a literary agent to handle his business affairs. By this time he was thirty years old, divorced and remarried, and had struggled for the best part of ten years to make ends meet and to find some means of making his way in the world. Now the London literary critics were beginning to notice him.

How good Wells was as a writer of fiction is something that will be forever debated by students of literature. There is no question that he was at the right place at the right time with an enviable talent, but even some of his contemporaries insisted that he couldn't live up to the comparisons that critics were making with the work of Daniel Defoe, Jonathan Swift, Rudyard Kipling, Charles Dickens or Conan Doyle. In fact some of these writers outsold Wells ten times over. Wells was moving ahead quickly, but he was not yet in the league of well established English writers.

Writers and critics have often compared Wells to Jules Verne, but neither Wells nor Verne considered themselves to be made in each others image. In fact biographers Norman and Jeanne Mackenzie have pointed out that Jules Verne was reported in an English periodical to have said 'I do not see the possibility of comparison between his work and mine…his stories do not repose on very scientific bases…I make use of physics…he invents.'[3] Perhaps Verne was right, and perhaps this inventiveness was one of the appealing things about Wells' work. Wells would certainly have read most of Verne's work. Verne was a generation older than Wells and was already widely translated. On the other hand Verne could not have read more that the early *fantastic romance* novels that Wells produced. Wells would certainly not have been impressed with Verne's remark since he spent most of his life insisting that his student work in biology made him a scientist and Verne's implication that his work does not repose on a scientific basis would not have been appreciated.

Near the end of 1897 Wells and Jane moved to new quarters in Worcester Park. This was a new home and new circumstances. He was making new friends and was being exposed to a part of the literary world he had not seen before. In early 1898 he and Jane made their first trip to Europe to visit their friend George Gissing. Wells later suffered a couple of minor setbacks in health but continued his writing at a furious pace. He had found his occupation and his stride.

In early 1900 Wells committed to a major investment. He purchased land in Sandgate near England's south coast with the intention of building a house. He hired an architect and proceeded with what would come to be known as Spade House. The home was designed to meet Wells' vision of a family home and a writer's home. It eventually cost him about three thousand pounds, a handsome sum at the turn of the twentieth century. They moved into their new home in 1901 and in July of 1901 their first child, George Phillip Wells, was born. Two years later their second son, Frank was born. Wells was now a family man earning substantial income and ready to settle into a new environment. During the period between 1897 and 1901 Wells had published, *The Invisible Man*, *The War of the Worlds*, *When the Sleeper Wakes*, *The First Men in the Moon*, and several collections of short stories including *The Plattner Story, and Others, Thirty Strange Stories* and *Tales of Space and Time*. Several other books were already in preparation and his entire approach to writing was about to change.

A new era began in England as the twentieth century dawned. As indicated in Chapter 4, the significance of the jump into the new century can't be underestimated. No less a change was occurring in Wells' life. His circumstances were stable, he was settled in a new and much more comfortable home and he began to think about voicing some of his social and political opinions. His first major effort in this direction was a new book entitled *Anticipations of the Reaction of Mechanical and Scientific Progress Upon Human Life and Thought*. This is more commonly referred to as simply *Anticipations*. The book was the outgrowth of a collection of articles previously published in the *Fortnightly Review*. It turned out to be a substantial success and required several reprints from the publisher. Many of the details of the book are considered later in Chapter 28.

Anticipations is a significant work in many respects. It immediately established Wells as a prophet in the new century, and it convinced him the he could write successfully about social reform. Hitherto he had made his living writing imaginative adventures and supernatural tales. Clearly he could do other things and gain an even wider audience. The success of *Anticipations* puffed up his ego and he quickly moved into a new path where he felt he needed to be teaching the world about its mistakes and pointing out what would have to be done to remedy them. In many respects this was the most important turning point in his career. It was the point at which Wells stopped his contribution to literature and began to pump out lengthy, repetitive political tracts that were read with topical interest and then largely ignored.

It was becoming clear to Wells, as it was to his publishers and his critics, that ever greater numbers of people were reading his books and his newspaper articles. He was convinced that his audience was not only interested in what he was saying, but they probably were in agreement with most of his ideas. A fascination with new writers and new ideas was a common phenomenon in the new century. The irony is that Wells knew full well that book publishers, periodical owners and politicians were starving for fresh ideas and quickly gobbled up the work of any new writers and academics that could attract an audience. Wells was good at what he did, and his work was absorbed by the expanding world of literary journalism. Wells' folly, if any, was that he paid little attention to his own sermon. Over the first few years of the new century he became so thoroughly impressed with his own abilities that he changed his entire approach to writing. The story teller, the dreamer of worlds to come, the interpreter of social folly, gradually began to metamorphose. He became the instructor, a pompous autocrat, and an artist overly certain of his own ability. Wells had fallen victim to the notion that his own brilliance was the foundation of his success rather than the changing social system around him. He was also oblivious to the common success of other writers and populists who were gaining notoriety with even less promise and talent than he had.

In 1903 he joined the Fabian Society and became deeply involved in socialism. He migrated towards Beatrice and Sydney Webb and Charlotte and George Bernard Shaw who were already on a one-sided political bent. Here was one of the new audiences Wells needed to hear his ideas. In the minds of his biographers Wells immediately saw the Fabian Society as a vehicle that he could change and mold to promote his personal views of socialism. Although he and the society's social principles were in general agreement, many of the members, especially the old guard, were less than impressed with an upstart who pretended to instruct them on the principles of socialism and the administration of a political organization. Wells' relationship with the Fabian Society became almost comical in its immaturity. He was miffed when they paid little attention to him. The Society's old guard was miffed when Wells called them names and had the nerve to suggest that change was a requirement of the Society. Typical of a young upstart, Wells would go off in a huff when he was reprimanded, often leaving the country, and not speaking to his detractors for an extended period of time. His response to criticism was commonly a long written treatise that he would carefully manufacture at his writing desk. He would have it signed or supported by whomever he could muster to his cause and then submitted it to the directors of the Society. Perhaps in retrospect it was George Bernard Shaw who demonstrated the most patience with this young upstart. Shaw saw the brilliance of youthful ideas and the necessity of quiet encouragement. In the end Wells proved to be far too self-centered and impetuous for the organization, and he resigned his membership in 1907 to go on to other things. The entire Fabian issue was at once a blow to Wells' ego and a fertile seed for his future thinking. Wells involvement with the Fabians had a major impact on his writing, some of which is considered in Chapter 6.

Wells imaginative writing did not suddenly terminate as his thinking shifted towards social and political issues. He wrote and published *The Food of the Gods, A Modern Utopia, Kipps, In the Days of the Comet* and *The War in the Air* between 1904 and 1908. These were all imaginative novels that played on the social issues of the day. The latter novel, *The War in the Air,* is a bright and entertaining account of aerial warfare written several years before aircraft were used as fighting machines in the First World War. Much of Wells' enthusiasm about flying machines was encouraged by a friendship that he had established with J.W. Dunne. Dunne developed experimental aircraft and was a strong advocate of the use of flying machines and other mechanized contrivances in warfare. Dunne had apparently entrusted Wells, on one occasion, with some of his papers while he was abroad and helped arrange Wells' first flight in a seaplane in 1912. As Wells often did he nobly professes that his ideas were developed from the fertile minds of others, but he does not hesitate in other circumstances to flaunt his originality. For example, in his autobiography he comments, 'Already in 1908 in *The War in the Air*, written before any practicable flying had occurred, I had reasoned that air warfare, by making warfare three dimensional, would abolish the war front and with that the possibility of distinguishing between civilian and combatant or of bringing war to a conclusive end.'[4] Wells also points out in the same breath that '…early in 1914 I published a futuristic story *The World Set Free*, in which I describe the collapse of the social order through the use of 'atomic bombs'…'[5] As often happens in the world of journalism, a written statement is paraphrased by an admiring journalist, reinterpreted by another, and very soon enthusiasts had Wells inventing the tank, aerial warfare, and the atomic bomb. There is little doubt that Wells had the means to promote ideas, and the ideas were eventually associated with him even though he had no part in their origin. At the turn of the new century, the whole world was interested in new ideas, especially aircraft. It was only logical that Wells would write about current and popular topics, and that such topics could be easily attributed to him whether he later claimed credit for them or not.

Wells' social activities were beginning to attract attention as the year 1908 began. It was clear to some that he was a walking contradiction who preached morality and socialism out of one side of his mouth and professed the worst kind of hypocrisy out of the other. Journalists were now firmly poking Wells with the same literary stick that he so freely used on others. He recognized that this controversy was costing him book sales and that he might have to adjust his attitudes. The importance of money in his life was now well established and his disdain for those of lesser stature was growing. He points out in his autobiography that the financial impact of his social problems on book sales might have to be taken into account since he saw no sense in '…cutting myself off from association with any but the working class & risking the lives & education of my children by going to live in some infernal slum or other at a pound a week or so.'[6]

Wells' home life during this period of controversy was tense and busy. He had freed himself of the Fabian Society and was writing at a frenetic pace. His family was important to him and he spent as much time as he could playing with his two boys. Two children's books, *Little Wars* and *Floor Games* resulted from their common war game activities on the floor of his study at Spade House. Jane Wells hired a Swiss governess for the boys named Matilde Meyer who later wrote a small biographical account of Wells covering her five years with the family.[7] Although the book is often overly enthusiastic about Wells' character and stature, it does contain insights into the family and its workings during the period prior to the First World War.

Wells was gaining continued success with novels like *Tono-Bungay*. This was a popular book and he was doing everything he could to generate as much revenue as possible from its wide distribution. This included arguments with Macmillan, his publisher about serial rights to the book. His exuberance resulted in an agreement with Ford Maddox Ford to republish the novel in six parts with Wells earning a portion of the profits. It turns out that the enterprise lost money and Wells received nothing. Meanwhile Macmillan was becoming unhappy about their arrangement with Wells to publish his next novel, *Ann Veronica*, since they didn't considered it the kind of novel purchased by their customers. This was a good example of the bad judgments and petty disagreements that were often the cause of Wells shifting from one publisher to another, sometimes at the expense of profits.

In 1909 Wells was facing what would today be called a middle-age crisis. He was 43 years old, very successful, and beginning to have some doubts about the value of his accomplishments. His wandering eye got him into a lot of trouble with old friends and family alike. His activities could probably be described as childish and irresponsible reactions to a perceived need to prove himself at middle age. His decision to move to France for a while and sell Spade House was an impetuous act in response to what he called 'domestic claustrophobia'. The home he had designed for himself and his family was sold for about 3200 pounds, and they moved into London to apartments at 17 Church Row in Hampstead. The children were old enough at the time to wonder what was happening and why it was happening. Typical of Wells' literary habits, he continued to write and plan furiously through one crisis after another and published *Ann Veronica, The History of Mr. Polly*, and *The New Machiavelli*, all in the space of two years. Today's critics consider these novels to be some of Wells' best work in his post *fantastic romance* period. *Ann Veronica* in particular was a controversial work about a rather free spirited young woman who moves to London to find her own way in the world. Because of the close association of the characters in the novel with well known social figures, Macmillan would not publish the book as they had previously agreed, and they contracted the project out to another publisher. This brought Wells and Macmillan close to litigation, but both parties eventually came to an agreement and went their separate ways. This would not be the last of Wells' arguments and misunderstandings with his publishers.

Wells began to spend much more of his time in France and Switzerland, often for periods of several weeks at a time. In 1913 he spent enough time in Switzerland to complete writing *The World Set Free*. This novel is a controversial story about a group of self appointed leaders who take control over the world after an uncompromising war. As noted in Chapter 8 some of the ideas he is beginning to adopt lean towards world domination by a superior intelligence. As often becomes obvious in his novels, Wells is logically a part of the superior intelligence.

After a couple of years Wells had again tired of living in London and began a search for new quarters in the southern countryside. In early 1912 he moved, dragging his family behind him, to Little Easton in Essex. He kept the apartments in London to provide quarters for his work and his social life while in the city. The move to Easton provided a slightly more settled feeling for Wells and he began to take a serious look at the direction of his writing. Around this time he began to realize, and agree with many of his critics, that he was not a novelist that could ever be compared to Henry James or Rudyard Kipling. As he came to accept this position it pushed him towards the type of treatise and political novel that promoted his ideas about saving the world with socialist governments and improvements in man himself.

A great portion of his income was now being generated by agreements for one group of articles after another with the major London newspapers. He was much in demand for his political slant on imperialism and the growing controversy in Europe. Many of these articles and essays were reprinted in collected editions or rewritten as pamphlets and small books. Titles like *The Great State: Essays in Construction, The Labour Unrest, Liberalism and Its Party, War and Common Sense,* all appeared between 1912 and 1914. The novels *Marriage* and *The Passionate Friends* were added to the mix. Wells commanded a huge audience and his writing produced both financial rewards and controversy in similar proportions. Like many well known personalities of the period he was admired and despised at the same time by all levels of society and across a wide portion of the English speaking world.

The coming of The Great War was a shock to Wells. Although most of the nation could see it coming, and Wells had written prophetically about its approach, it was still frightening to see a war of such magnitude and terror descend upon the world. In 1914 Wells published a group of eleven essays under the title *The War That Will End War.* This title became a much repeated mantra during the war and seemed to voice the consensus of the allied nations that a war of this magnitude would destroy the ability and the will of the world to ever wage war again. Many agreed with Wells' distaste of the war and the reasons for fighting, but that didn't make any difference to the conflict. It raged on for four years until the German monster was beaten back within its borders and subjected to a humiliating settlement.

The war did not place a damper on Wells' work or his social activities. He wrote articles, essays and small books at a furious rate. They were mostly meaningless political tracts that delivered pompous statements about the unquestionable rights of the western world and the inevitable end that would be faced by Germany. He managed a visit to Russia with a colleague in 1914 and had a number of talks with Maxim Gorki. Wells seemed to be impressed with the type of socialist elite that was springing up in Tsarist Russia at the time. His liberal leanings would pull him back to Russia again in later years, but he was already close enough to this tenuous war-time ally that he reacted strongly to accusations of Bolshevik tyranny made by his friends.

Wells placed himself in the thick of the war effort and made the best possible use of his literary pulpit. When he had the opportunity he visited the front where he could see for himself the difficulties that troops had to face. He fired verbal volleys at anyone who did not believe in the just cause of the war, or at any pacifists who considered themselves above the fray. This continued to irritate many of his former friends and a substantial segment of his audience, but it also had the benefit of exposing him to a new and broader audience who were interested in his war time journalism, if not in his previous political writing.

As the war thundered onward Wells' involvement grew more intense. He was convinced of the incompetence of politicians and the idiocy of the generals conducting the war. He offered advice in great quantities to anyone who would listen and was convinced that he ought to be given a job in the war effort where his experience and knowledge would do the most good. Since he fully believed that he had invented the 'tank', he could not understand why he wasn't consulted on its use and design. His frustration probably went a long way toward fueling his latent hatred for the monarchy, the titled elite, and conservative politicians. Wells never understood that the people he so disliked may simply have viewed him as an outspoken journalist rather than as God's gift to the British Empire. Wells was not a scientist, he wasn't an engineer and he didn't possess any special talents that would be of value to the war effort. Neither had he ever been involved in warfare beyond the war games he played with his children. But this didn't seem to deter him from offering advice in the conduct of the war or from incessant public criticism of the military leadership for their 'routinely idiotic decisions'.

As busy as he was, Wells still found plenty of time for other women, and in 1914 Rebecca West gave birth to a son whom Wells acknowledged as his own. Rebecca named the son Anthony West. This was his second child out of wedlock and he made little effort to hide the relationship with Rebecca. A few years earlier he had struggled to keep an affair with Amber Reeves under wraps after she gave birth to a daughter out of wedlock. His wife had long since given up any protest about his extra curricular activities and they had come to an agreeable living arrangement. Thus Wells put himself in a position where he could have his cake, and eat it too. He and Jane agreed to some major remodeling of their house at Easton Glebe. They had leased the home on the estate of Lady Warwick in 1912. It provided them with a large well finished home where they could entertain guests from London and put up friends for extended visits. Wells continued to maintain apartments in London where he did a great portion of his work. During the early years of the war he wrote the novel *Mr. Britling Sees It Through*. This is a semi-autobiographical account of Wells and his family and their life at Easton Glebe. It became the most successful of his works in several years and generated substantial income in England and in the United States.

As an end to the war became a realistic vision, the government of Lloyd George had to make a number of changes to hold its position while slipping in popularity. These changes included offering Wells a job in the Ministry of Information as a contributor to the preparation of enemy propaganda. He didn't last long at this position. As might be expected he considered the effort to be a waste of time as he did with most projects that he had not initiated on his own or that he was not controlling. He could see that Europe had been torn apart by the First World War and that previously centrist governments were now highly factious and supported only by an increasingly dissatisfied public. Wells was becoming more and more certain that a revolution of some sort was the only answer to the world's ills. He believed that this revolution had to be a quiet and peacefully organized revolution that would change the way people lived and worked. This was the seed from which much of his writing over the next few years would grow. It was also the reason for his enthusiastic participation in the movement to create The League of Nations. Wells deserves substantial credit for his work in the effort regardless of how hard he tried to stamp it with his own political goals. The League was established after the end of the war, and was the precursor to the United Nations. It turned out to be a powerless and inept organization and was considered a failure by many. It certainly didn't come close to providing the world government that Wells believed was necessary for continued peace.

After the war Wells began work on *The Outline of History*. He was financially independent and was able to commit large blocks of time to a project that he'd been thinking about for many years. He wanted to produce a definitive textbook of mankind's history that could be used to educate the masses for years to come. Writing the book would quickly become a monumental task and he had to enlist the help of several others, including his old friend Gilbert Murray. Wells worked long hours on the project throughout 1918 and 1919. When the work was completed it first appeared as a serial publication in twenty-five separate parts. The serial publication sold approximately 100,000 copies. It was then bound and reprinted by Cassell in 1920. There was little doubt about its success and it began to earn substantial sums in royalties. The book was republished in numerous editions over the years and became one of Wells most successful publications, both financially and as a contribution to his literary legacy. Wells followed this work with what he insisted was a 'completely rewritten summary' entitled *A Short History of the World*.

Wells didn't place his other interests on hold while he worked on *The Outline of History*. Much to the concern of others he was beginning to show an increasing sympathy for the newly established Bolshevik government in Russia. Many years later it would become clear that he was in full agreement with removing imperialist regimes by force and establishing socialist utopian governments in their place. As often happens to idealists, the corruption and brutality of the Bolshevik movement was completely masked from his mind. Wells had previously met Gorki and the two kept up a correspondence throughout the war years. Gorki invited Wells to visit him in Petrograd, and of course requested that he bring whatever aid in foodstuffs that he could collect.

Wells made the trip to Russia with his elder son Gip. They were pleasantly treated by Gorki who escorted them on a tour of Petrograd and introduced them to a number of local dignitaries. Gorki also arranged a trip to Moscow where he met Lenin and Trotsky. Wells seemed to be duly impressed with the efforts of communism to modernize Russia and pull it out of poverty. When he returned to England he published a series of newspaper articles which were later collected in book form as *Russia in the Shadows*. At the time the English were not particularly happy with the Bolshevik concept of government, so Wells' writing was not well accepted, and he was forced to defend himself on several occasions. Winston Churchill made it clear in an oft quoted article in the London *Daily Express* that any defense of Lenin or the system he represented was pure foolishness. Furthermore the fact that Wells was presenting himself as an expert on the government and intentions of Bolshevik Russia was pure arrogance. In a slanted reference to *The Outline of History,* Churchill wrote 'When one has written a history of the…human race from protoplasm to Lord Birkenhead in about a twelve month, there ought to be no difficulty in becoming an expert on the internal conditions of Russia after a visit of fourteen days.'[8] Wells could not let this tantalizing slight go without an equally demeaning retort. This was a good example of a case where Wells didn't recognize Churchill's greater wit and wisdom and his quick response in defense ensured that he and Churchill would never have much in common.

It was soon after this visit to Russia, in November of 1921, that Wells was asked by a number of friends and colleagues to stand for the parliamentary seat at London University as a Labour candidate. He accepted the candidacy and became involved in a short and low key campaign that included a number of speeches and public appearances. He ultimately finished last in the polls and a tenuous Tory government was re-established at Whitehall. The government lost a vote of confidence and fell the next year and Wells was asked again to stand in the 1922 general election for the same seat. He lost the election for the second time but the Labour Party gained enough seats to form the new government. Very little has been written about Wells' reaction to his humiliating double defeat, but as noted in Chapter 14, he quickly bowed out of political life and went on with his other interests.

Wells was now a wealthy man and lived an almost independent life. He traveled and lectured widely, wrote newspaper articles, and churned out book after book. His family still lived at Easton Glebe and he maintained his own flat in London. He remained active in the social circuit and worked incessantly. Novels still flowed from his pen and *Men Like Gods, Christina Alberta's Father,* and *The World of William Clissold* came out of the mid-1920's. His old health problems began to surface again and they took a toll on his work. Much of this work became repetitive and his ideas were becoming a bit old and tiresome. In 1926 Wells turned sixty years of age and was loosing his grip on originality. He was in the middle of an argument with Hillaire Belloc over *The Outline of History* and was thoroughly entwined with a number of mistresses. This was in addition to the usual demand of deadlines, and what had become a number of excessive financial commitments.

If things could not get worse, they did. His wife Jane, who still maintained the central Wells household at Easton Glebe became ill and died in October of 1927. Wells returned from France as soon as he learned of her illness and remained at Easton Glebe to be with her as her health declined. He had begun work on *The Science of Life* with his son Gip Wells and Julian Huxley, and spent his spare time working on this popularization of the zoological sciences. After Jane's death he began work on a memoir which he tied together with some of her writing and diary entries. He published it as a small book entitled *The Book of Catherine Wells,* using her given name rather than the pet name he'd given her many years earlier.

Wells returned to France where he had just completed work on a villa near Grasse that he named Lou Pidou. He needed change, and change was coming. He sold the London apartment and moved to another one. He also leased an apartment in Paris to accommodate his social adventures in France. In 1928 *The Open Conspiracy* was published, and soundly criticized in print by G.B. Shaw. He hounded his son, G.P. Wells, and Julian Huxley into helping him complete *The Science of Life,* which was finally published in 1930. His writing was becoming less original and new sales were not exciting enough to attract the interest of the many publishers who knew him to be demanding and difficult. To make things worse he was becoming immersed in legal problems with his collaborators and antagonists as noted in Chapter 18. One of these detractors actually accused him of plagiarism and took him to court.

As often happened in Wells' life, he was again assessing his accomplishments and failures. He was probably not as satisfied with his work as he might have been. In particular his social and political philosophy had not gained the following he would have liked. After twenty years of writing and lecturing on socialism and utopian government during a period of domestic injustice and major political change, it was difficult for Wells to understand why he had not attracted more interest and active support. Without a doubt Britain was a hotbed of socialism and underground communist sympathizers between the two wars. In many cases these organizations saw the great Bolshevik movement as the savior of a world gone amuck. Both Oxford and Cambridge were a breeding ground for communist organizations and Bolshevik collaborators, many of whom were to maintain their underground influence well into the Second World War. Certainly this atmosphere encouraged Wells in his thinking, and made it easy for him to write and publish his ideas however avant garde they might seem. Why he didn't have a greater social impact remains a mystery to many but on closer reflection it may not be so puzzling. It wasn't the message that was being rejected; it was the messenger that was being ignored.

It probably never dawned on Wells at the time that his lack of impact was not a disagreement with his point of view, but a declining interest in Wells himself as a social and political proponent. He was arrogant, difficult to work with, and often created venomous disagreements with those friends who were most likely to support him. He was a hypocrite in his treatment of women, and like many socialists, he loved to hobnob with aristocrats and the rich and famous in spite of his constant thumping of capitalists and the privileged.

Wells may have misjudged his reception in many quarters, but he wasn't oblivious to the market for his books and articles. He could see that regardless of the number of people who were reading his work in Europe and America, political events and changes in government were not going the way he thought they should. Time was getting short. He was getting older and there were unsettling rumblings coming from Europe. Persuasion didn't seem to be working. Out of frustration Wells began to turn more toward a prophesy of doom that he believed was inevitable if political changes were not forthcoming. He picked up his sharpest weapon and began writing with a new furry and with a more threatening voice. The world could not continue on its present path, he postulated, without eventual social, political and economic collapse. In some respects there is an almost pathetic appeal to his writing. He would soon be forced to leave the world behind and he couldn't imagine doing so without having molded it a bit closer to his own image of perfection. If he was not going to be successful in his efforts, then he believed he was almost duty bound to inform anyone who could read that the world would surely collapse as soon as he left it.

Wells continued to write at a furious pace even though h
the world of literature behind. Most of his books were collec
articles and long tiresome manifestos of social imperatives. He
klin D. Roosevelt's New Deal in America. A nation that had been devastated by
economic recession and massive crop failures was building its recovery on a vast
investment in make-work programs and guaranteed cradle-to-grave social security. In 1934 Wells made a trip to America and arranged a visit with Roosevelt.
He was impressed by what he saw and believed that Roosevelt's administration
embodied the ideas presented in his earlier book *The Open Conspiracy*. In typical
Wells fashion he later wrote 'I do not say that the President has these revolutionary ideas in so elaborated and comprehensive a form as they have come to me'.[9]

Wells believed his social formula represented a superior approach to world
government and it needed to be understood by the world's leaders. A planned
economy was an important part of this formula and he believed that the new
leadership in Russia needed his help in understanding this. Later, in the same
year as his visit to America, Wells was off to Moscow with some of his colleagues
where he had arranged a visit with Stalin. The discussions he had with Stalin were
recorded by a secretary and Wells later published an edited version as *Stalin-Wells
Talk: The Verbatim Record*. It became clear to Wells that Stalin's vision of the
machinery required to power a socialist system was not the same as his, and that
Stalin's view of the bourgeoisie was less than condescending. What Wells didn't
know, of course, was that Stalin was in the process of planning a wholesale liqui-
dation of those he considered undesirable in his reformation of government.
Although Wells was never foolish enough to publicly suggest the use of a firing
squad to change the government, he certainly thought in those terms when he
penned his screenplay *Things to Come* in 1934. After years of patient writing and
preaching had produced no results, what better way to move things along than to
gas the populace into submission, and to give the gas the almost Orwellian name
'The Gas of Peace'.

Wells interview with Stalin did not go unnoticed by the British press. Nor did
Wells' opinions agree entirely with those of G.B. Shaw who had also been part of
the group that met with Stalin. The result was another public argument based on
the exchange of letters to newspaper editors. The letters contained a colorful,
original and forever entertaining collection of barbs, unkindly adjectives and
snobbish put-downs.

In 1936 Alexander Korda and his brother finished production of the film version of *Things to Come*. They had previously produced *The Man Who Could
Work Miracles* as a low budget film. Wells was becoming very enthusiastic about

the film world and made a trip to Hollywood where the editing and final production of *Things to Come* was being done. He met a long list of movie stars, including Charlie Chaplin who was a well known soviet sympathizer. He dined with producers and was flattered by starlets wherever he went. There is little doubt that he was enamored with Hollywood and could easily be persuaded to spend his time writing movie scripts rather than books. The ease with which his head could be turned was just a tiny indicator of his loss in direction.

Wells arranged a lease on new premises at 13 Hanover Terrace overlooking Regents Park. It provided him with convenient access to his London publishers and comfortable quarters for writing and entertaining. His work still included the occasional novel, although they were usually allegorical or carefully crafted satire. True to form he found time to attack old friends and acquaintances whenever he felt justified. The novel *Apropos of Dolores* was published reluctantly by Macmillan, since they feared possible repercussions from Odette Keun, one of Wells' old and intimate acquaintances whom he was now quite ready to pillory with his pen. In the three years prior to the start of the Second World War he produced *The Croquet Player, Star Begotten, Brynhild, The Camford Visitation,* and *The Brothers.* At the same time he continued his work for newspapers and ensured that his opinions were constantly in print.

He began to formulate his concept of a World Encyclopedia while keeping up with the rest of his writing. Although the concept was not a new one, Wells was convinced that it would provide the means to a uniform world wide educational system. Education was an issue that was dear to his heart and he believed it was one of the cornerstones to world peace and a stable global government. He published several articles on the subject and collected them, with other ideas in *The Idea of a World Encyclopedia,* and *World Brain.* Much of this writing remains interesting reading today and as noted in Chapter 22 it is a good example of how Wells could develop an idea and create its justification without ever producing a single fact or practical example. This ability is analogous to his enviable talent for creating adventurous fiction. In fact he worked his World Encyclopedia into a couple of his novels, which tended to place the concept in the same category as his other fictitious speculation. Taking him seriously when he came up with some of his more imaginative ideas was difficult, even for his most devoted readers. Today there are some that wonder whether or not his World Encyclopedia project may have been just a bit tongue-in-cheek.

When the Second World War erupted over Europe Wells was fast becoming a bitter and frustrated man. He was convinced that mankind, as a species, was rapidly becoming extinct and the only way to save the race was through world government. This resulted in lengthy treatises like *The Fate of Homo Sapiens* and *The New World Order*. Throughout the war he remained at his Hanover Terrace apartments and continued to write and publish under wartime restrictions. His message became repetitive. He was reworking the same old song over and over again with what seemed like less and less effect. *Guide to the New World* and *The Outlook for Homo Sapiens* continued his repetitive drubbing of old subjects to whomever would listen.

As the war raged in Europe he continued an effort to convince the world that nothing short of World Revolution would avoid mankind's imminent destruction. In 1945 he produced his last book entitled *Mind at the End of Its Tether*. It was published by Heinemann, the same publisher that had originally produced *The Time Machine,* the novel that had thrust him into public view. The new book was a continuation of his exposition on the extinction of mankind. It included a revision to the last section of his *A Short History of the World*. To Wells, the complete history of mankind would logically include a chapter on man's demise, and he was going to ensure that it was added to his work on history before he left the world.

How serious Wells was about the extinction of mankind is difficult to know. He never really explained exactly what he meant by extinction. Would man descend into the Stone Age with a complete collapse of the social system? Would the race truly die out completely, or would man kill off every member of the species through war and pestilence? Wells was certain it would happen, but that certainty may have been more akin to the religious fanatic waiting for the end of the world. He is not too sure how it will come, or when it will come, but it surely will come. Wells was indeed at the end of his tether. He knew that he had made little progress in convincing other people to believe in his ideas. His influence was dwindling and world politics were moving well past his ability to keep up with them.

Wells lived just long enough to see the end of the Second World War in Europe and the atom bomb dropped on Hiroshima. He died in August of 1946 at 80 years of age. Had he lived for another fifty years he might have learned that many of his ideas about social reform would never have worked and that war would be an ongoing occupation of man. It would change its shape and location every few years, but it would continue ad infinitum. Socialism would clearly be as corrupt and decadent as every other form of government and those practicing socialist states formed after the turn of the last century would collapse into rubble requiring another generation to rebuild them. However, Wells would never sit back in disbelief, admitting that he was wrong; he would simply change his tune to fit the circumstances and find a new harp to strum.

Wells was one of the most prolific writers in the English language. He wrote on a wide range of topics including educational textbooks, social tracts and world government. He excelled at story telling and produced both classical Victorian novels and memorable science fiction. He was in constant demand as a speaker and produced hundreds of pieces of editorial material and opinions for the London and American newspapers.

As we look back at his life from the early part of the twenty-first century Wells memory has faded substantially. New generations have appeared and they are faced with new problems that bear little resemblance to those of the previous century. Wells' ideas were not universal and they were not timeless. So it's logical that very few contemporary readers will be familiar with any of his work written after 1901. Today he is remembered by science fiction fans as the creator of *The Time Machine.* Perhaps a few movie buffs remember the *War of the Worlds* and *The Invisible Man.* This lack of recognition one hundred years after his early success is not just the result of passing time. In the years after *Anticipations* Wells became involved in many different activities and worked with a great many people on a great many different projects. His interest in producing timeless literature was not one of these projects. The following chapters will discuss some of the reasons why Wells stirred up animosity, offended many readers, and became little more than a drone spouting the same political speech to the same listeners over and over again.

3

H.G. Wells' Finest Hour

During the waning years of the 19th century Wells produced the novels and short stories that would endear him to his public for the rest of his life. Some of these early novels would remain popular long after his death and probably will continue to be popular well into the future. He matured quickly as a writer and his natural talent for creating and presenting a story came into full bloom before the turn of the century. Combining political controversy or popular sentiment with a literary adventure can often compromise the public reception of a novel but Wells was able to artistically wrap the two into an unforgettable package. This talent undoubtedly helped him in later years to spread his message and his ideas over much of the world.

Because the period between 1894 and 1901 was so important in Wells development as a writer it can easily be considered his finest hour. In fact this short period made both the man and the writer. This chapter will look more closely at his work and his personal life during this period since it was perhaps the most important time in his literary career. It only takes a glance at Appendices One and Two to see when his most recognizable work was produced. It doesn't stretch a point to suggest that all of the work that provides H.G. Wells with the recognition he retains today, was written during this early period. A twenty-first century straw poll among booksellers, the general public, and movie goers in the English speaking world might produce some surprising results. Booksellers should recognize perhaps a dozen of his early novels since there is still a small market among readers and collectors. The general public, on the other hand, will reflect disappointing results. When asked to name two or three novels written by H.G. Wells, very few will be able to produce a single title, let alone two or three. Those who can list more than one novel will often respond that Wells wrote *The Time Machine, The Island of Dr. Moreau*, and perhaps *The War of the Worlds*. When the question is reversed and the man on the street is asked to name the author of the novels that appear in this list, the response is perhaps more likely to be H.G.

Wells than another writer. Either way, the unfortunate truth is that few people are aware of Wells voluminous output, and even those that are aware probably cannot name more than a few of his titles beyond those named above.

The early short stories and novels that Wells produced were created in an era when literacy was expanding dramatically and the principal form of communication was through newspapers and periodicals. The improving economic situation combined with a new artistic enthusiasm that was developing at the end of the century was reflected throughout Europe and writers were quick to benefit from the demand for printed copy. In Wells' own words 'The last decade of the nineteenth century was an extraordinarily favourable time for new writers and my individual good luck was set in the luck of a whole generation of aspirants.'[1] After muddling through a number of things in his early life Wells saw the opportunity before him and picked it up. A little bit of practice and a few shillings in revenue provided the boost he needed to be off and running.

Wells married his first wife Isabel in 1891 and after three years of marriage their domestic situation became very tense. They were living on short funds and his intermittent health problems served only to interrupt the flow of income from his teaching duties. He discovered that he could supplement his teaching income by writing articles on a wide range of subjects for newspapers and the new weekly magazines that were becoming so popular. Occasionally he submitted short stories or humorous anecdotes, some of which were published under a pseudonym.

In 1895 Wells left Isabel and took up residence with Amy Catherine Robbins, one of his former biology students. His work writing literary and entertainment reviews was generating enough income to pay the guinea a week required for their rented London flat. He was asked by the *Pall Mall Budget*, a weekly news and features magazine, to write a series of short stories for which he would be paid five pounds per week. The first of these stories was *The Stolen Bacillus*, which remains today as one of the best known of his short stories. His enthusiasm for this kind of writing is evident in the number of stories he produced in the three years between 1894 and 1896. Wells quickly broadened his scope as soon as the demand was evident and he began writing short stories for other London serial publications and magazines.

Wells and Miss Robbins left London during the summer of 1895 and took temporary lodgings in Sevenoaks, a few miles south of London. Medical advice had indicated that his frequent health problems needed the benefit of rest and country air for a short period. He carried with him a good stock of work including a commission from editor and publisher W.E. Henley for a serialized story based on previous material entitled *The Time Traveler*, which in turn, was an expansion of *The Chronic Argonauts* that he had published in *The Science Schools Journal* while studying biology in Kensington. As noted in the previous chapter, this short story was the source of *The Time Machine*. The first installment of the serial was published in the January 1895 issue of Henley's new magazine called *The New Review*. Wells was paid one hundred pounds for the complete story. This was more money than his writing had ever earned previously. With further help from Henley, the story was published a few months later in book form by Heinemann.

While writing material for serial publications in London, Wells successfully made arrangements with John Lane to publish a small collection of anecdotes entitled *Select Conversations with an Uncle*. He was proud of this little book and it convinced him that it might be possible to earn a living as a writer. It contained twelve humorous anecdotes in the form of conversations with an anonymous uncle. This was his first collection of fiction. Only 650 copies were printed and it was not a big seller. It is now a rare collector's item and has generally been forgotten or overshadowed by his other work.

In January of 1895 Wells had taken a job with *Pall Mall Magazine* as a dramatic critic. The editor had promised him the first salaried position that became available on the magazine, and it happened to be the drama critic's position. Wells points out in his autobiography that this was the only 'regular job' that he ever had. This introduction to the theatre was a bit of a shock and he admits 'None of the criticism I wrote was ever anything but dull. I did not understand the theatre. I was out of my place there. I do not think I am made to understand the theatre...'[2] But the job had its long term benefits in exposing him to the work of playwrights like Henry James, Oscar Wilde and George Bernard Shaw. His lack of enthusiasm about writing critical reviews of dramatic entertainment eventually got the better of him and he resigned from the position after a few months.

Wells was already developing his determined work habits in 1895. As soon as he had established contacts with the publishing world he began work on another novel, *The Wonderful Visit,* which was published by J.M. Dent, a well known publishing house in London. His short stories were popular enough in weekly magazines that another publisher arranged to produce a collection entitled *The Stolen Bacillus and Other Incidents*. This is perhaps his best known book of short stories and is a fine illustration of his ability to spin highly imaginative yarns on a wide range of topics.

In the Fall of 1895 Wells and Jane moved to Woking in Surrey. They wanted to get out of London where they could spend more time outdoors and enjoy the country air. The bicycle had recently become a popular form of transportation.

There were no cars on the roads and the bicycle had evolved from a primitive novelty to the conventional two-wheeled tubular frame we know today. However, the development of brakes and gears would still require a number of years. The bicycle played a major role in his novel *The Wheels of Chance,* a story about a bicycling holiday in the south of England. This novel was published the next year in 1896. At the same time he had begun work on *The Island of Dr. Moreau.* This popular and enduring novel was published by Heinemann who had previously published *The Time Machine.*

As fast as Wells could produce new work it was being accepted for publication. His sales were encouraging enough that they began to produce a reliable source of income. Three more collections of short stories appeared in 1897 and he completed work on *The Invisible Man.* The success of his earlier work in producing serial publications for *Pearson's Magazine* spurred his creative talents and he reached an agreement with the editor to produce *The War of the Worlds* in serial form. Heinemann again published this work as a book the following year.

In 1898 Wells and Jane made a trip to Italy with their friend George Gissing and his wife. It was the first time that either Wells or Jane had been abroad. Gissing was a writer who lived a tragic life and died an early death. The two couples spent a month in Rome touring the city and its environs. Wells and Jane later proceeded to other parts of Italy on their own. When they returned to London they took up residence in Worcester Park. Here he began work on two more novels. *When the Sleeper Wakes* was published in 1899 along with another collection of short stories entitled *Tales of Space and Time.* The following year *Love and Mr. Lewisham* was published by Harper & Bros.

Wells and Jane frequently toured the countryside on bicycles while he worked on new writing projects. On one of their outings he became ill and was forced to rest at the home of Dr. Hicks and his family whom he had met through George Gissing. He never returned to their Worcester residence. Jane packed up their belongings while he was convalescing and found them new lodgings in a semi-detached home named Arnold House, at Sandgate on the south coast of England near Dover. By now Wells divorce from Isabel was complete and he was free to marry Jane. The move to Sandgate was thus a symbolic milestone in his life. Here he worked through the remainder of the nineteenth century. He had quickly evolved from a fledgling novelist to a well respected writer and journalist. Wells was now at the point in his life where he could look at his financial position with some confidence. He was earning a good living as a writer and could afford to lease larger quarters or take a holiday to escape the world of manuscripts and deadlines. Wells was very aware of his commercial properties by this time and was using them to the best of his ability. 'My commercialism is not, I think, innate, but my fight with the world for Jane and myself and my family, had set a premium on money making. I was beginning to like the sport. I was beginning to enjoy being able to pay for things. I was getting rather keen on my literary reputation as a saleable asset.'[3]

His commercial efforts were paying off in 'spades'. By 1899 he had accumulated enough money to begin construction on a large house at Sandgate and still hold a surplus of 1000 pounds sterling. At the time 1000 pounds was easily a years' income for a well heeled London businessman. Their new house was named Spade House (for unusual reasons) and was home to his family for over ten years. Wells was pleased with himself. His health was improving and the thought of settling down in a new home with his wife and first child was very appealing. 'I became a Borough magistrate and stability and respectability loomed straight ahead of us.'[4] While the work of supervising the construction of his new home was in progress Wells was working on *The First Men in the Moon* which was published in 1901. The same year he produced a significant piece of work for the *Fortnightly Review*. It was published by Chapman & Hall as *Anticipations of Mechanical and Scientific Progress upon Human Life and Thought*. This three hundred page book was his first work of non-fiction and was to become a major work of future expectations. Prophesy had become a byword of the new century and Wells intended to play his part in the adventure of the future.

It's not difficult to see how much Wells had accomplished in the brief space of seven years between 1894 and 1901. In his autobiography he considered himself 'Fairly Launched at Last'. From this point he began to look at what he considered some serious work, and was confident that his improving health would now allow him the time to write at a more leisurely pace. His poor health was perhaps one of the primary reasons for his desire, and his ability, to work at a furious pace producing from one to three books a year, year after year. His writing career spanned a period of about fifty years between 1895 and 1945. During this time he published dozens of novels, collected essays and speeches, and hundreds of newspaper articles. Although much of his work was highly repetitious, and a number of his books were little more than pamphlets, the continuous flow of material from his pen has seldom been equaled.

Many biographers and literary critics have looked at the large collection of Wells' work and have given it less than rave reviews. There are a number of reasons for this lack of enthusiasm by some critics ranging from political differences to simple disagreements about the literary value of his writing. In truth Wells inability to gain a place in the hallowed halls of English literature is probably because he is treated more as a prolific journalist with a lot of strange and often unrealistic ideas.

But that is not to say that he didn't produce memorable work. Perhaps one of the most interesting facts about Wells' work is that the material that remains popular in the twenty-first century all comes from the same period in his life. It's well accepted that he matured quickly as a writer and produced some monumental writing after 1901, including novels like *Tono Bungay*, and non-fiction work like *The Outline of History*. In fact many academics will profess that his finest writing was done well after the turn of the twentieth century. However, this is not the work that is remembered today. In fact many students of Wells' work including present day scientists and writers will admit that their first exposure to H.G. Wells was through his science fiction. Noted Wells biographer Bernard Bergonzi makes an important comment about Wells' work after 1901. 'In that year Wells published The First Men in the Moon, which I consider his last genuine novel-length romance, and Anticipations, his first major non-fictional work, where we see him ceasing to be an artist and beginning his long career as a publicist and pamphleteer.'[5]

It's not difficult to find a few simple adjectives to describe his early work. It was imaginative, adventurous, romantic, brilliant, and memorable, and there were perhaps countless other things that endeared the work to its readers. The work he produced in this short period was also a product of the times. Wells was young and adventurous, and he badly needed a way to make a living. He had married early and was forced by circumstance to learn a craft very quickly. Newspapers and periodicals; were demanding new novelists, short story writers and topical journalists. Wells quickly found that he could 'dash off' a short story, and produce a return of five pounds sterling. This produced enough to cover room and board for a month and leave some over for the tailor and entertainment. He was soon in the position of being able to talk to editors and become involved in larger projects. Although life was a struggle for much of this period he slid easily into the role that allowed him to produce *The Time Machine*.

During Wells' early years writing short stories was an enjoyment and they often represented ideas that he would later expand into a novel or screenplay. The market for short stories and essays was immense and the best writers of the time were generating copious amounts of written material for periodicals. At various times Wells was writing for *Pall Mall Magazine*, *Pall Mall Budget*, *The Pall Mall Gazette* (the Astor empire), *The Strand Magazine*, *Pearson's Magazine*, *The*

National Observer, The Saturday Review, Vanity Fair, Fortnightly Review, The New Review, and others. Periodicals came and went. They changed editors often and competed strongly with each other for readers. They sold alongside the daily newspapers and produced the fodder demanded by a public that was now highly literate and absorbing entertainment in a world without radio, television, automobiles, airplanes, movies or other twenty-first century innovations and distractions. Appendix Two is a list of most of the short stories Wells published during his lifetime. It's clear that after 1901 his short story output declined abruptly. In many respects this is a terrible disappointment to his contemporary readers. They will never know what additional work could have emerged from such a fertile and imaginative mind. Instead, that mind went off into other less productive and often questionable pursuits.

Jules Verne preceded Wells in the world of imagination and *fantastic romance* and Wells had read translations of Verne's work. The end of the nineteenth century was demanding adventurous fiction as a form of entertainment and Jules Verne was every bit as good at the art as Wells. Almost certainly Wells gained a few ideas and much enthusiasm from Verne's work. Verne was older than Wells and had already established the significance of scientific and engineering accomplishments in works of fiction. Wells' work, as opposed to Verne's, was often considered as much folklore as it was scientifically based fiction. Wells has often been called 'The Father of Science Fiction' but there are masses of Jules Verne fans that would take great exception to this title. However, this was a new literary genre and the field was vast and uncluttered. New writers were welcome and they were absorbed quickly by the marketplace. A case in point is Arthur Conan Doyle who competed for print space right alongside Wells and delivered imaginative science fiction by any standards. It is perhaps as regrettable that Conan Doyle is know today only for his *Sherlock Holmes* novels as it is regrettable that Wells is known only for *The Time Machine*.

Wells impact on the world of English literature will probably be felt for several more generations, but only because of the work he produced in his *finest hour*. Contemporary science fiction writers regularly generate a continuous flow of highly imaginative work, but none are likely produce more original and memorable work than H.G. Wells produced between 1894 and 1901. Had he not been so successful in such a short period of time he may not have turned to other types of writing. Bernard Bergonzi aptly states what is often thought of Wells later work. 'Wells, at the beginning of his career, was a genuine and original imaginative artist, who wrote several books of considerable literary importance, before dissipating his talents in directions which now seem more or less irrelevant.'[6]

Were his talents dissipated? Was his later work more or less irrelevant? Sadly this statement is probably true and with the exception of a few gems that emerged from his pen in later years, H.G. Wells was a flash in the pan and never regained the brilliance of his early years. Like striking a match, his fire would die almost as quickly as it flared up. After forty years he would look back and express dissatisfaction over his accomplishments. This dissatisfaction was not over his writing, but over what he considered his inability to teach the world how to survive.

Wells had his ego stroked too often for him not to believe that he was anything but a great writer, a prophet, and a leading social reformer. It took many years before he understood that, although he had become a highly visible figure, very few people beyond his socialist colleagues were paying much attention to him. In the next few chapters it will become more obvious why he gained notoriety, rather than respect, as a writer and why most of this notoriety disappeared within a few years of his death.

4

Le Fin de Siecle

It is difficult to look at the historical period between 1850 and 1950 without bumping into Le Fin de Siecle (The End of the Century), especially if the literary climate of the era is being considered. Shortly after the Germans left Paris at the end of the Franco-Prussian War of 1871 a new era of radicalism in the arts was born. Literature, painting, architecture and the theatre gained a new and often decadent complexion. Thus was born the Avant Garde in Paris that would soon manifest itself as fin de siecle. The term was again applied loosely at the end of the next century when the world marched apprehensively through the year 2000. However, in spite of the comparisons, the reluctant leap into the twenty-first century was nothing like the grand rush from the nineteenth century into the twentieth century.

In France this was a time when everyone had read Victor Hugo and his influence on French literature at the end of the century was substantial. New writers like Guy de Maupassant and Stephen Mallarme began to flourish. Arthur Rimbaud, the poet with a dark and brooding personality had just published *A Season in Hell.* Thereafter he left his wife for the company of a man who subsequently died of a drug overdose. This was considered to be a rather chic way for an artist to live and die in the 1890's.

The German influence at the time was epitomized by Friedrich Neitzsche who was considered one of the era's most dominant intellectual figures. His work was being translated into English and the impact of his book *Thus Spake Zarathustra* was not only felt at the dawn of the twentieth century, but it surfaced again with Arthur C. Clarke's and Stanley Kubrick's projection of Zarathustra into the far future of science fiction. Neitzsche also invented the *Ubermensch* or Overman. This foreshadowed the coming of everything from Nazism to the concepts of eugenics and the elite ruling classes of Wells' socialist utopias. The seeds of art, literature, politics and social philosophy pushed deep roots back into the nineteenth century.

Contemporaneously the French judicial system became immersed in the Dreyfus affair. This was the saga of the French army officer, Alfred Dreyfus, who was falsely accused of spying for the Germans and sent to Devil's Island. In 1898 Emile Zola who wrote an open letter to the courts entitled *J'accuse* citing the terrifying injustices of the French judiciary. The Dreyfus case was reopened and the courts set him free. At the same time and place, was the birth of the Pantomime and Art Nouveau. Hector Guimard and Victor Horta were the architects that created the new fluid style that not only set standards for the wold of architecture but permeated art and design for years to come. Art Nouveau was originally considered anti-establishment and a bit shocking to a world that grew up with Gothic Cathedrals and highly ornamented rectangular stone apartment blocks and business edifices.

The fin de siecle movement in France was gone within a few years after the turn of the century, but its mark remained on art, literature and design for decades. In testament to its impact, most of the English speaking world still uses many of the original French terms and phrases of the era. A century later, throughout Europe and North America, we can still see the architecture born during fin de siecle. It is a great misfortune that these French language extracts have been so encased in their English meaning that few people are even aware of their origins. Bernard Bergonzi has said that 'In its widest sense fin de siecle was simply the expression of a prevalent mood: the feeling that the nineteenth century—which had contained more events, more history than any other—had gone on too long, and that sensitive souls were growing weary of it.'[1]

The impact of this period in art and literature could not help but be felt in England, on the other side of 'la Manche', the channel that the French could never bring themselves to call 'English'. This was particularly true for H.G. Wells who not only read the work of French writers but spent many of his holidays in France. He eventually built a vacation home in southern France at Grasse where he entertained friends of all types and persuasions, usually without the company of his family.

Opportunity for writers in England was everywhere. The explosion of commerce, rail systems, manufacturing and global investments produced an emerging middle class of educated and trained tradesmen. The Boer War was in progress and The Great Empire stretched around the world. Like everyone else, Wells began to think about the future. The questions asked by writers and the reading public were often about the prospects and appearance of the next century. The twentieth century!

Wells responded to his own futuristic enthusiasm with his novel *When the Sleeper Wakes: A Story of the Years to Come*, published in 1899. This is a science fiction novel, or in Wells words, '...a story of the future...' in which he creates a character named Graham who is awakened from a deep sleep some 200 years hence. This is one of Wells' more practical novels of the future wherein he describes many of the engineering, design, and construction accomplishments his hero sees after his awakening. In spite of the novel's appeal to some futurists, Wells stated that he was never very satisfied with the book and he had it republished in 1910 with substantial changes under the title *The Sleeper Awakes*. Interestingly, the illustrator who prepared drawings for the first edition of *When the Sleeper Wakes* clearly thinks that the architectural features of cities in the twenty-first century will draw heavily on the round buildings and circular tower concepts of Art Nouveau design. The spiritual fire of the Industrial Revolution was still upon the minds of the public at the turn of the century and its effect was not lost on H.G. Wells. *The Sleeper Awakes* is in stark contrast to his later novels where the physical world of the future that surrounds his protagonist gets short shrift, and the politics of utopian socialism take over.

This period at the end of the nineteenth century was also a time of prophesy. Not only were writers telling stories of imagination and accomplishment, but they were producing opinions and non-fiction work about their visions of the future. As noted in Chapter 28, Wells states in the fourth volume of the Atlantic Edition of his work, '...and stimulated perhaps by the fact that everyone about him was summing up the events of the past hundred years, the writer set himself, with such equipment as he possessed, to work out the probabilities of contemporary tendencies as thoroughly as possible...'[2] Thus was born *Anticipations*, one of Wells' favorite and most successful efforts at prophesy. In his mind, this was a fitting cap to the end of the century and a logical road into the next one.

The concepts of fin de siecle were not governing factors in controlling the shape of Wells' novels or in shaping his political ideas, but they were certainly underlying currents that subtly bumped him in one direction or another. Throughout the last half of his life and for decades after his death Wells was considered a prophet. Had he been born 50 years earlier, or 50 years later, he probably would never have gone in this direction. Wells was also an expert at writing short stories and he published dozens of them at the turn of the century. At any other time in history, there would have been little market for short stories since neither the media nor the readers would have existed. Similarly, at any other time the educational system would not have been available to Wells. Prior to 1880 there would have been few scholarships for students of his background, and the world of biological sciences that fascinated him had not yet experienced the revolution created by Darwin and Huxley. After this time the educational system would have establish schools in Bromley that would ensure that he never left the suburbs for London. The end of the century was the time of H.G. Wells. He saw the changes, he agreed with the changes, and he picked up on the changes. Prophesy, looking and thinking ahead, thoughts of the future, new social concepts, and above all a more sophisticated and mature political system were all to grow out of fin de siecle, and Wells would help to see that it happened.

These were the times that shaped Wells early writing, the things that helped him develop his ideas and the things that consistently changed the way he thought about political and social events. Once he was well established as a writer he had the resources and the freedom to pursue issues that were not always popular or productive. In the following chapters some of these issues will be addressed by looking at his work and tracing his ideas through many novels and non-fiction publications.

PART II

His Fall Into Socialism

5

Changing Direction

Wells didn't make an instant left turn at the end of the century and suddenly begin expressing his ideas on new and more controversial topics. While he was writing his most memorable novels and short stories at the end of the nineteenth century, he was also generating a supply of articles for newspapers and periodicals. These articles provided a substantial part of his income for several years, and for the most part he was allowed to write as he pleased as long as he filled the assigned commission. In London he appeared routinely in *The Fortnightly Review*. The *Cosmopolitan* magazine in New York was another lucrative source of revenue on the other side of the Atlantic. The topics of these articles were usually political, and in many cases controversial, issues that were being aired frequently at the beginning of the new century.

Wells claimed to have received large volumes of laudatory correspondence from readers of his articles. This prompted him to correct and revise a number of them for publication in book form. The result was *Mankind in the Making*, published by Chapman and Hall in 1903. Collections of previously published newspaper and magazine articles were to become a common book format for Wells. He retained copyright to most of his periodical work and selected those articles that he considered topical and those that best illustrated his current thinking. In *Mankind in the Making*, his first major effort at publishing a collection of previously printed material, he chose eleven articles from *The Fortnightly Review* and prepared two new appendices. The purpose of the articles and the reason for their choice is outlined by Wells in a preface he prepared for the book.

Wells' first non-fiction work after the turn of the century was *Anticipations*, published in 1901. It was an effort to predict the future of the new twentieth century without too much emphasis on the political aspects of the changing scenery. *Mankind in the Making* was his first social and political non-fiction work and it bears many of the hallmarks that would appear in Wells' work throughout the rest of his career. Firstly, he considers this work '…an attempt to deal with social and political questions in a new way and from a new starting point…'[1] This is one of the first places in Wells' writing where we can begin to suspect the veracity of his vision. It probably never entered his mind that his book really did not have any new ideas and was simply a rehash of old socialist concepts and political controversies. Wells was still too low on the journalistic horizon to attract the attention of those best qualified to point out his lack of originality. Secondly, he politely informs the reader that he is unqualified to be doing what he is doing. 'He is remarkably not qualified to assume an authoritative tone in these matters and he is acutely aware of the many defects in detailed knowledge, in temper, and in training these papers collectively display.'[2] Wells then hastily proceeds to explain to the reader that he can view social and political issues 'in a new way' because he possesses a freshness that is uncharacteristic of an experienced specialist. And thirdly he assures the reader of his scientific bona fides by pointing out that he is '…a man who knows a little of biology, a little of physical science, and a little in a practical way of social stratification…'[3] This attempt at some measure of scientific justification will appear over and over in his writing, even though he never pursued advanced scientific studies and at no time in his life did he ever practice in any field of science or engineering.

In *Mankind in the Making* Wells has selected newspaper columns that cover a broad range of issues, including education, the concept of a common language, the physical makeup of mankind, and the organization of political and legal systems. These were becoming pet topics for Wells as his audience expanded and they were controversial enough to be addressed individually in later chapters of this work. Perhaps the first article in the book, entitled *The New Republic,* best represents the flavor of his thinking and his reasons for preparing the book. Although he talks around the topic for many pages, Wells seems to be trying to convince the reader that the New Republican is one who believes in a continuous rebirth of religion, politics, social relationships, and in changes to long established ideas. This thinking was common to many writers in several languages as the new century dawned on Europe. It was Wells' ability to put these ideas of rebirth into words that provided him with an audience, not any unique concepts or new developments.

As noted in the previous chapter, Wells' vision of newness fits with the image of fin de siecle, a new generation, new politics, and even a new and better homo sapiens, the product of a new and better birth. Each succeeding generation assumes new responsibilities, including the production of a new generation markedly better than the last. All old things like tradition and obsolete customs must be abandoned or replaced, especially institutions as backward and decadent as the Monarchy. Even national loyalties, patriotism, and local party adhesions are less than productive. 'I do not see how men, save in the most unexpected emergency, can be content to accept such an artificial convention as modern patriotism for one moment.'[4] Wells will write many future books that try to convince readers of the futility of nationalistic concepts. He could justify the notion to himself by seeing it as a solution to conflict, and a way of bringing people all over the world into a more uniform system of education and commerce. Wells seems to have abandoned everything he learned in his 'scientific training' about the nature of man. It would only have taken a glance from a different vantage point to understand that tribalism is a fundamental characteristic of mankind. No matter how futile Wells thought nationalism might be, from small tribes to vast nations, it would not go away in the new century, and is not likely to go away in centuries to come. However, any attempt to convince Wells otherwise would only have met with animosity rather than the enlightened argument he professed to enjoy.

His *New Republic* was a product of his youth, a product of the new century, and a product of his search for something new and dramatic to say. The balance of *Mankind in the Making* is devoted to justifying one or more aspects of his New Republican philosophy. In some places it gets a bit frightening to the contemporary reader, but a century ago things like socialist states, utopia, eugenics, rewriting history and state controlled educational systems were fodder for journalistic machines.

Wells closes his book with a chapter entitled *Thought in the Modern State*. After presenting a number of arguments about improvement of the population, about changing the education and aspirations of a new generation, he wraps things up with a general outline of how people should think in the new and modern state. In particular the literature available to the public should be critically assessed by a review board. This will save the public from its inability '…to judge any new literary thing or to protect itself in any way from violently and vulgarly boomed rubbish of the tawdriest description.'[5] The reader is then treated to a long and detailed description of the quality of art and literature and the questionable value of classical literature.

To Wells' credit he continually emphasizes the importance of education in his New Republic, although he is unfamiliar enough with the history of education to understand that the better informed a population becomes, the less likely they are to tow the line of a socialist state. Although academic institutions were, and still are, centers of New Republican thinking, the general public, or the New Republican proletariat, will respond to academic elitists only for a short period of time.

When this new proletariat sees the shaky foundations of their elitist leadership they become factious and often go in many separate directions with little fore-warning. The result is a collapse of the very foundations of the socialist state. What is most upsetting to Wells and his fellow socialists is that the most durable and long lasting systems of government in history have been the well established monarchies. Not dictatorships, not democratic republics with their elected presidents and legislators, not military despots, but dynastic monarchies with vision, education and a fundamental desire to biblically 'lead their people forth'.

6

The Fabian Society

The Fabian Society is a peculiarly British type of organization. It was formed in 1884 by a small group of left leaning socialists including George Bernard Shaw, Sydney and Beatrice Webb, Graham Wallas and a number of their friends and political colleagues. The Society took its name from the Roman general Fabius Cunctator whose patience in dealing with the invasion by Hannibal only resulted in a military stalemate. It remained for another general to take the war to Hannibal and drive him out of the country. The founders of the Fabian Society considered themselves the intellectual elite of the London social scene at the end of the nineteenth century. By the standards of the time it's probably true that they were both intellectual and elite. They busied themselves in writing tracts and giving lectures about a new social system that would rid Great Britain, and ultimately the world, of its inequities and inefficiencies. As often happens in circles across the political spectrum, those who have a need to govern will make the rules and the great public masses must fall into line. In the case of the Fabians they lauded many ideas ranging from those slightly left of center, to those extreme and overtly socialist scenarios with government ownership of all private property, utilities, institutions and industries. According to one of Wells' biographers they '...substituted the State for God as the means by which they were to live, move and have their being.'[1]

Socialist ideas were becoming more popular in Great Britain around the turn of the century. The class system often made it impossible for large segments of the population to gain an education, or to avail themselves of any public services and facilities. The expansion of the British Empire and the aloofness of the monarchy did not seem to help matters. Those who were stuck at home, chained to the land, or born downstairs saw little chance to break out. The introduction of Fabian idealism into the social and political life of the lower class British citizen was a refreshing change. The Independent Labour Party was born in this same environment and was supported by the Fabians as a practical solution to changing the government.

After nearly 20 years the Society began to lose much of its aim and conviction. The political goals of the Society seemed to be more influenced by the dinner parties arranged by Sydney and Beatrice Webb than by the activities of the membership. G.B. Shaw was an astute thinker and an exceptionally perceptive organizer. He saw the gap between the Society and its outside audience widening and knew that something was needed to restore the fire in the organization.

Into the gap stepped H.G. Wells. He and G.B. Shaw had been friends for some time and Shaw was willing to sponsor him for membership. In February of 1903 Wells became a member of the Fabian Society. Thus began an interesting period in Fabian history characterized by the two prominent and vocal personalities, Wells and Shaw, using each other to further their own ends. Shaw was casting about for something to inject a greater interest and vitality into the Fabian Society. Wells saw a way to gain a public platform for his socialist philosophy and the Fabians represented the intellectual elite that he saw in his New Republic. Wells had already shown both his flair as a writer and his political colors in his books *Anticipations* and *Mankind in the Making*. However, he had demonstrated in his newspaper writing '…his distaste for trade unionism, and his ignorance of the realities of industrial life…'[2] This effectively reduced the number of communication vehicles he had to promote his brand of socialism since labor unions, at this point in his career, were loath to support him. In the Fabians he saw an opportunity to promote some of his ideas and to put them into practice with the support of an elite group of intellectuals. The match between Shaw and Wells seemed timely and appropriate.

Wells poor performance as a speaker and his inexperience in working with organizations did not help get him off to a good start. He was not a particularly dashing public figure. He spoke with a falsetto voice and was erratic in his presentation. He disagreed regularly with others and was easily miffed when his ideas were ignored. In March of 1904 he disagreed with a Society tract on free trade and tendered his resignation in the Fabian Society. He was chastised by other members for his inability to accept any ideas that weren't his own. In particular Shaw wrote to him saying '…I believe you are so spoiled by living in a world of your own invention, peopled by your own puppets, that you have become incapable of tolerating the activity or opinions or even the phrases of other individuals…'[3]. After Shaw and the Webbs had met with him and had convinced him of his value to the Society, Wells withdrew his resignation and returned to the work of developing his own political and social ideas for governing the world.

During the early years of the 19th century Wells writing was ～～～～ ～～ ～ ～～～～ found popularity. His books were being widely read, newspaper editors were requesting his articles and statements, and political allies and foes alike would stop and listen when he spoke. There can be little doubt that this notoriety went to Wells' head and was largely responsible for the arrogance noted by so many of his friends. He was not yet 40 years old when he joined the Fabians and had come a long way for a boy from the High Street in Bromley. It was natural that his work with the Fabians would be closely entwined with his socialist views and his writing. If anything, his ideas had a certain radical appeal to the reading public who responded enthusiastically to anyone who was prepared to stir up the status quo. It was Wells' daring more than his courage that kept him pushing the limits of his utopian views

His writing soon begins to show embellishment by some of his more controversial ideas such as his attitudes towards women and marriage, his belief in eugenics and some of his antagonistic views about religion. Wells also was beginning to promote the concept of an elite Samurai to act as the governing body of the utopian state. Perhaps some of his most terrifying propaganda comes in the form of his World State '...that maintains a central index system in Paris which keeps track of every person in the world...[and]...is directed towards the improvement of the race.'[4] He also believes that the ordinary citizens (who are to be ruled by this improved race) '...should be less constrained—on condition that they breed only according to the rules.'[5] Often he would attempt to change the interpretation of his statements in later publications, and in later years his more extreme ideas mellowed substantially. Regardless of changes in his method of expression, many of his beliefs in world government, eugenics, and total state control, remained with him throughout his life.

Some of these dramatic changes in ideas and attitudes did not escape the notice of his reading public, his friends, and certainly not his critics. His artful writing was beginning to show signs of strain. In particular he was losing his magnificent ability to build characters in novels and to present colorful situations that convinced readers they were virtually present in the story. If he was not losing his descriptive abilities, then he was setting them aside for what he thought was a more important issue. His writing suffered. Wells '...felt compelled to talk at his readers through his characters rather than to allow them the room they need to emerge as personalities.'[6]

Nevertheless, Wells popularity as a writer and speaker showed little sign of diminishing. He was emboldened by his notoriety and in December of 1905 he confided in Leslie Haden Guest, one of his colleagues, that he would be '…having a go at the Fabians…to make things hum in a business-like way.'[7] Indeed he did start a tempest by asking the Society executive to set up a committee to review the organization's finances and activities. The executive reluctantly agreed on the assumption that Wells might produce some welcome reforms, and if he didn't the failure would reflect only on Wells himself.

Wells attacked the old guard with a vengeance and made himself extremely unpopular with the Society executive in the process. Shaw, again, chastised Wells for his lack of amiable behavior. Beatrice Webb noted in her diary that Wells '…showed an odd mixture of underhand manoeuvers and insolent bluster when his manoeuvers were not successful…' She later wrote that Wells has '…grown in self-confidence, if not conceit as to his capacity to settle all social and economic questions in general, and to run the Fabian Society in particular…' However he did claim a large amount of support from the rank and file membership. He published a tract entitled *The Faults of the Fabian* and attempted to use it as a draft proposal for reform of the Society. He was planning to leave on a two-month lecture tour in the United States and wanted to establish his views to avoid being preempted during his absence. The Society executive, however, would have none of it and Wells headed across the Atlantic on March 27th, 1906 knowing he would have to pick up the sword again on his return.

In the Fall of 1906 Wells delivered a speech to the Fabians on the subject of socialism and the middle classes which he later published. It established many of his ideas on how much involvement the state ought to have in the family and the daily life of the middle classes. The London press picked up on his discourse by pointing out a number of apparent contradictions or 'changes of convenience' in his speech. At the same time Wells new novel *In the Days of the Comet* was nearly a total failure at the book shops. He did not like criticism and he did not understand that one of his books could be a flop when he had become so well established as a writer. It was in this atmosphere that Wells and his group of revisionists delivered their report to the executive of the Fabians. It was presented simultaneously with a report from the old guard that sat on the executive. Wells was proposing changes in the society all the way from a new name and new premises to a complete organizational change. It was a bad move from a political perspective and some last minute maneuvering by Shaw robbed Wells of many of his followers and placed him in a position where he could not win a vote between his followers and the stodgy old executive.

Wells backed down and quietly removed himself to a corner where he continued to exhibit the self-righteous attitude implied by Beatrice Webb. Wells was not a good loser. The affair demonstrated at least two basic failings that would dog him for most of his life. First, he was an amateur when it came to maneuvering into position and presenting his ideas. Shaw was able to dance around Wells, easily lead him into a trap, and then let him make a fool of himself. Secondly, Wells exhibited the worst of bad manners by ignoring etiquette, throwing unkind remarks at friends and enemies alike, and figuratively stamping his feet when confronted or defeated. Wells was not drummed out of the Fabian Society, nor did he resign in a huff. He maintained a low profile for a number of years and looked for other avenues to promote his brand of socialism. But he would remember this short period of conflict for the rest of his life. It was his first experience in working within a formally constituted organization and his first real public defeat. He learned how little he liked to play by rules established by others, and just as important, he was beginning to learn that others were not always going to listen to him.

The Fabian Society still exists today, after more than 120 years of activity. If nothing else, they are tenacious and prepared to change with the times to meet the demands of new ideas in socialism. They bill themselves as an organization that is '…slightly left of center…' which, in the best political tradition, avoids frightening potentially new members but maintains their credentials. In contemporary literature they also claim to be '…affiliated with the Labour Party but editorially independent…'[8] It remains for the Fabians to demonstrate that this is not a contradiction in objectives.

The Fabians claim both Wells and Shaw as 'founding' members. Although that stretches a point in regard to Wells, it is certainly true of Shaw. Both Wells and Shaw are now long gone and their memory is fading, especially with respect to their Fabian activities. When they are remembered outside the United Kingdom, Shaw is usually associated with the theatre and H.G. Wells is equated to *The Time Machine*. The Fabian Society is virtually unknown outside the United Kingdom, and those who are familiar with its activities are universally left of center in their political leanings. Much like Wells himself, the Fabians can change chameleon-like to suit the current political climate. When socialism is out of favor, they are simply left of center. When socialism is in vogue, they are the center of the western world's social conscience.

7

Downstairs Misery

When Wells joined the Fabian Society in 1903, they were a strictly socialist organization that used books, pamphlets, lectures and other means of communication to spread their version of the socialist ideal. During his membership he had a number of arguments with Fabians over the meaning and direction of socialism in Britain. He made himself particularly unpopular with George Bernard Shaw and with Sydney and Beatrice Webb, some of London's best known social figures. When Wells joined the Fabians he fully believed that he could reform the stodgy old organization but as we've seen in the previous chapter, his efforts were largely unsuccessful. He was repeatedly out maneuvered by political minds much brighter than his and he eventually resigned his membership in September of 1908 under less than amicable circumstances.

The merits of the Fabian Society, questionable or otherwise, are fodder for a different cannon. However, one piece of Wells writing during his membership in the Society is of substantial interest. In December of 1905 he published a tract in the *Independent Review* entitled *This Misery of Boots*. It was reprinted with some alteration by the Fabian Society in 1907 as a small 48 page pamphlet in a plain green paper cover designed for distribution to its members. A black and red title plate was pasted on the cover. Five pages of Fabian advertising were included in the back of the booklet[1].

In spite of its small size this publication represents an important stage in Wells political thinking. It clearly illustrates the development of his hatred of the British aristocracy and his resentment of anything successful, especially businessmen and capitalists. Firstly, he presents his case for socialism by illustrating the inequities among the various classes of people living in Great Britain at the turn of the twentieth century. The title of the tract reaches back into his youth when he lived with his parents below their china shop in Bromley, south of London. Wells was able to watch the pedestrian traffic on the street from the family's below-ground residence by looking up through a grating on the sidewalk. The quality and condition of the shoes worn by different pedestrians became the talisman around which Wells developed his thesis of class inequity. He implored the reader to '...keep in your mind, if you can, some sort of talisman to bring you back to that essential gospel, out of the confusions and warring suggestions of every-day discussion.'[2] He then devotes an entire chapter of this little pamphlet to his explanation of how and why the wealthy ride on the backs of the poor.

Wells' belief that the rich are evil and the poor are the deserving masses is a very real one. He is clear in stating that the under classes are justified in taking all private property from the wealthy and turning it over to the state to be used, not for profit, but for service. He proposes that '...the State should take away the land, the railways, and shipping, and many great organised enterprises from their owners, who use them simply to squeeze the means for a wasteful private expenditure out of the common mass of men, and should administer, all these things generously and boldly, not for profit, but for service.'[3] It never entered Wells' mind after rising from his basement hovel, that he might now be one of the organized enterprises, or that he might be involved in wasteful private expenditure. Pompous political pundits of all generations are commonly plagued with undeniable hypocrisy, and Wells was no exception.

At no point in his discussion does Wells allow that his proposed socialist state might be even less capable of managing property for service, or for that matter, managing property for any purpose, than the capitalists he mercilessly flogs. If he had looked around himself, even at the time he wrote *This Misery of Boots*, he could have found examples of socialist states that had accomplished little more than the total destruction of utilities, transportation systems, and productive agricultural institutions. Had he been alive at the end of the twentieth century he would have seen even more persuasive examples of the socialist ideal being corrupted by the incompetence of greedy reformers who stooped even lower than Wells' own despised landowners and capitalist exploiters. Further, he would have seen wealth and privilege dealt to political cronies rather than the masses that were supposed to be the beneficiaries of the great social redistribution.

Wells was so convinced that the abolition of private property was the answer to the social evils of the world that he truly lost sight of the principles he was supposed to be advocating. He is categorical in stating that the elimination of personal ownership would result in a new and better society. 'That, and no less, is the aim of all sincere Socialists: the establishment of a new and better order of society by the abolition of private property in land, in natural productions, and in their exploitation—a change as profound as the abolition of private property in slaves would have been in ancient Rome or Athens.'[4] In using the term 'private property' Wells goes beyond the issue of simple land ownership to include any type of business development or exploitation. In effect this thesis maintains that the entire foundation of western civilization over the last two centuries has been all wrong. He maintains that business, finance, insurance, shipping and manufacturing industries that built empires in the eighteenth an nineteenth centuries should really be in the hands of the socialist despots that destroyed nations and started the bloody revolutions that would be remembered throughout history.

Naturally Wells expects most greedy capitalists to object to the expropriation of their property, and he has a ready-made answer for them. The answer is not based on the experience of discussion with capitalists, or on the evidence of statistics, or even popular press coverage. Rather, he simply puts words in the mouth of a hypothetical capitalist by saying that 'He would probably either embark upon a long rigmarole, or, what is much more probable, lose his temper and decline to argue.'[5] For one as insightful as Wells usually is, this is a particularly poor and immature rebuttal to what he assumes might be the objections to socialism.

Just as short sighted is Wells' attempt to describe a practical example of exploitation. He cites the capitalists who control private enterprise, and as part of their business they obtain leather from abroad to make the boots of the underprivileged masses. He continues by neatly bringing the rest of the world into his sphere of indignation by importing the leather from South America. Along the way the leather is processed, shipped, distributed and made into boots by enterprises that ride on the backs of the poor. Although the shape of industry is now much different from that of the late nineteenth century, it was true then, as now, that private enterprise provided the greater volume of employment, and certainly the most financially rewarding employment, for the world's labor force. Naturally Wells must assume that the State could do substantially better than private industry and corrupt capitalists, or the basic premise of socialism would begin to fray.

Wells insists that most, if not all, real property and industry is privately owned. 'And your workers all round you, you find, cannot get house room until they too have paid rent—every inch of the country is somebody's property, and a man may not shut his eyes without the consent of some owner or other.'[6] He sees no merit in this situation. But he fails to provide, at least in this tract, any logical method for accomplishing his aims, or for ensuring that his socialist ideals will actually be achieved by confiscation of private property. Historically this has been one of the downfalls of socialist revolutions. In the end, when put into practical terms, the new order often destroys more than it creates or remedies.

By 1905 Wells was a reasonably successful writer and was earning a substantial income from his work. This put him in a position where he had to defend himself from criticism, real or imagined, about the accumulation of wealth and property, in conflict with the ideals of socialism. This is a potential source of guilt among wealthy leftists who have inherited or created enough wealth to do just about anything they please. Only greedy capitalists are supposed to accumulate wealth, and when they do, it is on the backs of the poor, and their wealth must inevitably be used to exploit people and resources. There are many wealthy socialists in the world and they commonly lean towards hypocrisy in justification of their own wealth and substantial property ownership.

Wells uses a particularly empty, and almost amateur, justification of his own wealthy position by explaining early in the pamphlet that 'The thought of the multitudes so much worse off than himself in this matter of foot wear gives him no sort of satisfaction. Their boots pinch him vicariously.'[7] It seems that he considers himself forgiven if he had also experienced the misery of ill fitting boots himself, and certainly Wells had to wear miserable boots when he was a child. Perhaps he is salving his own conscience by assuring us that he has an intimate understanding of their plight. Wells certainly didn't spend great quantities of his time and money on charities directed toward feeding and clothing the downtrodden. Justification of his own wealth seems almost comical in the context of the serious issue he's trying to bring to our attention. To the contemporary reader this is just an early version of the 'I feel your pain' platitude.

To send his point home Wells closes the pamphlet with a particularly challenging remark. 'I want to change everything in the world that made that; and I do not greatly care what has to go in the process. Do You?'[8] History has demonstrated that socialists are not always pacifists, nor are they always patient enough to wait for change brought about through legitimate or due process. Although in a volatile situation this remark might well be taken as a threat, Wells probably was doing no more than trying to make his arguments memorable. Certainly the Fabians were impressed enough with his thesis that they underwrote the printing of this little booklet and sponsored its distribution.

The early years of Wells childhood are always given credit for the part they played in his emotional development and in the effect they had on his literary thinking. For example, the tunnels at Uppark[9] that ran between the main house and the outbuildings were part of his youthful playground and probably contributed to the Morlock underground habitat in *The Time Machine*. His abortive apprenticeship to a chemist in Midhurst made a major contribution to his novel

Tono Bungay. But perhaps his early years as a small boy in Bromley made a deeper impression than most critics acknowledge. Wells resented being poor. He resented having to look up at people through a grating in the sidewalk. He resented the failures of his father and the excessive workload that fell upon his mother. This resentment was a major contributor to his thinking as he grew up and began to make his way independently in the world.

When Wells began to earn enough money to ease his concerns about food and rent he began to formulate his political ideas. He quickly leaned towards socialism and delighted in pointing out the injustices of the world. He was a mature writer when he wrote *This Misery of Boots,* but he still had a long way to go in developing a cohesive political philosophy.

This small pamphlet is a good illustration of some of Wells' literary assets. It's mildly humorous, and carries the unique turn-of-phrase that he became so adept at producing. However, it's politically weak and unimpressive when compared to some of his later work. Perhaps it was intended more to attract the attention of the Fabians than to be definitive of his political thinking. In spite of this, *This Misery of Boots* is probably overlooked as an important milestone in both his thinking and his publication history. He remained bitter for the better part of his life and may have often been embarrassed by his lowly beginnings. He was born into the under classes and spent a lifetime trying to break into the upper crust of a highly stratified English social hierarchy. As an old man Wells was frustrated by how little he had accomplished beyond his writing, and how small an impression he had made upon the world. Although *This Misery of Boots* can't be considered a focal point in his writing career, it is a very telling example of his personal feelings and of the type of work that he would produce. After writing this tract he was less likely to expose his unvarnished bias and his thoughts were more carefully worked out. His political justifications became much more realistic and issues were supported with concrete, or at least more logical, examples.

8

Setting The World Free

By the time the Great War was about to descend on the world Wells had gained most of the huge audience that he would hold for another two decades. In addition to his novels and his articles for newspapers and magazines, he delivered lectures to various political and literary groups. He used this audience to promote his belief in socialism. He was convinced that a version of socialism could rid the world of the coming apocalypse. As Wells' ideas about the world and its people began to mature, his writing would reflect these more carefully considered concepts. He again chose the novel as the best medium to illustrate a whole scenario of life in a socialist world.

In 1914 Wells published a novel entitled *The World Set Free*. It reflects both his changing political ideas and a significantly different approach to writing novels. He was clearly shifting from the *fantastic romance* to what would eventually become his *discussion novel*. As a novel, *The World Set Free* leaves a lot to be desired. It's a weak story around which Wells builds a new world in his image of the ideal society. Like many of his other novels and social tracts, it tends to show impatience with those who don't conform to the new order and often attempts to ensure this conformity by the use of force.

In this novel he uses atomic bombs to subdue the masses, or at least what he considered at the time to be an atomic bomb. His story was written on the eve of the First World War in Europe and was a prediction of an atomic holocaust in the late 1950's. The bombs were delivered in a rather precarious manner using an open biplane with a pilot and a companion who performed the job of a latter day bombardier. 'His companion, a less imaginative type, sat with his legs spread wide over the long, coffin-shaped box which contained in its compartments the three atomic bombs, the new bombs that would continue to explode indefinitely and which no one so far had ever seen in action. Hitherto Carolinium, their essential substance, had been tested only in almost infinitesimal quantities within steel chambers embedded in lead.'[1]

After successful use of the hypothetical bomb much of Europe lay in waste and the stage was set for a new ruling order. Military superiority was now in the hands of a self appointed group of elitists who met in a mountaintop retreat and laid plans for a new world government. Many literary scholars have credited Wells with predicting the use of atomic bombs in warfare, however this is not a credit that he ever claimed or really deserved. He dedicates *The World Set Free* to Frederick Soddy's book *The Interpretation of Radium*[2]. Soddy was a chemist who had worked with Sir Ernest Rutherford in Montreal on radioactivity and later moved to London to work at University College with Sir William Ramsay. Soddy went on to win the Nobel Prize in Chemistry for his work on radioactivity

Wells has reinterpreted some of the concepts of atomic energy for use in applications ranging from electric generators to automobile engines. He was certainly correct in his suppositions, but by the turn of the twentieth century these were already well recognized concepts. Further, Wells' understanding of nuclear power was limited as evidenced by his confusion of nuclear fission with radioactive decay, i.e., his bombs didn't explode, they burned 'cherry red' at a rate determined by their half-life. The bombs were made from a new fictitious element named Carolinium. His description of how the element releases its energy appears early in the story. 'What the earlier twentieth-century chemists called its half period was seventeen days; that is to say, it poured out half of the huge store of energy in its great molecules in the space of seventeen days, the next seventeen days' emission was a half of that first periods outpouring, and so on.'[3]

As he often does, Wells manages to drop a few more predictions of future accomplishment into *The World Set Free*. The use of atomic energy to power automobiles, trains and aircraft was certainly a common prediction that hasn't yet been realized. Since predictions that miss the mark are seldom publicized, the practical atomic engine does not currently rank as one of Wells' inventions. He was a bit more successful with his comment about the Channel Tunnel albeit not entirely original. 'At every convenient place upon the line on either side of the Channel Tunnel there were enthusiastic spectators, and the feeling of the regiment, if a little stiffened and darkened by grim anticipations, was none the less warlike.'[4] A number of genuine proposals for a tunnel under the English Channel had been made decades before Wells was born, including a scheme by Napoleon. As it turns out this prediction was spot-on, and subsequently dozens of people have been given, or have claimed, credit for originating the idea.

The story line in *The World Set Free* proceeds along a scenario that Wells used many times in his novels of the future. The world is in chaos, nations are fighting, people are starving and all organization has fallen into decay. Not only does he reuse this theme in *Things to Come* twenty years later, but Cabal, the hero of this later novel expressed exactly the same sentiments as the soldier Barnet in *The World Set Free*, 'Damned foolery! It was Damned foolery. But who was to blame? How had we got to this?'[5] Tedious repetition was one of the tools Wells used to get his point across. If there wasn't a new novel churning in his head, he would just rewrite an old one. To some extent this added to his loss of popularity in the 1930's and 1940's when the reading public become less than enthusiastic about his new books and articles. It didn't take a brilliant readership to see that he was thumping the same old drum. New novels and fresh ideas were not regularly forthcoming from H.G. Wells

The antagonists in *The World Set Free* are subdued by force, and a group of world leaders begins to assemble to re-establish government. Wells necessarily shifts his tale to a number of new personalities, one of whom is named Leblanc. Leblanc was an intellectual idealist and a literary reflection of Wells' ideas. He was totally convinced that a new world government had to be formed. 'He was possessed of one clear persuasion, that war must end and the only way to end war was to have but one government for mankind.'[6] Perhaps the characters in Wells' novel were not aware that some of the bloodiest wars in history were civil wars that came to a boil under the control of a single government.

Leblanc attends the mountaintop conference where a large number of people have gathered to discuss the issues of world government. Wells gives us a list of the people who attend the conference. It includes '...monarchs,...presidents,...ambassadors,...powerful journalists,...and influential men...' Although Wells describes only a few of the personalities in this list we can't help but assume that this is a laundry list of the people he believes should rule the world. With little doubt Wells will place himself among the powerful journalists and influential men who are ordained to form the new government.

Another of the attendees at this leadership conference was King Egbert. In a noble turn of mind Egbert indicates that he is prepared to give up his monarchy in favor of a new and just world government. Further, he is specific about the form of this new government. 'The whole world has got to be a Republic, one and indivisible.'[7] During the period between the two World Wars there were many writers and politicians that lauded the concept of world government. Indeed Wells' deep involvement in promoting the League of Nations was based on his enthusiasm for some form of global administration. It did not take a lot of deep thinking to understand that a single governing body, global in its scope, might well find a way to stop to the slaughter and hypocrisy of war. Perhaps the public were grasping for the promises being made by advocates of world government because, as this novel was being published, the drums of war were being heard once again across Europe.

We cannot disagree with motherhood and apple pie, and it is similarly difficult to disagree with any effort to still the violent waters of war, to eliminate famine, or to improve the life of those less privileged than ourselves. But Wells' story soon takes an ominous turn and King Egbert shows us the true color of the new government being formed. In a conversation with Firmin, his aide, he declares that they should simply take over world government, without election, and proceed with the job of governing. 'Firmin, we are just going to lay down our differences and take over government. Without any election at all. Without any sanction. The governed will show their consent by silence. If any effective opposition arises, we shall ask it to come in and help. The true sanction of kingship is the grip on the sceptre. We aren't going to worry people to vote for us. I'm certain that the mass of men does not want to be bothered with such things…'[8] Apparently we have gone from one dictatorship to another in the space of fifty pages. However, the new dictatorship, according to Egbert, is really a Republic, and its rulers will have a just and understanding character. How just and understanding soon becomes clear when Egbert declares that lawyers and private property will be abolished. 'All over the world we shall declare that there is no longer mine or thine, but ours.…Then we shall declare that every sort of property is held in trust for the Republic.'[9] In the twenty-first century there will be difficulty in agreeing with the former abolition, and the latter will certainly cause some upset, even among left wing socialists who covet their personal wealth and business assets as much as the despised capitalists.

Wells closes his discourse on the new world government by outlining many of the things that would become mandatory regulation. This includes who gets voting rights and how, the number of constituencies into which the world is divided, and a neat and tidy hierarchy for workers and businessmen with the intellectuals at the top. Shades of utopia filter in when he states that 'The majority of our population consists of artists, and the bulk of activity in the world lies no longer with necessities, but with their elaboration, decoration and refinement.'[10] Perhaps it's fortunate that this kind of utopian thinking is a relic of the past. It may be wonderful to have someone talented enough to paint flowers on your toilet seat, but if there is no one to manufacture the toilet or install the plumbing, then the entire system collapses. Wells tends to contradict himself in describing and explaining the basic mechanism of the human social system. He writes readily of 'aeroplanes', rail systems, manufacturing and agriculture, but seems to forget how intricately our economy and social fabric are entwined in the design, construction, and maintenance of these physical requirements. When he decides that the majority of his utopian population consists of artists, then heaven help the remaining minority who have to feed, clothe, and shelter the great artistic majority.

The last chapter in the novel seems to be an unnecessary appendage to the book. This afterthought is used to get few more political ideas into the book that may not fit with the original storyline. It's a common failing in Wells later novels, and perhaps one of the reasons he isn't placed high on the list of literary icons. The extension to his story shows us how parts of his ideal world will work. In a medical research center high in the Himalayas, and accessible only by air, he has a number of new personalities discussing world affairs. Although Wells does not explain where this research center came from it must have been financed and staffed by the minority who are not artists of one form or another, and its design and construction would have to be carried out by the remaining few workers. There is no need to justify the balance of nature in a novel, and certainly Wells has no obligation to be logical when he writes a story. But he demonstrates a significant lack of contact with reality when he promotes his ideas in the public forum with the same vigor that he uses in writing a novel. A good example of this is his promotion of a world encyclopedia, a subject addressed in a later chapter. In the final chapter of *The World Set Free* he has devoted workers maintaining what amounts to an index of the world's knowledge by updating its paper pages with new sheets every week. 'Here—I must show you it to-day because it will interest you—we have our copy of the encyclopaedic index—every week sheets are taken out and replaced by fresh sheets with new results that are brought to us by the aeroplanes of the Research Department.'[11] Even in 1914 when this novel was being written, Wells could have put pencil to paper and determined that maintaining an encyclopedic index of the world's knowledge would have required a huge staff, working continuously twenty-four hours a day on thousands of volumes. We can't fault Wells for promoting global education and supporting an index of human knowledge, but we can be puzzled that his solutions are often far from practical reality and especially narrow in vision.

Wells has set the world free from war in his novel but promptly places it under the management of a group of benevolent dictators who impose a new government, of their own design, on the entire world population. This is a simple, effective, and efficient way to manage the world's affairs but an inevitable difficulty arises when somebody disagrees or prefers to take a different route. The remedy exercised by the newly constituted state might well be prison or the firing squad. Dissent is not permitted. Wells repeats this theme again in other novels, sometimes changing only the characters and the location. The scenario is world domination, usually by force, the rise of a benevolent dictator, world peace and eventually happiness for all mankind. Seldom does he attempt to explain how much work it takes to achieve the world peace and happiness or how long it lasts. But when is a utopian ever connected to the real world or concerned about mundane details?

9

Putting the Science in Socialism

Wells had always considered himself to be something of a scientist because of his early training in biology. By most academic or industrial standards of the time there was little chance that he would have been recognized as such. His aptitude for physical and mathematical sciences was very low and he preferred those studies where he could learn by rote and pass exams by cramming. He never followed through with graduate studies or became engaged in any field of research, and he was never employed as a scientist. This didn't stop him from including himself in the ranks of academia and portraying himself as a writer and speaker well versed in scientific methods. Later in life he had aspirations about joining the Royal Society as a social scientist, and was bitterly disappointed when told that he did not have the qualifications, nor would the field of social sciences be considered a science by the Royal Society. His interest in science is evident when he writes about engineering projects in the United Kingdom such as the rail system, quarrying, aeronautics, the machinery of war and many other mechanically oriented developments. He also spends much literary capital on vivisection, surgical procedures and other biological issues prompted by his early studies. But, an interest in science is a long way from being a practicing scientist, and it was often difficult for Wells to separate the two.

Wells was a member of the University of London Club, an exclusive group of academics to whom he proffered political advice in large quantities. In March of 1923 they held a dinner in his honor and asked him to speak '…on some aspect of the political situation…' His speech was reprinted as a four page folded pamphlet under the title of *Socialism and the Scientific Motive*.[1] Although this publication is far from being a milestone in his literary career, it does reveal much about his social and political thinking at the time. The following short quotations are taken from that same four page pamphlet and make it clear that Wells places himself high on the scale of learned academics.

He begins much like a contemporary politician by moderating his position and declaring that the argument of Socialism and Capitalism should be '...not one of opposites at all, but an argument of more or less...' He follows by declaring emphatically that private ownership of property is not the best way to run a community. Once he has established his necessary connection with socialism he proceeds to inject what he sees as Scientific Motives. In particular, to be scientific, Wells suggests that farms be amalgamated into large scale agricultural enterprises, and he proposes planned operation of transport systems and the development uniform mass purchasing and distribution systems. In other words, operation of the social infrastructure and the logistics of consumer goods have become the scientific motive for socialism. Wells never saw the irony or contradiction in his proposals. These were exactly the things that industrialists and capitalists of the period were beginning to do to improve efficiency and profitability of a rapidly expanding economy. In Wellsian terms, when efficiencies are created by the hands of a conservative businessman they become vile capitalist tricks, but when placed in the hands of an educated socialist, they were simply a scientific means to the improvement of socialism.

To emphasize the need for science in socialism he carefully folds the issue of efficiency into his argument. Without question Wells sees the '...enormous waste and inefficiency...' in production and distribution as the fault of '...the present fragmentary ownership...' that existed at the turn of the century. He envisions '...scientific production...' as the answer to those existing difficulties. Although he does touch on many aspects of civil engineering, he doesn't propose or develop any firm scientifically based motives to explain why socialism is such a fine solution to a problem that usually exists only in the minds of socialists. In fact this speech is a good example of how Wells often develops a complete social scenario without the least bit of evidence to support his conclusions or without any figures or documents to confirm his assumptions. Further, he exudes an aura of expertise on subjects that he has, at best, a shallow understanding. It was as common a political tactic 100 years ago as it is today. Find a problem or an injustice, and present it to your audience as something that needs to be cured immediately. Then create a scenario that will solve all of the problems and right all of the wrongs without ever having to produce examples, evidence, or documentation of its efficacy. Any effort to gather and present facts is entirely directed towards demonstrating some apparent evil or injustice that pervades society and then convincing the audience that a remedy is most urgent.

Wells ends his speech by summing up many of his convictions about socialism. Other aspects of his ideas and writings also slip through to his summary. In particular, he uses the words 'we' and 'our' when he refers to his Labour Party and to the University of London constituency. Wells wants badly to be considered part of the elite, even an aristocrat. He points out that it will be '…the necessary leadership of professionally trained men…' that will become the '…aristocracy of the new world…' He does not hesitate to include '…men of letters…' in his list of those he considers qualified to administer the new order of things. Not only has Wells put himself into class of academics and professionals, but he has also joined the social group that he criticized so aggressively not twenty years earlier. Neither does he hesitate to condemn the profit motives of the capitalist when, by this time, he has amassed a substantial fortune of his own from journalism, something that would never have happen under his own socialist manifesto. These contradictions never seem to deter Wells from pressing on with his goals. In the twenty-first century he would probably have been quickly roasted by the tabloid press, but in the early twentieth century, communication was much slower and memories were much shorter.

Throughout Wells literary life he wrote newspaper articles and published collections of non-fiction essays containing statements and opinions on a wide range of social and political issues. For one who constantly inserts the '…scientific motive…' into his writing he conspicuously avoids the facts, the details, and the documentation that constitute the scientific method he claims to have learned so well at Imperial College. This literary arm waving and verbal manufacturing does not go unnoticed by other contemporary critics. In 1914 Wells wrote a series of articles for The Daily Mail on politics and labor issues in England. Biographers Norman and Jeanne Mackenzie have noted that 'They contained few facts, but they were packed with the rhetorical generalizations which H.G. employed whenever he wrote on politics.'[2]

A continuous lack of concrete facts is perhaps one of Wells greatest failings, and it's a failing that will dog his work far into the future. During his lifetime few people, other than avowed socialists, could take him seriously for very long. His writing became fanciful and he produced nothing that would have a lasting impact on the socialist movement in Europe, or on the history of socialism. Indeed, as Wells himself pointed out so often, writers without a lasting impact simply fade into the dustbin of history.

10

Visions of the Future

In 1933 Wells published a lengthy novel called *The Shape of Things to Come*. The book takes the form of what might be called a 'history of the future'. It was an effort by Wells to put into prose some of his ideas about a world state and how this form of government would be imposed upon mankind. In 1935 he followed this with a screenplay entitled *Things to Come*. The screenplay carried the same theme with different characters and expresses at least one version of Wells' vision of the future. It was produced and distributed as a motion picture the following year by Alexander Korda.

This was not the first of Wells' novels or short stories that were rewritten for the movie screen. Authorized screenplays and movies were produced for *The Time Machine, The Invisible Man, The Man Who Could Work Miracles, The War of the Worlds, The Food of the Gods*, and others. In fact the *Time Machine* and *The War of the Worlds* have gone through at least three iterations plus a couple of animated efforts. Some of Wells' short stories have also been used as seeds in the production of various 'based-on' films. In 1929 he wrote and published a screenplay for a film entitled *The King who was a King*. It was never produced and he later wrote that he was not very satisfied with the work. 'His previous effort in film writing, a silent film, *The King who was a King*, was an entirely amateurish effort which never reached the screen.'[1] This was perhaps an understatement. Wells' attempts at writing screenplays usually produced poor results and his talents in the movie world were far better expressed as a contributor or consultant rather than a as writer.

Things to Come, however, is unique partly because of Wells personal involvement in the film's production. He got to know the producer, Alexander Korda, very well in the mid-1930's. This relationship helped Wells ensure that his vision of the story was appropriately translated to the screen. The film had impeccable credentials when it was released. It was an H.G. Wells screenplay, produced by Alexander Korda, directed by William Menzies, starring Raymond Massey and

Ralph Richardson. But, regardless of its initial impact, it did not have the staying power that some of Wells other film adaptations have had. Leon Stover has published an excellent account of this film story and its production,[2]

The film is now over 70 years old, so it's important to avoid judging its production qualities by today's flamboyant standards. We can forgive most of the film's inaccuracies and a few minor contradictions in the screenplay. We can also forgive its technical failings even though Wells, in 1935, had access to more accurate engineering and astronomical help than he was inclined to use. Clearly anything bordering on science fiction, even today, takes substantial risks in predicting the future. Even the dialog in its repetition and condescension can be set aside as being typical of film making in the 1930's. It seems that the writers were never very confident that the film-watching public would get the point, or understand the grand meaning of the film, so they were pummeled repeatedly with trivial dialog and inane imagery. Many of these shortcomings have contributed to the film's slide into oblivion. It is now virtually unknown except to those movie and history buffs who reach into the past for milestones in film and science fiction. In the case of *Things to Come,* accounts of the film can be readily found on the internet. The half dozen contemporary reviews are amusing and often insightful in their criticism of this aging motion picture.

What is more interesting from a contemporary point of view is the method Wells uses to get his political and social ideas of the future into the film. By the time this screenplay was written, Wells had been writing furiously for years about solving the world's problems by imposing a benevolent socialist government on the populace. The terror of the Great War was something that Europeans in general, and the English in particular, did not want to ever see repeated. Nor did the rest of the world want to live under the shadow of other large military powers while they were locked in deadly conflict. It was a time when everyone had opinions on how to correct the social and political ills that plagued the world. Wells believed that war could be eliminated by world government, and the just rule of wise and even-handed administrators. This belief was, and still is, a bit fanciful, but Wells could quickly gloss over most of the major problems and objections to the formation of his world state.

Wells' vision of the structure and administration of his proposed world government is partly addressed later in the movie, but the methods used to accomplish these aims hit the movie-goer squarely in the face as soon as the film opens. After the exposure of troops to poisonous gas in the Great War, the entire issue of gas in wartime became a major social and political issue. How could such terrifying methods of warfare be eliminated? The world's leaders came to both a moral and contractual agreement on the use of gas after the First World War, but the integrity of these agreements rested entirely on the shoulders of the signatories. Then along comes Wells with his dream of the future, and his method of enforcing this dream is by gassing the world's populace. But Wells' gas, of course, is a good gas. In fact it's called the Gas of Peace. 'This gives us a chance of trying this new anaesthetic, the Gas of Peace...I wish I could go...'[3] Little is said in the movie about the fate of the war lords and local tyrants who were gassed. Presumably they awoke to a new and better world, or perhaps the gas convinced them of the evil nature of their ways and they immediately became useful and productive citizens. Either way their military might simply disappeared when the gas was administered

Clearly Wells was presenting a hypothetical path to a better world through his screenplay. For that matter most of the journalists and novelists of Europe were developing antidotes to the conflict mentality that plagued the continent. But in getting to the better world Wells has no other means than the use of gas and the introduction of a new brand of dictatorship. As one of the characters in the novel indicates, 'You are the great grandson of John Cabal, the air dictator—who changed the course of the world.'[4] If the story is passed off as science fiction, the political overtones are soon forgotten, but the consensus among movie goers of the 1930's, fresh from the terror of the world's most vulgar war, might have been much different from ours. Europe had already seen the carnage produced by decadent monarchies and self appointed planners of new worlds. The public was thus not ready to view a new savior with a kindly eye, especially one who established his credentials by gassing the population. The screenplay's hero explains how he assumed his new position, and makes it clear what that position is. 'I've walked into it. I—the planner of a new world...'[5] Later in the novel when the hero's grandchildren ponder the benevolence of their grandfather it becomes apparent how quickly Wells has re-established a monarchy. The only difference is that the new monarchy is created in his own image.

Throughout the screenplay Wells creates a number of descriptive labels that easily remind us of the things that George Orwell parodied so clearly in his *1984* characterization of double speak. We see terms like 'World Communications', 'Pax Mundi', 'Wings Over the World', 'Gas of Peace', and 'Controller of Traffic and Order' used repeatedly. As Wells jumps one hundred years into the future to the year 2055 he develops descriptions of the populace and portrays them as little more than sheep who respond to anyone who waves a flag or makes a speech. Certainly perspective makes a difference. Our vision from the twenty-first century will bear little resemblance to Wells' view of the future from the early twentieth century. Similarly a contemporary of Wells' might view the future of a socialist society from an entirely different perspective. Perhaps George Orwell had a chance to see the movie *Things to Come* before finishing his own seminal work.

There are hints of other fundamental concepts in the screenplay, some of which did not make it to the movie screen. Wells' severest critics have often used his leanings toward eugenics to beat him into disgrace. Although the issue of eugenics doesn't arise directly in the screenplay, the concept is presented with unquestionable clarity in a scene of the far future. As the film's hero, Cabal, and a companion are watching young people fly down a water chute for entertainment, his companion remarks at the number that have been hurt or killed in the process. Cabal, the master aviator, asks 'But how are we to save the race from degeneration unless this sort of thing goes on?'[6] This is followed immediately by a remark from one of their children pointing out that '...it isn't nearly dangerous enough for a properly constituted animal...' The issue resurfaces later in the screenplay with another scene that didn't make the final cut. Three old men are congratulating each other on their mutual longevity and freedom from 'Diabetes and body rot. Deafness and blindness, the pitiful lot.'[7]

At least two other screenplay scenes are devoted to improvements in health and fitness. One scene lauds the reduction in infant death rate, and another professes the latest thing in canine genetics. The atmosphere around which these improvements are made is not one of better medical care but rather an improvement in breeding and an effort to reach and maintain the 'properly constituted animal'.

The screenplay culminates in another conflict between groups of people who are at odds with the management of the future society. This time the conflict is not the classical war between the 'Haves' and the 'Have-Nots', but rather it's a conflict between the 'Doers' and the 'Do-Nots'. It's not clear that the reason for the conflict, or the final result, is any different from the one at the beginning of the screenplay but Wells carefully adds a few instructions for the director and costume maker that helps to illuminate the intent. He points out that the mob must be well dressed and have the well groomed look that is universal to the new world. 'This mob, by the by, is as well dressed as any other people in the film. It has the well groomed look which is universal in the new world.'[8] Probably dressing the mob in fine clothes and grooming them appropriately justifies their presence or their purpose. We will never be entirely sure how Wells made this justification in his own mind, but he clearly changed the purpose and reasons for mob insurrection. This was faint consolation for those 'Controllers of Traffic and Order' who were required to stay a mob armed with clubs, regardless of the century from which they come.

The screenplay closes, as does the film, with Cabal's line 'Which shall it be, Passworthy?' As he gazes off into the stars, he is asking whether our world will be '…all the universe—or nothingness…' The answer to this question is no more obvious today than it was a century ago. However, we are left with the impression that the desired solution, in which man claims 'all the universe' requires us to agree with most of the other things that Wells paints into his story of things to come.

Wells was trying to project his thinking one hundred years into the future when he wrote this story. Considering how much has been written about his ability to foreshadow the future, he scores poorly in this screenplay, perhaps because he was projecting a political and social concept well beyond its practical limits. There were a few small things worked into the story that have had some practical manifestation, such as a reduction in infant mortality, and tall air conditioned buildings. But, the major theme about airmen gassing the world into submission, and a world of central government and global equality are fiction with limited science, and no more probable today than they were one hundred years ago.

PART III
Designing Utopia

11

The Shadow of Eugenics

The history and principles of eugenics are seldom discussed in today's politically correct social environment, but there are few people who do not have a volatile (and largely negative) reaction to the very concept of human breeding. However, a critical review of the history and practice of good breeding in the human race suggests that much of this criticism is hypocritical. There are few societies that do not have traditions and rites associated with the choice of a mate. There are even fewer parents that do not have a prejudice or preference toward certain characteristics in the choice of a man for their daughter, or in the choice of a woman who will produce the next generation in their dynasty.

Throughout history parents have devised customs and traditions to ensure that their offspring are married to others from the best possible families. As eligible children gained more influence in their own marriage decisions, they made choices that were heavily biased towards obtaining the brightest and the fittest mate that could be found. Every animal in the forest thinks or reacts in a similar manner, and the human race has always leaned towards certain perceived biases in the choice of a mate. To pretend that people lean towards the least attractive and least fit in selecting a marriage partner is completely unrealistic. Thus it's hypocrisy to deny that humans consider genetic features or that humans tend toward well established physical attractions when choosing a mate.

The work of Mendel in the 1860's produced firm evidence that plant and animal characteristics are inherited. This added fuel to the research efforts on human genetics, and by the turn of the 20th century it was clear that breeding programs were able to produce domesticated animals like dogs, cattle and sheep with a variety of characteristics that were predetermined in a small but measurable way. Compared to today's standards the methods and background knowledge was rather primitive but the basic science had become established. Inevitably some research would be done on the possibility of human breeding.

During the early half of the 20th century the concepts of eugenics were much talked about and the demands of parents trying to assure that their children 'married into good stock' were well established. In fact most races and cultures tended to marry within their own system of beliefs. This maintained consistent physical characteristics that became obvious to most observers. What then, placed eugenics in such disfavor? There are probably many answers to that question but perhaps two reasons float to the top. First, there is the social and religious issue. Humans of all cultures consider themselves far removed from animals, and indeed in most religions human beings are the children of God. To suggest that God's children might be subject to breeding for improvement of the race is sacrilege. Even without the firm conviction of religion, the concept of human breeding leaves a bad taste in the mouths of most people. Secondly, there is the political issue. Needless to say, Adolph Hitler perhaps has done the most in recent history to stir up this pot. The very thought of a government of any kind, dictatorial or elected, establishing a human breeding program, whether optional or compulsory, is not just distasteful to most people, its terrifying. This implies that there was little chance for eugenics to get much past the Second World War. However humans continue to practice their own more tasteful form of selective breeding in choosing a mate.

An historical review of the thinking that surrounded eugenics up to the Second World War indicates that it's not unusual that H.G. Wells would consider its potential value in establishing his utopian dreams. Wells' ideal socialist society was to be ruled by the intellectual elite. What better way to ensure the continued presence of the elite than to see that they are properly bred for the task? The fact that Wells himself was far from an attractive or well breed personage did not deter him, either from his utopian designs or from his pursuit of women.

The previous chapters have examined some of the changes in Wells writing as he moved to the left of the political arena and began to express a number of socialist concepts that he believed could improve the world. As his thinking matured he designed his own utopian systems, and they inevitably included the concept of eugenics in one form or another. Sometimes there was only a casual mention of an individual coming from a family of good stock. In other cases there was a description of a carefully planned breeding program designed exclusively for improvement of the race. Often the latter expressions are buried in lesser known essays or newspaper articles and are seldom read by the contemporary reader. The next chapter examines some of this lesser known writing and the context in which it was written.

12

The Birth Supply

Chapter 5 provided an introduction to a series of articles Wells wrote for *The Fortnightly Review* in 1902. He collected and republished the articles the following year in a book entitled *Mankind in the Making*. As Wells states in the introduction to this 1903 publication he considers this book to be 'An attempt to deal with social and political questions in a new way and from a new starting point.' The new starting point may have been debatable, but the book was a marketing success and was reprinted with a new introduction in 1914. Two of the articles or essays included in the book appeared again in the Atlantic Edition of *The Works of H.G. Wells* published by Fisher Unwin in 1924. These articles were entitled *The Case for Republicanism* and *The Problem of the Birth Supply*. The former article expresses Wells' intense dislike of the British monarchy and the second article took a close look at how mankind perpetuates itself through the supply of new offspring.

The latter essay is an early and straightforward discussion of Wells' views on the issue of eugenics. This was an open and frequently debated issue around the turn of the twentieth century and Wells was not alone in his favorable comments on the subject. Indeed, his general philosophy of controlling the birth supply and the methods he suggests for improving mankind are the same logical thoughts and concepts that many people recite today when they're reasonably sure of being in private company. History has pushed the entire issue of eugenics into the depths of the politically incorrect waste-bin and as a result we are often unable to objectively view thoughts and essays published over one hundred years ago. The delicate political climate of the twenty-first century makes it difficult to even turn the page on issues of racism and class structure, let alone offer quotations from a long buried journalist. When Wells wrote his essays on eugenics he did not live in such a restrictive environment, nor did he have the hindsight of two world wars where the destructive power of political oppression, human breeding and brain washing had been brought to a terrifying reality.

If Wells suffered failings in his writing, the failings were not in his choice of topics. Many controversial issues that would frighten a contemporary politician were in open discussion around 1902. His failings were more likely to have included a lack of vision with respect to the potential consequences of his comments and ideas. This lack of foresight was not uncommon in Wells' essays, criticisms and *discussion novels*. He would present an argument or concept and laboriously explain its fine characteristics, but fail completely in understanding its long term consequences. This flies in the face of his reputation as a prophet which be began to establish with his publication of *Anticipations* in 1901. Although we now understand that his belief in the inevitability of an idealized socialism and the accompanying philosophy of eugenics was off the mark, many of Wells contemporaries disagreed with him at the time he was publishing. Wells possessed a thin skin when it came to public criticism and he often resorted to venomous responses in the pages of books and newspapers.

In *The Problem of the Birth Supply*, Wells simply states his fundamental agreement with others who have written pamphlets and periodicals before him. 'It seemed to me then that to prevent the multiplication of people below a certain standard, and to encourage the multiplication of exceptionally superior people, was the only real and permanent way of mending the ills of the world. I think that still. In that way man has risen from the beasts, and in that way men will rise to be over-men.'[1] An interesting historical footnote can be added to this quotation. Exactly one hundred years after Wells published this statement in The *Fortnightly Review*, his great-grandson, Simon Wells, was directing another remake of the enduring story *The Time Machine*. The screen play included a number of variations from the original novel that upset many of the Wells purists. One of these variations was the introduction of a supreme ruler over the race of Morlocks. This ruler was the Uber-Morlock, or the Over-Morlock, a clear breeding of a superior being to rule the underground race of Morlocks. Perhaps the appearance of the Uber-Morlock, as brought to the movie screen by actor Jeremy Irons and director Simon Wells, would have been enthusiastically approved by H.G. Wells himself.

One of the most obvious contemporary concerns about the issue of eugenics is the selection or appointment of the people who make the decisions about who might be below a 'certain standard', or who is considered 'exceptionally superior'. This issue did not seem to concern Wells. He was more inclined to spend page after page in a complicated discussion of what characteristics should be preserved or enhanced in the selective breeding of human beings. His presentation creates an air of expertise and he incorporates a few of his classic scientific terms and phrases to add authority to the essay. What is remarkable is that the essay is completely devoid of scientific facts, evidence, quotations or research. Wells does not hesitate to contradict the voices of other writers without presenting any reasons for his contradiction. When Lord Salisbury tried to point out that the average of a species was raised by the interbreeding of individuals above the average, Wells was ready with the comment, 'Lord Salisbury was no doubt misled, as most people who share his mistake have been misled...'[2] Wells had developed his own concept of the benefits of human breeding programs, without any research or evidence, and the opinions of others were often dismissed out-of-hand. The race card was not even worth playing in 1902 because it was clear that 'The 'perfect' health of a negro may be a quite dissimilar system of reactions to the 'perfect' health of a vigorous white; you may blend them only to create an ailing mass of physiological discords.'[3]

By 1902 Wells was 35 years old and many of his life-long prejudices and his writing techniques were well established. His air of authority was becoming more pronounced in his journalism and in his novels. He commanded a large newspaper and periodical audience and his success allowed him to puff up his personal credentials to levels that might be almost comical in contemporary circumstances. He has no hesitation in passing himself off as a psychologist, anthropologist, zoologist and sociologist, all in the same article. He presents his own work as evidence for the benefits of human selection programs in the development of bad habits. 'My own private observations in psychology incline me to believe that people vary very much in their power of acquiring habits and in the strength and fixity of the habits they acquire. My most immediate subject of psychological study, for example, is a man of untrustworthy memory who is nearly incapable of a really deep-rooted habit.'[4] One can't help but wonder how Wells determined that his work was 'psychological study' and what tests were done on the man's memory and habits. When this kind of pompous authority was demonstrated by a writer circa 1914, it usually went unchallenged. Today the writer would not be invited to write or speak again.

Wells doesn't hesitate to mock the work of other psychologists who '...take measurements...' by comparing them to phrenologists. Others are unreservedly disparaged when he points out that '...the public mind suffers from the imposition of theories and assertions claiming to be 'scientific'...'[5] Certainly Wells has no hesitation in being creative about his own definition of the term 'scientific'. He draws again on his short baccalaureate study of biology to convince himself that he would be, for the rest of his career, a scientist of some merit. Much later he would attempt to become a member of the Royal Society. Fortunately for the integrity of the Royal Society, he would be disappointed by their lack of interest in his so-called scientific work.

Wells devotes much time and space (in this essay and others) to discussion of those aspects of human character that should be preserved by careful breeding. Some of his discussion appears to be imminently logical. He asks rhetorically, who could not be in favor of reduction or elimination of disease, crime, poverty and ignorance? Who could not agree? For one who professed a scientific background in the biological sciences he seemed to be especially ignorant of the ability of a breeding program to reduce or eliminate social problems. However, the goals of eugenics and the issues surrounding eugenics were often based on the political aspirations of the issues' proponents. In his attempt to be fair and considerate Wells leaves the reader to determine which inbred characteristics are the most desirable. This is one of the aspects of eugenics that have made it so unpopular today. In particular no one in control of a human breeding program is going to politely ask the public about their breeding preferences. Those preferences have been well established since the beginning of time. The concern is that anyone in a position of power will attempt to change these long-standing preferences to suit their own requirements. One hundred years ago many believed that strictly controlled breeding was an important, if not necessary, part of the utopian society they were trying to create. The general public disagreed with these alarming ideas and this alarm was partly responsible for the popular reception given to Aldous Huxley's *Brave New World*. Huxley pointed out the similarities between a brutal totalitarian society in which humans were created to order in incubators, and Wells' idealized totalitarian society in which a state of perpetual bliss was the result of near perfection in breeding.

To some extent it's surprising that Wells spent so little literary capital supporting his arguments with research, facts, or other experimental evidence. What's even more disturbing is the fact that Wells spends even less time trying to anticipate the effects of a planned birth program on government in particular and mankind in general. A number of Wells' novels reveal his ideas about the future of mankind, and we can assume that part of this future included a well planned breeding program. But he carefully avoids any anticipation of the long term results of planned procreation. His attempts to be technical or scientific about the issue are quickly dissolved when he agrees that undesirable people are those who are '…weak, silly, mischievous people…' The scientific method is further debased by opinions on how the ideal citizen of his New Republic would embrace selective procreation. 'The New Republican, in his private life and in the exercise of his private influence, must do what seems to him best for the race; he must not beget children heedlessly and unwittingly, because of his incomplete assurance."[6]

It's difficult to avoid falling into a trap by quoting Wells' opinions out of context. When removed from their social environment these opinions sound more like the ranting of an extremist. It is also difficult to ensure that we don't mix fact and fiction, especially in quoting the work of a novelist well known for his imaginary creation of future societies. However, much of what Wells created was far from imaginary and he repeated his opinions many times over in a public forum. He collected newspaper articles and produced newly edited books with a special introductory preface. He would later revise or rewrite these books as his opinions changed and as he garnered support from new organizations and political factions. Even some of his novels were reshaped and republished as new books because he thought they needed improvement. A case in point is his early novel *When the Sleeper Wakes* published in 1899. It was republished in 1910 as *The Sleeper Awakes* with substantial changes. A decade after its first publication he decided that he was unhappy with the book and rewrote it to accommodate his changing views. Popular novelists are at liberty to do whatever they wish with their ideas and opinions, but the process begs comparison. How often did Kipling or Dickens decide that they didn't like a novel they wrote a decade earlier, and then proceed to publish a rewrite of the story?

Over a century has passed since Wells first expressed his opinions on human breeding programs. In the current social environment much care must be taken in supporting or criticizing arguments on the subject, regardless of how or when they were made. The issues are largely ones of politics or religion, or both. They are felt so strongly that the possibility of contemporary research on eugenics has been virtually eliminated. Even some of the more popular periodicals and technical journals that might have addressed the issue fifty years ago are now very careful in their treatment of genetic or racial issues. Financial support for research that might affect the treatment of disease or inherited conditions is allotted carefully and monitored by both governments and special interest groups. Perhaps, if history agrees to repeat itself, we may see the reverse situation arise in another one hundred years.

13

Modern Utopia

The amount of material Wells wrote about utopian societies and idealized social systems probably exceeds that of most contemporary writers. This was not because of any special expertise on the subject. It was simply the result of Wells amazing ability to turn out thousands of words on short notice and to maintain two or three active projects simultaneously. During his lifetime he wrote a dozen novels that dealt with utopian systems in one form or another and he produced countless newspaper and periodical columns on various aspects of the subject from education to industrialization.

In 1905 he published a novel entitled *A Modern Utopia*. It's an imaginative piece of fiction but it can stretch the reader's patience with excessive and often meaningless dialog. Wells was beginning to develop his technique of establishing a setting or a situation and talking around it for dozens of pages before any new action occurs. He explains in an introductory chapter that he arrived at this approach to the book after rejecting several other formats. It would later become what he called a dialog novel or a *discussion novel*. Regardless of the literary impact of the novel its significance lies in the fact that it's his first major effort to put his newly developed concepts of utopia into a novel. He also provides references to many other works on utopian subjects including the historically significant *News From Nowhere* by the socialist William Morris[1]. The references provide little support to the story but may convince the reader that Wells has done substantial background reading on the topic before writing this new book.

When *A Modern Utopia* was published, Wells had been a recognized writer and novelist for fewer than ten years. Although he had not established the body of work he would later produce, he was financially stable, confident, and ready to launch himself into new subjects he thought the public should be reading. This novel is a substantial side step from his previously successful *fantastic romances*. Although gripping novels like *The Island of Dr. Moreau* were based on pointed social comment, they contained an exciting plot and a fast paced narrative. None of this comes through in *A Modern Utopia*. But as Wells explains, he chose this method of presentation explicitly. It certainly gets his concept of utopia across, but it fails as a novel with literary impact and lacks the ability to stand the test of time. The novel is now one hundred years old and seldom appears on any reading list except perhaps in the halls of academia.

The story is based on the experience of two travelers hiking in the Italian Alps. As they hike over a mountain top and into a cultivated valley they are transformed into what might be described as a parallel universe where the populace lives in an entirely different social environment. Each individual, and every place, in the real world has a counterpart in the new universe. How the travelers arrived in the new world is of little importance. What they see and describe thereafter becomes the new, and not yet mature, thesis of the Wells utopia. It is born of his newfound success, his socialist ideals and the grand entrance of the new century.

Each chapter in the book addresses a different aspect of utopian society including the topics of freedom, economics, women, race and many others. In some chapters Wells is clearly producing nothing more than a long list of opinions rather than a well thought out design for utopian development. It's also clear that his knowledge of economics, and the commercial impact of other non-European societies, is decidedly limited. When he winds up his novel by sending the two travelers back to their London home he has done little more than speculate about what might be if he could place the world into a framework designed by whimsy.

Some of the specific issues Wells addresses are interesting both in their naiveté and in their sweeping scope. As is the case in most of Wells writing about idealized social systems, he omits the detail describing how the world arrived at its state of perfection. He also ignores most issues that address the infrastructure required to feed and shelter the population, to provide transportation, communication, power and water. However this is not the obligation of a successful writer who is simply presenting some of his concepts of utopian life.

The issue of freedom is always a personal concern whenever our social structure is being changed dramatically. Wells believes that there will probably be a lot of things that we can't do, but few laws telling us what we must do. 'In this Utopia of ours there may be many prohibitions, but no indirect compulsions—if one may so contrive it—and few or no commands.'[2] With a bit of thought one could certainly make a long list of prohibitions that would suffice to restrict activity to the point where life would be intolerable. There is no better way to design a command or an order than to restrict the recipients to the point where they have no other choice but obedience.

The fundamental issue of privacy arises very quickly. Wells method of restricting privacy is novel, to say the least, and in some respects suggests that he really hasn't thought the issue through. In particular he honors the sanctity of the private household but he develops an intricate system of taxing privacy elsewhere. If we need more space, we pay more money. 'Privacy beyond the house might be made a privilege to be paid for in proportion to the area occupied, and the tax on these licenses of privacy might increase as the square of the area affected.'[3] He flogs the issue further by suggesting that walls around ones house should be taxed by height, and that private gardens might not be taxed so dearly if '...a well behaved public...' could come in and enjoy them on occasion. Naturally these freedoms are all appreciated by a busy public. A quick glance at the people walking the streets in Utopia tells us that '...they walked well and wore a graceful, unfamiliar dress...' When they spoke, they spoke in '...clear, fine voices...' The reader will have difficulty in deciding whether the walk and the voice are the result of prohibitions or commands. Certainly Wells does not agree with prohibition of all alcoholic beverages. In particular his opinion of other non-alcoholic beverages suggest that they are '...solutions of qualified sugar mixed with vast volumes of gas, as, for example, soda, seltzer, lemonade, and fire extinguishing hand grenades—fill a man with wind and self righteousness.'[4] Such is the stuff of freedom in Utopia. Wells methods of taxation and his regulation of alcoholic beverages are self-righteous and comical enough that many a chuckle would have been heard, even as far back as 1905.

If Wells approach to utopian freedom seems a bit light, he tends toward the naïve when he begins to describe the ideal economic system. He proposes dropping gold coinage and substituting 'energy units' as a means of trade. This may sound like an advanced concept in a future world plagued by energy shortages, but Wells didn't stop to consider that something as nebulous and unwieldy as 'energy units' might have to be converted to gold or silver simply for practical convenience, let alone economic efficiency.

In his utopian designs Wells makes certain that the state will control trade and commerce and he will not permit business or personal wealth to exceed certain limits, or to be passed on beyond two generations. Real property laws would allow a man to accumulate wealth until it abridges the freedom of others. Then of course someone in Utopia has to decide which freedoms have been the most abridged or violated. To avoid getting further into a subject that he doesn't understand Wells turns the whole business into something that allows him to speculate with little chance of protest from the reader. 'In Utopia there is no distinct and separate science of economics. Many problems that we should regard as economic come within the scope of Utopian psychology.'[5] Thus Wells closes the complex subject of economics and neatly writes off objections by categorically stating that there is no distinct science of economics in Utopia. Although Nobel prizes did not exist at the turn of the nineteenth century, there currently exist a few Nobel laureates who might simply smile in knowing amusement at this pronouncement. As noted in Chapter 19 Wells was absolutely incensed that The Royal Society would not accept his brand of socialism as a science but he seemed unaware of his own hypocrisy in writing off economics as a science.

When discussing the evils of allowing personal wealth to be passed on to following generations Wells seems to be blissfully ignorant of the notorious 19th century English Chancery court and the infamous ability of licensed solicitors to pocket the last farthing of vacated estates, leaving nothing for the heirs, let alone the exchequer for Queen and Country. Charles Dickens makes it clear in more than one of his novels that the cold and carefully calculated business of economics controlled large segments of the English population and was at its most rude and primitive when family fortunes were being passed on to the next generation. Only those dynasties that carefully passed control of their estates to living offspring or trusts were able to retain their wealth. Perhaps Wells considers all economic and legal aberrations such as this to be the result of greed, which could be classed as a psychological problem requiring hospital confinement for the offender. Under these circumstances fraudulent behavior or the mysterious shortage of pension funds might be solved by the construction of a few new hospitals. Regardless of what it was called or what laws controlled it, turning personal wealth over to the state would require much more than simply prohibiting inheritance for more than two generations.

Almost as a justification, where the exception proves the rule, Wells admits that there is such a thing as failure in his utopian society. In fact he collects a large number of issues under the chapter entitled *Failure in a Modern Utopia*. At a minimum he requires the utopian government to feed the starving poor, to clothe the ragged, and to house the homeless. The state will also provide jobs for all indigent and unemployed persons at a livable minimum wage. There may be some choice available in these jobs, but they are clearly not optional unless the individual is physically incapacitated. Wells seems to be aware that he will have a large number of people in this category because he provides a great list of manufacturing, construction and other public service jobs that will be done by this class of citizen. Things get a bit more disturbing when Wells provides his long-term solution to the problem of indigent, unhealthy and disinterested people. The state will simply prohibit such persons from marrying or having children. Although he doesn't discuss the issue of punishment for those who disagree with his methods, he does point out that all drunkards, criminals, diseased and insane should probably be confined to an island where they might cause the least interference with the rest of the population. He must have been attracted to the French Devil's Island prison colony established in 1884. The great advantage to this expulsion program is that it ensures that less desirable folk do not reproduce, and thus the quality of the population as a whole will improve with each generation. 'By such obvious devices it will achieve the maximum elimination of its feeble and spiritless folk in every generation with the minimum of suffering and public disorder.'[6] Wells refines this idea further in later novels but seldom reveals the methods his utopian state must use to enforce the rules. It would probably have been a shock for Wells to learn that his future society would have been even less able to deal with unwanted births than his Victorian society of 1905.

The chapter in *A Modern Utopia* on failure includes lengthy discussions of the labor force, how it is trained, and how it is disposed of when it's too old to work. Since Wells will provide everyone with a job, he recognizes that it may be necessary to reduce the number of work hours provided to each individual in order to ensure jobs for everyone. He ignores some of the obvious complications. Specifically, the reduction in work hours automatically reduces the total income of minimum wage employees to a level below the minimum wage. However, rather than dealing with the issue, and its ramifications he simply assures us that this will probably not be necessary. 'But with sane marriage and birth laws there is no reason to suppose such calls upon the resources and initiative of the world on more than temporary and exceptional occasions.'[7] The organization and control of the work force is to be managed by ensuring that every citizen is fingerprinted and issued an ID number. This ensures that everything runs '…like a well oiled engine…'

How Wells sees himself in his modern utopia is usually left unsaid, but occasionally, in this volume and in some of his later work, he leaves a generous opening for critics who see his two-faced approach to rules and regulations. As noted above he allows that it should be acceptable to inherit money, but it must be limited to one or two generations. Thus the state would not confiscate Wells fortune, or that of his children, when he died, but future generations were on their own. Further, those who inherited large sums of money should not be required to work because '…a certain portion of men at ease is good for the world…'[8] It was incredibly easy for Wells to rationalize the right of himself and his family to be citizens of leisure, but anyone beyond his vision would have to forfeit their fortunes. Many of Wells readers had long memories and could clearly see how he disliked the wealthy and elite when he had to look up at them, and how fiercely he protected himself when he became the object of his own aversion.

The rules imposed on the reproduction rights of women are important to Wells and he devotes many pages to women's issues. He usually treated women as second class citizens and his attitudes were well established by the time he wrote this book. In order to reproduce in his utopian society women must have the permission of the state. To obtain this permission they cannot be diseased, in debt, imbeciles or criminals. If men are subject to similar prohibitions in the modern utopia he never provides the details. The inferiority of women in Wells' mind was typical of nineteenth century thinking. It was a male dominated society and woman were just beginning to gain the advantages of education, employment in business, and the right to vote. Wells paid lip-service to the women's movement but he carried the typical male attitude toward their innate abilities. It seemed clear that a woman was a lesser person for many reasons including '…her incapacity for great stresses of exertion, her frequent liability to slight illness, her weaker initiative, her inferior invention and resourcefulness, her relative incapacity for organisation and combination, and the possibilities of emotional complications whenever she is in economic dependence on men…'[9] In addition to the burden of these liabilities and inferiorities women might also be guilty of other gross offences against the social system, such as marital infidelity. In his modern utopia Wells made sure that such activities were dealt with summarily. 'Her infidelity being demonstrated, [she] must at once terminate the marriage and release both her husband and the State from any liability for the support of her illegitimate offspring. That, at any rate, is beyond controversy; a marriage contract that does not involve that, is a triumph of metaphysics over common sense. It will be obvious that under Utopian conditions it is the State that will suffer injury by a wife's misconduct, and that a husband who condones anything of the sort will participate in her offence.'[10] If similar restrictions or requirements exist for men in the modern utopia, they are difficult to find. Wells' attitude went beyond mere regulation of activities into more personal habits and customs. For example, he assures us that women would be '…disarmed of their distinctive barbaric adornment, the feathers, beads, lace, and trimmings that enhance their clamorous claim to a directly personal attention…'[11] It's not difficult to see why few women admired and supported his work. This negative feminist reaction hasn't changed much in the last century. Women still do not read Wells' work. He did little to help the nineteenth century women's movement other than to encourage their involvement in open marriages and free love. Such activity was far more to his benefit than it was to women. As time passes Wells is justifiably being judged more as a self-centered bigot rather than a great writer with advanced ideas about social systems.

His views about the racial makeup of mankind were not much different from his ideas about women. He usually treated the subject with a delicate and conde-scending hand by assuring readers that there should be some value in all races. 'Utopia has sound sanitary laws, sound social laws, sound economic laws; what harm are these people going to do?'[12] The reader doesn't have to go far to under-stand what people he's talking about. In a generous manner he assures us that he doesn't consider it necessary to exterminate inferior races as the English did in Tasmania, or as the Americans did to the indigenous natives. After all, they must have some value '…that justifies God in creating them…' Before he completes his justification of various races in Utopia he inserts a terse proviso to ensure that there is no possibility of infection by inadequate people. 'Suppose then for a moment, that there is an all-around inferior race; A Modern Utopia is under the hard logic of life, and it would have to exterminate such a race as quickly as it could.'[13] Its not difficult to see that this might have a chilling effect on the minds of a good many of Wells' readers who might perceive themselves as being attached to 'inferior' racial groups. Even more chilling is the possibility that the new utopian state might decide that they belong to an 'inferior' group. The chill will be more than equaled a few years hence when Wells decides in his novel *Things to Come* that the best way to bring a dissenting populace under control is to render them temporarily unconscious by gassing them. These attitudes, at the turn of the twentieth century, were not unique. Although Wells alienated people of all races, religions and political colors he also attracted large blocks of sympa-thizers who saw another war on the horizon and readily blamed the specter on differences in race and religion.

Who then is going to rule this Modern Utopia? What form of government controls such a successful social enterprise? Wells does not provide much infor-mation on the structure of government but he does introduce us to the ruling elite that he calls the Samurai, named after the Japanese warrior class. Clearly the concept of the Samurai governing class appeals to him because he addresses the same issues and describes the same Samurai in dozens of other works throughout his career. Anyone can become a Samurai. It is a voluntary class of governing men and women of all races and religions who exercise universal control over the laws and activities of the Modern Utopia. All volunteers must meet a number of criteria before they are accepted. These criteria include minimums for education, health, moral and social standing and some unspecified but clearly demonstrated talent. All Samurai must obey the Common Rule. This Common Rule is really a collection of rules that certainly could not be obeyed by anyone but the selected elite. 'The Rule was planned to exclude the dull, to be unattractive to the base, and to direct and coordinate all sound citizens of good intent.'[14] Wells has once again rebuilt the class system he despised as a young man, only now he is the one who controls access to the upper classes and has put himself in the position of judging who is a sound citizen. The Common Rule ferrets out the unsound and the weak through prohibition. 'Many small pleasures do no great harm, but we think it well to forbid them, none the less, so that we can weed out the self-indulgent.'[15]

Wells has many illusions about the reality of utopia, and in a gesture of self justification he admits that utopias are fragile things and that this novel represents only his personal prescription for *A Modern Utopia*. The Samurai and his utopian ideals will appear many times in novels, public addresses and newspaper articles. Indeed *A Modern Utopia* is his first attempt to publicly promote his views on the ideal social system. It was also one of the books that writers like Aldous Huxley had in mind when they wrote their own satirical novels or antagonistic newspaper articles condemning Wells thinking.

14

Creating Men Like Gods

By 1923 Wells was a well established writer with a broad and influential readership. He was routinely quoted in the press and translated into at least a dozen other languages. Wells had changed publishers a number of times, always trying to get a better financial deal or a marketing advantage. In some cases he abandoned a publisher in a huff because he didn't like the way a new book looked when it was bound and distributed, or he was upset with the size of the print run. Nevertheless he was a popular writer, in great demand, and commanded substantial advances and royalties. This financial position was solid enough that most publishers listened when he spoke. Success allowed him to write and deliver a number of novels designed specifically to promote his concepts of socialism and world government. *Men Like Gods* was one of these novels.

This novel can be said to contain examples of Wells best and his worst literary talents. Wells was a superb story teller and he began this story by setting up his characters and their personal environment, around which he begins to weave a tale. Once the novel's story line has been well established, he devotes great chunks of the novel to conversation among the characters. They expound upon Wells' personal philosophy of government, race, religion and education in a long series of conversations and lectures that rationalize his beliefs without the slightest hint of opposition. For the most part *Men Like Gods* can be considered science fiction. But it is not science fiction in the same sense as *The Time Machine* or *The War of the Worlds*. These latter novels were well orchestrated tales of adventure or *fantastic romances* in the phraseology of the 1900's. Any message behind the adventure was either optional or open to interpretation. *Men Like Gods* on the other hand, contains classical Wellsian adventure only in the first few chapters. Beyond its early chapters, the novel becomes pedantic and tiresome. Certainly Wells is entitled to spin a yarn when making a point, political or otherwise, but the story soon becomes a lecture by Wells on what the world of the future must become to survive. Further, the lecture often jumps out of the novel, leaving the story line and the characters to wait until Wells has finished pummeling the reader with the perfection of socialism and his utopian dream.

One major detraction from Well's ideas on socialism, especially when they are presented in the form of a novel, is their often contradictory and completely unrealistic nature. When his overt socialism is wound together with an adventurous story line, it becomes difficult to tell when Wells is serious and when he isn't. If the reader takes him at his word throughout the story, without tongue-in-cheek, then it appears as though Wells has not really thought out the practical issues of a utopian society. The more complicated and less desirable facts of human life don't seem to have been dealt with, they have just simply disappeared. The fundamental aspects of human nature, a subject on which Wells considered himself to be an expert, have been changed to suit the story. Wells was able to add or remove sexual desire, greed and avarice, or the competitive spirit, by simple education or training on the subject. It's only fair to allow a fine story teller like Wells to spin his yarn in any way he wishes, but it's also unfair to expect the reader to accept the fantastic as the real, simply because Wells is writing the story. The writer seldom gets to have it both ways.

Men Like Gods begins with an engaging description of Mr. Barnstaple who decides that he is badly in need of a holiday by himself. He circumvents his devoted but manipulating wife and spoiled teenage son and leaves London in his small yellow motor car. Along the way he is passed by two other large touring cars carrying what appear to be aristocrats. Suddenly Mr. Barnstaple finds himself transported into another dimension, along with the two carloads of aristocrats. Now the stage has been set and the story telling gradually changes to a series of long lectures on the nature of the new dimension in which Barnstaple finds himself, and the type of people who occupy the place. The batch of aristocrats that have fallen into the same circumstance as Barnstaple represent all that Wells dislikes about the world, and his description of the new utopian world they've fallen into represents all that Wells would love to see in a modern socialist state.

As the nature of this new found utopia unfolds we find that it's not run by any specific governing body, rather, all common decisions are made by the people best qualified to make the decisions. We are seldom told who these people are, and it's a segment of utopia that never really emerges from the novel. We can probably assume that these best qualified people are the intellectual elite that manage society in most of Wells novels of the future. What becomes a bit frightening is the utopian assumption that everybody will, without question, obey the rules. When one of the outsiders asks a Utopian how a rule might be enforced, the man answers with the following;

"It would not need to be enforced. Why should it?"

"But suppose someone refused to obey your regulation?"

"We should inquire why he or she did not conform. There might be some exceptional reason."

"But failing that?"

"We should make an inquiry into his mental and moral health."[1]

Wells never addresses the fact that his utopian mental hospitals might soon be filled by thousands of non-conformists, and other disagreeable people, who form the backbone of government, research centers, universities, businesses and financial institutions that are a necessary part of trade and commerce. The earthly aristocrats and business magnates that passed Barnstaple on the motorway and were transported into this new dimension with him certainly voice all of the popular disagreements with utopian logic, but they are quickly silenced by lengthy explanations that certainly belong in the domain of science fiction. Anyone familiar with current events in 1923 would have recognized their favorite politician or businessman in the characters so aptly thrown into the mix.

The novel quickly looses track of its plot and its characters and disintegrates into a series of discussions or lectures on diverse subjects including work, leisure, vegetation, food, science, religion, and other things commonly debated by well meaning people of all political colors. Any reader with some exposure to Wellsian logic might well expect the next rhetorical question. Why are the Utopians so healthy, so clever, so attractive and so successful in their endeavors? Clearly it's because of good breeding. 'For centuries now Utopian science has been able to discriminate among births, and nearly every Utopian alive would have ranked as an energetic and creative spirit in former days. There are few dull and no really defective people in Utopia; the idle strains, the people of lethargic dispositions or weak imaginations, have mostly died out; the melancholic type has taken its dismissal...'[2]

The antagonists who have been thrown unwittingly into Utopia with Barnstaple protest loudly and widely about most of the utopian concepts. They are dismissed again and again with simple replies. The issue of good breeding and planned parenthood is repeated in several different circumstances just to be sure that the reader is aware of the perfection that had been developed in the utopian citizen. 'The Utopians told of eugenic beginnings, of a new and surer decision in the choice of parents, of an increasing certainty in the science of heredity; and as

Mr. Barnstaple contrasted the firm clear beauty of face and limb that every Utopian displayed...'[3]

Inevitably Wells brings up the issue of religion in his ideal society. It seems that there is a priest with the group of aristocrats who speaks up occasionally on the Godless nature of the utopian system. Mr. Barnstaple, who is Wells' proponent in Utopia, berates the priest much as Wells has berated religion in England. In particular Wells' attacks on the Catholic Church, including his book *Crux Ansata*, were long and bitter. Further, Wells was known to play a bit loosely with women and those with a Christian morality who criticized his activities were not well liked or appreciated. All manner of complaints and disagreements with religion are caught up in Barnstaple's vocal tantrum. 'You make religion disgusting just as you make sex disgusting. You are a dirty priest. What you call Christianity is a black and ugly superstition, a mere excuse for malignity and persecution. It is an outrage upon Christ.'[4]

Barnstaple continues his support of the utopian system by explaining to the Utopian listeners some of the great faults of his earthly world. Businessmen and entrepreneurs are next in line for a verbal thumping. Naturally, one of the aristocrats from the outside is identified as a businessman named Barralonga. As must be the case with the profits generated by all businessmen, his gains were ill gotten. 'He made food costly for many people and impossible for some, and so he grew rich. For in our world men grow wealthy by intercepting rather than by serving.'[5]

The story turns from a criticism of all the ills of the earthly world to an explanation of the inner workings of Utopia. The whole land was like a garden. No one was ever short of food, fears had disappeared and seasonal festivals were regularly celebrated. Few laws were needed, and those few were seldom broken. Economic disputes had been abolished and the populace had freed itself from greed and avarice. Toil was never a part of daily life and the weather was perpetually warm and cloudless. It is not clear how Utopia had accomplished these wonders in the few score centuries Wells allowed for its development, especially the apparent compatibility of meteorological phenomenon with social tranquility. However he does tell us that 'Eugenics had scarcely begun here.'[6] The issue of eugenics is spread very thinly throughout the novel. Wells does make it clear that a well planned breeding program has helped in creating the beautiful people that his hero Barnstaple sees around him, and eugenics is largely responsible for creating the peace and tranquility of Utopia.

The entire concept of a human breeding program as an integral part of utopian society will offend the sensibilities of most people living in the politically correct and liberal thinking twenty-first century. But these ideas must be tempered by the times, and our view of Wells writing must necessarily be from the early twentieth century, the time during which this novel was written. Biology was a major part of Wells life, Darwin's work had become well established, and the English had pioneered sophisticated breeding programs for dairy cattle, grain crops and domestic dogs and cats. Eugenics was a popular topic of discussion and frequently appeared in newspaper columns and periodicals. It was not, therefore, a great leap for the well established concepts of breeding to be transferred to humans. From this perspective it's a bit difficult to understand why (and perhaps a tiny bit hypocritical) the western world became so aghast when they discovered the state sponsored eugenics practiced by Teutons between 1910 and 1945.

The scenes of order and tranquility in Utopia are broken up in what is often a Wellsian oversimplification of life and human nature. The outsiders, who have been thrust into Utopia by a break in the dimensional integrity of their everyday world, are quarantined in an effort to restrict the possible spread of disease brought in by the outsiders. In short order they plan an armed revolt, which is soon discovered, and they are consequently spun off into space by Utopian scientists. Barnstaple, of course, escapes any connection with the wayward aristocratic interlopers and takes up the Utopian way of life. He is allowed unrestricted access to the countryside, often with the help of a tutor to explain the workings of the perfect society. This literary scenario allows Wells to wander off into the prose he commonly uses to describe, and then to justify his political and social ideas. Wells is pedantic. He repeats his social concepts many times over, and expounds many of the same things he has presented in previous novels, and many of the things he'll repeat over and over again in future writings.

Perhaps the issues that are most questionable in Wells thinking are internal revolt, and economics. He touches on both items briefly but doesn't succeed in presenting anything that could ever be achieved in reality. Internal revolt is admirably addressed by the activities of the earthlings when they are quarantined. Utopians have no need to revolt. The spirit of antagonism has been bred out of them, and they forever live in peace and harmony. Perhaps this genetic lack of antagonism might be possible in some off-world civilization, but in our earthly environment it's a characteristic of mankind to engage in disputes. If disputes are not at a national level, then they are at a regional or personal level. When larger issues are solved, then disputes will arise locally over religion, territory, rules of law and social interaction. This is the nature of man. Man is a territorial animal and highly defensive of his resources, his assets and his family. Man will defend his right to gather his own food, feed his own kind and go his own way. In contemporary terms these are the basic freedoms we defend so vehemently. If Wells was more aware of the power of these basic instincts he might avoid many of the problems and contradictions he creates in his utopian world. If he was more aware of the power of human nature and its fundamental need for tribalism, he might have been more successful in his efforts to promote the League of Nations and other forms of world government.

The issue of economics and infrastructure is something that Wells never deals with in this novel. When he does bring up the issue he simply describes huge projects sponsored by the government, or the absence of money and banks. Like most writers Wells ignored the things that didn't matter to his story. However, the danger in dropping into his *discussion novel* format is that he touches dozens of controversial topics in a few pages. This includes, consciously or otherwise, items like economics and civil infrastructure. The electrical power, the communications systems, transportation and distribution all seem to be present without anyone being very concerned about their operation or maintenance. The bridges, roads, rails and shipping and other large scale endeavors all seem to look after themselves. All manufacturing is done to perfection since nothing ever seems to break. Perhaps more importantly Wells seems to dismiss any complications in economics and finance by suggesting that greed and avarice do not exist in Utopia. Perhaps they do not, but social interaction and commerce must exist in any social system. If money is only a method of keeping score, it must be present in one form or another, as paper or bank credits, in order to create and deliver the goods and services demanded by a functioning social system. Even the lowly ant hill must have a commercial balance or its occupants would starve, and much like Wells ideal socialist environment, greed is not a factor in the ant's social formula. In this respect Wells might have drawn on his training in zoology to understand that the things he tries to breed out of mankind are fundamental characteristics of all living things.

15

The New World Order

The year 1939 was a year of stock taking in most of Europe. By this time it was clear that war was only inches away even though some refused to believe it was going to happen. A few last minute attempts were being made by politicians to avoid the conflict, but they were destined to end in failure like Prime Minister Stanley Baldwin's 11th hour meeting with Hitler in Berlin. Wells was 76 years old in 1939 and he had watched the growing hostilities between nations since the end of the previous war. His frustration had increased over what he considered the inability of governments and politicians to see the folly of their ways. In many respects he was right in his assessment of the political ignorance and animosity that arose in Europe between 1918 and 1939, however his solutions to the myriad difficulties often fell upon deaf ears. Wells did not like being ignored, especially when he was so certain he was right.

His utopian ideals and his concepts of world government and international human rights were well developed after three or four decades of writing and lecturing. It's clear to most readers that *The New World Order* published in 1939 is one of the best and most lucid examples of his philosophy. He knew what he wanted to say and he believed he knew what was necessary to ensure that war would never happen again. Gone was much of the naiveté of his early ideas. However, he didn't seem to be any more aware of the potential problems in the realization of his socialist state. He continued to present *The New World Order* as the final solution and a panacea to world peace and social security. Wells left little room for compromise or accommodation of any kind.

There can be no doubt about Wells' perception of politicians and their political goals during the two world wars. It was clear to him that the rich and powerful were taking advantage of their status to settle old scores and to improve their position both economically and territorially. In fact one of Wells' statements is highly descriptive of the reasons for some of our current global conflicts over six decades later. In reference to the Spanish-American War at the turn of the 20th century he wrote '…the United States were irritated by the disorder of Cuba and felt that the weak, extended Spanish possessions would be all the better for a change of management.'[1]

The process that Wells used to get from a politically inept world to what he determines is the inevitability of socialism is not very clear. In previous work he has painted a picture of an open conspiracy that designs and develops a more efficient social system by open public debate and promotion. However he consistently avoids the mechanics of his political solutions. How do we get there, what happens when we arrive, and what do we do with those who disagree? The occasional reference to a gathering of states is always limited to the advanced industrialized nations of the world, and often limited to only the English speaking community. Wells perception of the European ability to compromise is also limited. In fairness, he does not have the advantage of several decades of hindsight, but some of his categorical statements clearly miss the mark. 'It would, I suggest, be far easier to create the United States of the World, which is Mr. Streit's ultimate objective, than to get together the so-called continent of Europe into any sort of unity.'[2] The current European Union and their common currency are real and tangible accomplishments, while the United States of the World is farther away from reality than ever.

The potential difficulties in getting from the political situation of 1939 to Wells' idealized society did not detract from his certainty of its eventual arrival. 'For in the world now all roads lead to socialism or social dissolution.'[3] His certainty of the arrival of socialism might have been frightening to some of his intended audience so he calms the reaction by expressing disfavor with the soviet model of revolution. 'We do not deplore the Russian Revolution as a revolution. We complain that it is not a good enough revolution and we want a better one.'[4] Thank goodness he didn't consider one of the world's cruelest, bloodiest and most barbaric revolutions to be good enough.

Wells provides one of the clearest and most succinct notions of his socialist world in his book *The New World Order*. His ideas are worth repeating because they are, in many respects, a clear distillation of half a century of socialism in the mind of H.G. Wells. This includes a continued effort to attach some scientific aspect to his revolution as though it would help improve its credibility. He states: 'This new and complete Revolution we contemplate can be defined in a very few words. It is (a) outright world-socialism, scientifically planned and directed, plus (b) a sustained insistence upon law, law based on a fuller, more jealously conceived restatement of the personal Rights of Man, plus (c) the completest freedom of speech, criticism, and publication, and a sedulous expansion of the educational organization to the ever growing demands of the new order.' He went on to express his disdain of the Bolshevik adaptation of socialism. 'What we may call the Eastern or Bolshevik Collectivism, the Revolution of the Internationale, has failed to achieve even the first of these three items and it has never even attempted the other two.'[5] Wells may have been certain of the coming Revolution, but his followers are still waiting, well into the twenty-first century. Certainly evolution will continue to shape the future of government and our social environment, but revolution is a destructive and often counterproductive process. The inborn impatience typical of social reformers is also part of the basic character of H.G. Wells. Thus he sees a need for revolution rather than reform.

As Wells established the makeup of his New World Order he tried to foresee the probable objections of his detractors. He drew on a technique that he used many times before. It's a weak technique often invoked by writers whose ideas can't stand up to on-the-spot verbal intimidation. Wells creates a third party who presents many of the probable arguments in a form that can be easily contradicted. He then presents a lucid contradiction of the third party objection and thus proves his point.

Interestingly, one of the publications of the time that made an impact on the public was Aldous Huxley's *Brave New World*. Wells was acquainted with Aldous Huxley and worked closely with his brother Julian when they collaborated on *The Science of Life*. Their grandfather, the grand old man of zoological science, Thomas H. Huxley, was briefly Wells' instructor at the Imperial College. As noted in the following chapter, *Brave New World* was a disappointment to Wells. He may even have felt it was a betrayal of the Wells-Huxley solidarity. Without inside information we can't judge how much of an impact Huxley's novel had on Wells, but Huxley certainly mocked Wells socialism and suggested that a society of cloned sameness would degenerate into a bland and stagnant system. The impact of the *Brave New World* was important enough to Wells that he presented an argument against its folly in *The New World Order*. As he summarized the creation of his new society he presented a vitriolic response to an imagined antagonist. 'He has been accustomed to associate "free" and "equal" and has never been bright-minded enough to take these two words apart and have a good look at them separately. He is likely to fall back at this stage on that Bible of the important genteel, Huxley's Brave New World, and implore you to read it. You brush that disagreeable fantasy aside and continue to press him.'[6] With that statement, Aldous Huxley is relegated to the sidelines of Wells social reforms and utopian ideals.

16

Huxley and Orwell

It is difficult to read about the concepts of utopian society in the period between the two world wars without being repeatedly exposed to the work of Aldous Huxley and George Orwell. Both Huxley's novel *Brave New World* and Orwell's novel *1984* were published well after H.G. Wells had established himself as prophet and designer of utopian systems, so they had little influence on his thinking. In fact Orwell's novel was published shortly after Wells had died. It's more likely that the reverse was true, that is, Wells' writing had some influence, however small, on the work of Huxley and Orwell. Although they didn't mix in the same social circles they were certainly aware of each others writing and thinking. The most interesting facts about the relationship between Wells, Huxley, and Orwell are not their personalities, but the contrasts in their writing and thinking. Not everyone agreed with Wells' view of the perfect utopian future. In fact some writers were certain that he was completely off base and expressed their disagreement in harsh and often bitterly satirical terms.

Huxley and Orwell had different attitudes about the future of the industrial world and the role of socialism, and they differed dramatically from the idealism and often unrealistic beliefs of Wells. There were also as many differences between Huxley and Orwell as there were between themselves and Wells. They came from different backgrounds, had different educational histories. They grew up with different values and had different friends. It's not surprising, in the fertile literary climate of the early twentieth century, that prominent writers could produce dramatically different literary views of socialism and utopian society.

Aldous Leonard Huxley[1] was born in Godalming, Surrey in 1894 and was Wells' junior by nearly thirty years. He was the brother of the biologist Julian Huxley who collaborated with Wells in writing *The Science of Life*. He was the grandson of the indomitable Thomas Huxley, well known in the nineteenth century as Darwin's most vocal proponent. Although Wells never knew Thomas Huxley well, he became friends with many of the younger family members.

Aldous Huxley studied at Oxford as a young man and managed to publish two volumes of poetry while he was a student. In 1921 his first novel *Crome Yellow* was published. It was a biting satire on intellectual pomposity and attracted enough attention to establish Huxley as a writer. He spent much of his latter life living abroad and he moved to California in 1947 where he remained until his death in 1963.

Brave New World was published in 1932 at a time when Huxley was becoming very dissatisfied with what he saw happening in the western world. His novel is a clever portrayal of a future society in which all humans are produced in a reproductive laboratory. This system generates human beings with various levels of intelligence from Alpha's to Epsilson's, each designed specifically for different levels of future employment. Children are conditioned to their working environment and job requirements as part of their childhood training. Everyone is content with their assigned tasks. The world in which they live is one of plenty with free sex, drugs, and a complete absence of discord. A small select group of rulers have absolute control over the management and direction of the society. This group is chaired by the World Controller.

The story that unfolds in the novel concerns the character Bernard, his friend Lenina, and someone called The Savage from a reservation in New Mexico. Bernard and Lenina have been created in the controlled environment of the new world where contentment is the most important requirement of life. Mass production and controlled consumption have always governed their life. The Savage is introduced to this society and is unable to adapt, eventually committing suicide. The novel relates the tale of contentment and conflict with everything from tongue in cheek humor to biting satire. Many of the concepts and situations created by Huxley to build his brave new world are hauntingly accurate when viewed from the present. In fact by 1959, after living through the terror or World War Two, Huxley saw enough of the brain washing and social control coming to life that he wrote another small book entitled *Brave New World Revisited* in which he expressed alarm at the number of social evils that had come to pass in the twenty-five years since he'd published *Brave New World*.

Without a doubt Huxley's concept of classified test tube births and total control of human activity from birth to death can be a terrifying concept. But in many respects it's as valid a prediction of a future socialist state as those that appear in Wells' novels. Huxley has simply taken breeding and control by the ruling elite off in a different direction. Wells undoubtedly read *Brave New World* when it was published. Although he seldom made written reference to the book, or to Aldous Huxley, it is clear that he didn't like the novel or the ideas it presented. He was probably very disappointed in the direction taken by someone he considered a friend. It's tempting to analyze Wells' and Huxley's different approaches to the future of socialism from a contemporary view point, and with the benefit of fifty years of hindsight, but it's important to view the work of Wells and the writers around him from his own time in history and in the environment in which he lived. In 1939 these men had very different beliefs and expectations.

George Orwell[2] was a different character entirely from both Wells and Huxley. He was born Eric Arthur Blair in 1903 in Bengal, India, the son of a British Civil Servant. He was sent back to England for his education and finished his formal schooling at Eton, graduating in 1921. Blair published a number of articles and essays under his own name before adopting the pseudonym, George Orwell. He was highly critical of the English class system, as was H.G. Wells. The class system limited the opportunities available to young and ambitious writers, but Blair grew up in the dynamic environment of the new century when talented writers were in demand. As a young man he joined the Imperial Police Force in Burma. Blair returned to England penniless and picked up odd jobs to support himself. It was well into the 1930's before he became a serious writer and began to earn small amounts of money. His first novel was *Burmese Days*, published in 1934 under the George Orwell pseudonym. It was well received by critics and provided him with some of the recognition he needed to get his work accepted by the public.

Orwell's exposure to the evils of the communist philosophy that began to flourish in the 1930's made him a strong opponent of communism and a believer in the English approach to socialism. His highly acclaimed novel, *Animal Farm* published in 1944 has become a classic portrait of the self-serving communist philosophy as it had been put into practice in the Soviet Union. When *Animal Farm* was published, the Second World War was nearly over and the evolution of the Bolshevik state into Stalin's Russia was nearly complete. The inequities and hypocrisy of Marxism in action was becoming obvious to the rest of the world. Even Wells pointed out that the Russians may be on to a good thing, but it would have to be done much differently in England. This is a good example of the English version of the 'we could do it better' attitude that is now more typically American in the twenty-first century.

Orwell made a mockery of the communist system in *Animal Farm*. Wells probably wasn't interested in taking issue with Orwell's work since he was approaching 80 years of age and losing some of his urge to scrap. However, we can be assured that he was not impressed with Orwell's portrayal of socialism, even though it was aimed at the Soviet Union. The novel was a financial success and provided Orwell with his first real income. In 1949 after the end of the war, and shortly after Wells' death, he published his classic work *1984*. This latter work is a finely crafted novel of the future gone bad. How mankind got into its terrifying political situation is of little concern to Orwell. Rather, he paints a picture of total social control, the rewriting of language and history, the evils of non-conformity and the terror of having every moment of one's life watched closely by the ephemeral Big Brother. Any deviation from the approved party line exposes one to the terror of the Thought Police. Punishment by torture and brainwashing is used to restore ones useful qualities as a citizen.

Orwell was pleased with the success of his novel and by 1949 he was well recognized as a writer and had become financially stable. But misfortune is never stayed by success. He contracted tuberculosis and died in 1950 at the age of 47, barely started on what was becoming a brilliant literary career. H.G. Wells died in 1945 at the age of 80 and did not see Orwell's *1984* published. Although we can assume that his reaction would probably have been negative, it would make interesting history if it were possible to read a book review of *1984* written by H.G. Wells.

The evolution of social concepts in the early twentieth century was very rapid. At the turn of the century writers, politicians and social scientists were enthusiastic about the dawn of a new economy, new opportunities, and the hope of a new political system throughout the western world. Everyone with an opinion expressed the promise of the new century. Wells was eager to participate in the speculation on future promise and his novels expressed opinions on almost every aspect of the coming revolution in social and political management. This was the time of *A Modern Utopia*. As the century began to mature it became clear that the future was still a long way off. The terror of the First World War passed, and changed the minds of many and renewed the determination of others. A good many doubts arose about the viability of European governments. This was the period in which *Brave New World* was written. Another war erupted very quickly and it quickly exposed the often rough core of man's inhumanity. It also exposed the dark side of the soviet system to the rest of the world. This was the era from which *1984* emerged. The idle luxury, plentiful food, informed discussion and easy consensus of the early part of the twentieth century, the era in which Wells thrived, was quickly becoming stained and diseased as the century aged and Europe passed through its Second World War.

The significance of the work of Huxley and Orwell, within the context of Wells' idealism and utopian social system, is their completely opposite view of totalitarian control. Wells believes that he and his intellectual elite are capable of governing in a benevolent and uniform manner. Once such a benevolent government is established, a world of plenty and good health will logically follow. Huxley and Orwell demonstrate that, whatever the intent of the original governors, total control of society by any man or group of men will ultimately have but a single result, i.e., a totalitarian dictatorship, the most terrifying and destructive form of government ever imposed upon man.

PART IV

Gaining Public Prestige

17

The London University District Election

The British Parliamentary system of government is one of the most fascinating systems in the world. It is a constitutional monarchy wherein the monarch reigns by the grace of Parliament. The British monarchy is the most widely recognized and one of the oldest reigning dynasties in the world. Like any political system the backrooms of the elected house are filled with intrigue, back stabbing, warring factions and questionable dealings. At the same time it is probably the most democratic and most often copied system of government in history. Americans will vehemently contest the idea that any governmental system could attract more superlatives than theirs, but when the American Republic was being designed, its makeup and purpose was often intended to be different from, as opposed to being better than, the British system from whence the bulk of its population came. The American result included a number of advantages and a few disadvantages, some of which did not become obvious for a couple of centuries.

The British House of Commons is currently composed of 659 Members of Parliament elected by the public from an equal number of constituencies established by population distribution throughout the Kingdom. There are several political parties participating in each election. The party with the most elected Members of Parliament forms the government and sits on one side of the house. The opposition or minority parties sit on the other side of the house. In the event that no party has a plurality, a coalition government can be formed by a collaboration of two or more parties or associated political groups. In a parliamentary system, the government must call an election within four or five years, but it may opt to call an early election at any time convenient to its purpose, or whenever a minority government, or coalition government, is overruled in the House. The number of Members sitting in the British Parliament, and the makeup of their constituencies, has changed frequently over the years as demographics and population changed. Perhaps one of the most significant benefits of the Parliamentary democracy is the fact the Prime Minister must be an elected member from a local constituency, just like all other members of the House, and he must sit in the House like any other Member of Parliament and defend his political initiatives. No excessive executive privilege here.

H.G. Wells was an active supporter of the Independent Labour Party throughout his career. This was the party that most closely represented his socialist views. Over the years he endorsed a number of candidates in their bid for election and routinely supported the labor movement with newspaper articles and pamphlets. In 1922 a general election was called and the Labour Party asked Wells if he would stand as their candidate in the London University riding. There were a few protests against his candidacy within the Party but they were quickly subdued. Wells agreed to stand as the Labour candidate and immediately began work on a rather brief campaign typical of the limited time period between the announcement of an election and the selected polling date.

Campaign activities in 1922 bear little resemblance to contemporary electioneering. Wells' campaign was largely limited to a couple of speeches and a few printed handouts designed to establish his position and present a list of prominently known supporters. This list was rather short, appearing on the back page of his first pamphlet, but they were elitists all, the very kind that Wells loved to hate as a young man. Interestingly the British Post Office refused to deliver one of his pamphlets because of the blatant promotion of his new book in the pamphlet. At the time it was strictly against BPO regulations to deliver promotional or advertising material under first class postage.

The election was held in November of 1922. Three candidates were standing for election in Wells' London University constituency. They represented Tory, Liberal and Labour parties. Wells finished last in the polls and was outstripped more than three-to-one by the Tory candidate Sydney Russell Wells (no relation). There can be little doubt that this defeat was a blow to his ego. He did not accept the candidacy without believing that he had a good chance of delivering the seat. Wells was also naïve enough to assume that his message would convince the largely conservative riding to change their vote in his favor. After the election he had to justify the thin support to himself as well as to his supporters. Wells concluded that the loss resulted from the fact that his message was not getting through to the electorate. After all, anyone who heard the message could not do other than to cast their vote in his favor. The more experienced politicians were probably less concerned about the loss than he was. The publicity he generated for the party was well worth the candidacy. The Party's satisfaction with his position and his campaign was confirmed by their request that he stand with them again as the Labour representative in the next election. The next election came sooner than expected.

The Liberal government of Stanley Baldwin was failing and they were forced to call another election within a year of the last one. Wells wasted little time in getting a much more active campaign going, including appearances on behalf of other Labour candidates. His campaign included speeches, pamphlets and dinner engagements. He had more political ammunition at his disposal from the abysmal performance of the Liberal government since the previous election. One of his speeches to the University of London Club was reprinted under the title *Socialism and the Scientific Motive* as noted in Chapter 9. The pamphlet included another list of his supporters substantially longer than the one distributed for the previous election. Copies of several of his pamphlets and position statements still exist in archives. The second election was a resounding success in many quarters. The Labour party gained a plurality and formed the new government. However, H.G. Wells again finished third in his riding. The same Conservative candidate, Sydney Russell Wells, won the seat. It was now difficult for Wells to rationalize his defeat. He had done his best to get his message out but he was just not wanted in the London University riding as a parliamentary representative.

This was the end of Wells' political candidacy. It was undoubtedly embarrassing to have suffered defeat twice. The defeat probably bruised his ego far more that it upset the Labour Party who now held the power in the House. It's difficult to understand how much it upset Wells to lose a second bid for a seat without knowing how he envisioned himself in the position of a parliamentarian. He was forward thinking enough to have made some plans for his political position if elected. He may have assumed he could promote major social and economic reforms and push the nation toward a new socialism more expediently from the ranks of the House than he could as a writer or newspaper columnist. But it was not to be. He continued to pick away at the policies of the new government in his writing and speeches, but his attempts to gain elected office ended and he moved on to other things. His support of the Labour Party continued for many years but active participation in political campaigns was a thing of the past

18

Disagreements and Disappointments

It's well known that Wells had many disagreements throughout his life with friends, colleagues, family members, and his publishers. More often than not, these were disagreements he started himself over some personal slight or trivial injustice he thought he'd been dealt. His position in the literary world provided him with the wealth, fame and social status to make others think carefully before they tangled with him. This allowed him to become something of a bully with little chance of being challenged by others.

There were, however, a number of people who were not in the least bit awed by H.G. Wells. One of them was G.B. Shaw. Wells often wrote vitriolic letters about political and social issues to the much older and more mature Shaw. This challenging and often offensive side of Wells' character began to appear as he gained public notoriety and considered himself worthy of attention. His efforts to apply pressure to the Fabian Society are a case in point. Shaw would reply to Wells' letters, often with fatherly sounding advice, telling Wells that he was being a fool. Wells would be characteristically miffed and then after an appropriate pause, he would write a long letter of apology for his bad manners or poor judgement, and the friendly relationship would resume much where it had left off. Sometimes arguments became more serious. Disagreements related to his work often went beyond the stage of a few nasty letters and got dangerously close to litigation.

As soon as Wells had finished *The Time Machine* and was paid one hundred pounds by Heinemann for the rights to the story, he became acutely aware of the price that could be demanded for a successful book. Wells quickly produced several successes in a row, and rather than being forever grateful for the contributions and revenue from Heinemann, he very quickly fell into a nasty argument over money and Heinemann's perceived lack of marketing effort.[1] Heinemann had also published *The War of the Worlds* and *The Island of Dr. Moreau*, both of which provided Wells with substantial revenue. During the same period Wells was having another argument with Bullen about how *Certain Personal Matters* was being published and marketed.

In many later instances Wells became a constant source of irritation to publishers by interfering in their plans for producing, marketing and advertising his books. He frequently believed that the publisher was not doing enough to promote the sale of his books, and he did not hesitate to offer his suggestions for improving their marketing program. On one or two occasion he was right in his criticism, and this simply fueled his efforts to demand more onerous agreements and greater sums of money. There is little doubt about the reason why Wells had so many different publishers. He dropped many of them quickly and others refused to do further business with him. As he neared the end of his publishing career many of his best literary bridges had been irreparably burned.

Wells personal dalliance is often reflected in his writing, especially the work he produced between 1905 and 1910. When he published *Ann Veronica* he faced some criticism about the novel's apparent advocacy of free love and the irresponsible actions of young women who were seeking independence by attempting to make their own way in the world. In 1909 he made an arrangement with Macmillan for the rights to *The New Machiavelli* which was about to begin serial publication in the *English Review*. When Frederick Macmillan read the proofs of the novel, he was upset by its sexual references and the social issues it dealt with, including obvious unflattering references to Beatrice and Sydney Webb who were prominent public figures and Wells former friends during his membership in the Fabian Society. If Macmillan went ahead with publication it would cost him readers and affect his reputation as a publisher. Wells agreed to some revisions of the manuscript, but Macmillan didn't consider them adequate. To honor the publication agreement Macmillan had made with Wells he put the manuscript out for offers. John Lane, a publisher who had often taken risks in the publication industry, agreed to take the book. *The New Machiavelli* was published in book form in 1911, and it immediately attracted the usual prurient interest that results from controversy. A few public libraries refused to stock the book, but generally it sold well and was a profitable undertaking for John Lane. Although Macmillan and Company did carry some of Wells titles in later years, this conflict was effectively the end of their association with Wells.

Wells had developed a friendship with Henry James over the years and the two met occasionally in London for dinner or social events. However their friendship became strained by a number of things James wrote in *The Times* in London. Wells, in response, collected a number of bits and pieces he had written earlier and pulled them together into a novel he published with the tedious title *Boon, the Mind of the Race, the Wild Asses of the Devil, and the Last Trump, Being a First Selection from the Literary Remains of George Boon, Appropriate to the Times.* The book is usually called simply *Boon*. The author's acknowledgement appeared as 'Prepared for publication by Reginald Bliss with an ambiguous introduction by H.G. Wells'. Wells, of course, wrote the entire book, and a later edition was published with his name as the author. It was published in 1915 by T. Fisher Unwin, shortly after war had broken out in Europe.

The book was a childish response by Wells to James criticism. It included satirical references to James as a pompous twit and it contained tasteless remarks about the literary culture in London. The literary circle in Britain was a closely knit group and its members immediately recognized the satire as an attack by Wells on the establishment from which he made his living. He made no effort in *Boon* to conceal his loathing for the upper class attitudes and politics of the literary elite. Not only was the book an immature expression of his indignation, but it was a good example of how Wells would often shoot from the hip when he believed he'd been slighted. In later years he would admit that he may have responded too harshly to criticism, but such concessions were inevitably made after the damage had been done. Many writers, including George Bernard Shaw who possessed a far sharper and brighter mind than Wells, were a bit cautious in dealing with Wells when he was on another of his campaigns to seek justice for some perceived personal offense. The results could be unpredictable and his friends never knew when they might be the next target, or for what reason. *Boon* is considered to be one of Wells worst books, poorly written, disjointed and lacking much sense.

Many years later, in 1925, Wells was accused of literary piracy and spent nearly five years defending himself. It seems that the case had only marginal merit, but nevertheless it consumed great amounts of Wells time and money. A writ was filed against Wells in the Appelate Court in Toronto accusing him and the Macmillan Company of Canada of plagiarism, receiving stolen goods and criminal conspiracy.

The source of this litigation was a woman named Florence Deeks in Toronto. She was an activist in the women's movement and had written a large book on the history of women entitled *The Web of History*. She submitted this to Macmillan for their review and possible publication. Macmillan's Toronto office apparently let the manuscript sit for a number of months before replying. During this same period Wells was hard at work on *The Outline of History* which was published by Cassell in London and simultaneously by Macmillan in Toronto. Florence Deeks immediately noticed the similarity between Wells work and hers, and she knew that Macmillan was in possession of both manuscripts at the same time. She decided that Macmillan had provided Wells with her manuscript, which he then used extensively in his preparation of *The Outline of History*. How else could Wells have produced such a large book in such a short period of time, Deeks argued.

The case went to trial after several uncomfortable years of preparation and accusation. The suit was to be heard in a Toronto courtroom. This put Wells at a distinct disadvantage in having to support his arguments and prepare his case by correspondence. During the trial Deeks' attorney presented a number of strong arguments and professional witnesses who listed dozens of similarities and apparent duplications in the two manuscripts. They argued that Wells could not have prepared *The Outline of History* in longhand in less than a year without help, and that help had to be the outline provided by Florence Deeks, which Wells then expanded with his own chauvinistic rubbish. They also insisted that when published, it effectively preempted any possibility of Deeks' work being published.

As convincing as the arguments may have been, the court decided in Wells favor and the plaintiff was subject to court costs. Florence Deeks was not in a financial position to support the legal expenses or to pay the costs. Wells' suspicious mind led him to believe that someone else was backing the action and simply using Deeks as a surrogate to get at Wells. Although there has never been any clear evidence of this published, it remains a good possibility simply because Florence Deeks did not give up her expensive quest, in spite of limited means. She followed up with an appeal to the Privy Council of the United Kingdom. This court heard the equivalent of Federal Supreme Court cases in Canada at the time. The appeal was dismissed in 1932 and Wells was eventually able to put the matter behind him. It was an upsetting and expensive issue in Wells life. Although he had little concern about his own innocence in the matter, it was a reflection of some of his earlier problems and tended to leave him gun-shy in dealings with other authors and publishers. Wells had often published material that caricatured and slandered other writers and public figures. On some occasions he came dangerously close to libel. He remained apprehensive for many years about the possibility of action over some articles in which he may have been less than discrete.

In 1928 Wells was working on *The Science of Life*, a monumental undertaking that was intended to be part of his massive trilogy providing an encyclopedia of mankind for readers of all levels. The trilogy included *The Outline of History, The Science of Life*, and *The Work, Wealth and Happiness of Mankind*. Characteristically he had taken on a huge work load that required the assistance of a number of people including Julian Huxley and his son G.P. Wells, both of whom are acknowledged as co-authors. In addition he enlisted the help of two other writers and researchers, E. Cressy and H.P. Vowles, to help fill out the material in his outline. While this work was in progress Wells had begun writing the final volume of the trilogy. This heavy commitment of his time and energy meant that he could not be present on a full time basis to supervise the work that was being done on *The Science of Life*. Much of the task of supervision was being handled by Julian Huxley and Wells' son. However after a year's effort Wells became very unhappy with the work being done by Vowles. In order to disconnect the two free lance writers from the project he suspended the work pending a review and a new approach to the book. Wells then promptly left London to indulge himself in a holiday for a couple of months.

When Wells returned to London he found that Vowles had gone to the Society of Authors and complained about the affair and accused Wells of breach of contract. The Society of Authors acted much like a guild or union and was empowered only by its members to take action against other members. Wells was a long time member of the Society but he was not informed of the action until he received correspondence in late 1929 from Herbert Thring, the Society Secretary. Apparently the Society believed that Vowles was entitled to damages and Thring asked Wells to present his defense of the charges. Wells responded with a reasonable compromise but couldn't resist inserting a few vitriolic remarks directed specifically at Thring for his interference in the affair by saying '…nothing seems to have mattered but the opportunity of annoying and bleeding me while I was ill and depressed.'[2]

In a typical flamboyant fashion Wells ensured that the argument became public by publishing a summary of the disagreement, and the related correspondence, in a small seventy-four page pamphlet entitled *The Problem of the Troublesome Collaborator*. About 175 copies were printed and they were distributed to the members of the Society of Authors. The mutual animosity that had developed between Vowles on one hand, and Wells on the other, had reached a point where it would be impossible to come to an amiable solution through The Society of Authors, so Vowles followed by having his solicitors issue a writ for breach of contract. This increased Wells irritation and he became intransigent. He would no longer allow Vowles to have any part of his writing project and he was determined to see Thring ruined and thrown out of The Authors Society. After more caustic correspondence between Wells and Thring, George Bernard Shaw attempted to intervene. Shaw, who was also a Society member, had been approached by Thring as an appropriate mediator. Wells had great respect for Shaw, even though they too had argued regularly in he past.

Fortunately Wells took the honorable road out if the issue, came to a compromise with Thring and allowed an arbitrator to asses a small additional payment to Vowles for his work. Wells also insisted that the correspondence be published for other members of the Society to read and he had it printed as another small pamphlet entitled *Settlement of the Trouble Between Mr. Thring and Mr. Wells*. He privately printed 225 copies and signed and numbered each of them. They were distributed to all Society members who had received copies of the first pamphlet. The matter did eventually come to a close, but not without upsetting a large number of people and creating a climate of bitterness about Wells and his work.

Wells had many arguments and disagreements throughout his career and many of them were hung out for public display, usually because he chose to do so. On those occasions when he may not have chosen to go public, he was probably involved in an unwanted and unnecessary scandal where he could not escape public scrutiny. Such arguments made him a number of enemies and a few serious critics. Perhaps more significantly, public disagreement and scandals affected his writing and his legacy. His reading public began to view him as an aging buffoon and a public irritant rather that a literary icon. Although Wells did not go out of his way to regain the lost affection of his readers, he no doubt was aware that he was alienating large segments of his audience. Even more devastating would be the long term effect on a future readership made up of people that Wells would never know and never see. These future readers will be less likely to pick up a Wells novel than a novel from another writer of the same period, simply because the work of other writers is much less pedantic and tedious.

19

Pursuit of Royal Society Membership

The intellectual elite were often the centerpiece of Wells' writings, either as objects of derision or as the absolute rulers of his utopian state. He always considered himself to be one of the elite. This was reflected in the social circles he frequented, the lectures he presented and his attitude toward women, labor movements and the moneyed industrialists. His many descriptions of utopia and his prescription for social reform invariably included a benevolent, educated and authoritarian leadership. Wells never imagined himself as one of the plebeians sweeping the floors, preparing the food, or constructing the buildings. In his mind, he'd done his downstairs duty as a youth while growing up in Bromley, and had no intention of going back. The mundane details of daily life in Wells' utopian dreams were always taken care of behind the scenes. In fact the Wells Utopia did not seem to need the mundane any more than did Lewis Carroll's *Alice in Wonderland*. The flowers were always fresh, tea always served on time, convenient transportation available, and the invisible, but required facilities always nearby. This was the way Wells thought, and to a large extent this was the way he lived. He earned a considerable fortune during his lifetime and it allowed him to assume a life style far beyond that of the rest of the populace.

Wells enhanced this elitist attitude at every opportunity, sometimes to his own detriment and disappointment. His vision of himself as a scientist kept reappearing in his work and in his conversations with others. Wells did gain a B.Sc. degree with honors in zoology in 1890 and he was the author, with his old friend Richard Gregory of a text book on zoology entitled *Honours Physiography*, published in 1893. Wells did some lecturing in zoology to earn extra funds and he used this textbook to assist students in their cramming sessions for examination. In later years he also undertook two monumental tasks in producing *The Outline of His-*

tory and *The Science of Life*. The latter was again written with the help of Richard Gregory.

In Wells' own mind, he was a scientist. In the mind of many scientists, he was a dabbler. He never pursued a degree beyond his baccalaureate and had never done any experimental research. He adopted no particular specialty and produced nothing for publication in scientific journals, or in any way contributed to the science he espoused. Although he was never derided for his lack of accomplishment, those accomplishments were not in any field of science. He was never considered part of the scientific community in Britain, or in the rest of the world. But technical requirements and peer recognition were never part of Wells definition of a scientist. His baccalaureate and his constant reference to the scientific method were the only credentials that he needed, particularly in times when science was blossoming and the British Empire was leading the world in discoveries and exploration. Wells wanted to be a scientific insider, and as he did in many other circumstances, he assumed he was qualified without ever realizing that the scientific community would never turn to H.G. Wells for references or advice. Perhaps this sounds like unfair treatment of a writer with a love of science, but when the shoe is on the other foot it's little different from the treatment the literary community affords perceived outsiders.

When asked by the scientific establishment for evidence of his work, his research papers, or his scientific accomplishments, Wells answer was that he was a social scientist and had produced a body of work worthy of the best scientists and research establishments. To confirm his position, in 1942 he returned to London University where he had obtained his original B.Sc. degree. The university had a program that would allow former students to earn a D.Sc. degree on the basis of their currently published work, if they presented a thesis or dissertation. The Ph.D. or D.Sc. degree was a basic requirement of membership in the Royal Society. This membership had been one of Wells secret desires for many years. Since he let very few personal challenges go unfulfilled, at the age of 75 he set aside some of his other work to write a doctoral dissertation. He presented this work with an extensive bibliography of his own publications, and was awarded the degree he sought.

His D.Sc. thesis was entitled *On the Quality of Illusion in the Continuity of the Individual Life in the Higher Metazoa, with Particular Reference to the Species Homo Sapiens*. Although it is difficult to assess its purpose, the kernel of the thesis suggests that man does not posses a single mental personality, but rather is a collection of behaviors or personalities. The view or concept of a single personality is an illusion. The thesis is very difficult to read and in places seems to be purposely obtuse. It is not backed up by any practical research and Wells references simply point to other work with similar statements about nature and mankind. An example of his obtuse logic, which is largely opinion rather than the scientific deduction he commonly agreed was an essential part of scientific training, appears in the introduction to section II, *The Elements of Human Ecology.*

'27. In asserting the illusory nature of the integrality of the human individual it does not follow that we sweep aside any idea of continuity in life. Rather does this recognition enable us to realize the real continuity of life to which the inflamed egotism of our self-consciousness has blinded us.'[1]

Further into his thesis there are sections where neither logic nor opinion seems to prevail. Although it may be unfair to pull a sentence out of context the following summary of section VI, *The History of the Idea of Gregariousness,* is an example in which it's difficult to understand what Wells is saying regardless of context.

'77. In the face of the hallucinatory quality of personality elucidated in this paper this, so far as it retains any validity, resolves itself into a demand for a new and broader education throughout the world in which a federal political and economic order and a common fundamental law of human rights may afford a protective screen (see paragraphs 40 to 43 ante) behind which the great impersonal society of the days to come, with its unprecedented range of variability, may develop to the best advantage.'[2]

With this work Wells considered himself to have established credentials as a social scientist. Although the D.Sc. awarded by London University, based on a body of published work, is a perfectly valid credential, it did not then, and does not now, assume that the recipient has generated any original work in a major scientific field. But this did not deter Wells. He was proud of his thesis and had it included as part of the appendices in '42 to '44, published in 1944.

Once his D.Sc. was in hand, his next challenge was to submit an application to become a Fellow of the Royal Society. There has never been any more distinguished and respected scientific credential than the simple FRS after one's name. This would be the jewel in Wells crown. To become a member one had to have earned a PhD or equivalent degree, be sponsored by another member of the Society and have your published work scrutinized by a learned review board. Wells now had the degree, and he once again approached his old friend Richard Gregory for sponsorship. Gregory had led a distinguished career in zoology and had been a member of the Royal Society for some time. When Wells presented his desire for fellowship in the Society, Gregory cautioned him that the Society was unlikely to consider any part of the social sciences as acceptable for membership. However, Gregory was a devoted friend and carried Wells wishes to the Society.

The membership committee did not produce a favorable response to his application. They would not admit Wells or the so-called social sciences to the Royal Society. Some biographers consider this rejection to be politically motivated by those opposed to Wells' rather liberal views on contemporary society. There may certainly have been some political disfavor among long standing members but more importantly, Wells just did not fit into the membership, and never would. The Royal Society was then, and is now, a distinguished body of scientists claiming dozens of members from Isaac Newton to Steven Hawking, all with impeccable research credentials. To have admitted Wells into this organization would have admitted someone who had obtained only a baccalaureate, had never done any research in his acknowledged field, had never published any scientific papers and had made no contribution to scientific knowledge. Although Wells viewed himself much differently he could have avoided setting himself up for a fall.

This rejection was a blow to Wells. Although we can never really know how he reacted, it was probably a more serious slight to his ego than is apparent in any biographical material. Wells had a habit of creating ideas or generating projects and then pursuing them to a satisfactory conclusion. He knew that success in his efforts to achieve and FRS would place a small crown on his distinguished career as a writer, a thinker and a prophet. It would legitimize Wells as a man of scientific means and qualifications. Wells health was failing, he was in his mid-seventies and he badly wanted this recognition. But it was not to be, and this disappointment may well have contributed to his depression in the last few years of his life. Wells admitted in later writing that there was one honor he would like to have achieved in his lifetime, but he was not prepared to reveal what it was. There is a good chance that it was membership in the Royal Society. Other honors to which he might have aspired were a Nobel Prize, as was awarded to his friend G.B. Shaw in 1925, or perhaps a knighthood, the acceptance of which would have made him the ultimate hypocrite. All these honors escaped H.G. Wells.

20

The Movie Business

Several of Wells novels and short stories were put into film productions during his lifetime. The movie business was a booming and glittering industry between the two World Wars and producers were constantly on the lookout for interesting and socially relevant stories to put on the screen. What better way to stroke Wells ego than to place him at the center of attention in a movie studio.

During the latter years of the silent film industry Wells sold rights to some of his work to movie producers, however he was not closely involved in any of the screen productions. This was to change when he met Alexander Korda, the ambitious Hungarian film producer. Korda had built a small studio outside of London and produced a film version of *The Man Who Could Work Miracles*. It was a low budget effort and not widely successful. When Korda asked Wells to participate in the production of *Things To Come* he eagerly agreed and began work on the screenplay. It was an ambitious and expensive production. It was released in 1936 and received wide distribution. Both Wells and Korda considered it to be an anti-war statement but its reception by the public was mixed at a time when war in Europe was once again a threat.

Things To Come was the most ambitious movie production that Wells became involved in. It came at a time when he was approaching seventy years of age and something new and refreshing had caught his interest. He began to think seriously about writing more screenplays and producing other films. A trip to California seemed to be in order and he ventured west as the guest of former countryman Charlie Chaplin and Paulette Goddard. Chaplin escorted him through the movie studios and introduced him to may of the well known figures in the film business. Wells loved the attention he received and relished the conversations with Chaplin on socialism and the emergence of Stalin's Russia. Chaplin was a well known communist sympathizer who believed that the Russian socialist state was the answer to many of the world's problems.

Wells visit to Hollywood ended quietly and generated no substantial interest in other movie projects. Although Wells writing would be used again as the centerpiece for several screenplays, *Things To Come* was the last movie in which he closely participated. After his death a serious effort was made to produce *The War Of The Worlds* and *The Time Machine* as movies. These two movies, released in 1953 and 1960 respectively, perhaps set the trend for science fiction films for the next couple of decades. The following list is compiled from a number of sources and represents most of the movie productions that were based on Wells novels or screenplays, both during and after his lifetime. Not included are a number of productions based loosely on Wells short stories, often bearing titles with little resemblance to the original.

The First Men in the Moon, 1919, Gaumont Films (SILENT)
The Wheels of Chance, 1921, Harold Shaw Producer, Stoll Film Company (SILENT)
The Passionate Friends, 1922, Stoll Film Company (SILENT)
Kipps, 1922, Stoll Film Company (SILENT)
The Island of Lost Souls, 1932, Erle C. Kenten Director, Paramount Pictures
Charles Laughton, Richard Arlen, Kathleen Burke, Bela Lugosi
This was a screen interpretation of *The Island of Dr. Moreau* banned in 1933 for its sadistic and sexual content. Wells didn't like the portrayal of Moreau as a sadist rather than a flawed idealist
The Invisible Man, 1933
The Man Who Could Work Miracles, 1935, Alexander Korda, London Films
Ralph Richardson, Roland Young
Things to Come, 1936, Alexander Korda, London Films
Ralph Richardson, Raymond Massey
The Passionate Friends, 1938, J. Arthur Rank
Kipps, 1941, Carol Reed Director
Michael Redgrave, Michael Wilding, Phyllis Calvert
The History of Mr. Polly, 1949, Anthony Pelissier Director, Two Cities Productions
John Mills, Sally Ann Howes, Finlay Currie
The War of the Worlds, 1953, George Pal Director, Paramount Pictures
Gene Barry, Ann Robinson
The Time Machine, 1960, George Pal Director, MGM Studios
Rod Taylor, Yvette Mimieux
Academy award winner for special effects in 1960

The First Men in the Moon, 1964, American British Production
Half a Sixpence, 1968, George Sydney Director, Paramount
Tommy Steele, Julia Foster, Cyril Richard
A film version of the popular London stage show
The Food of the Gods, 1976, Bert Gordon Director
Marjoe Gortner, Pamela Franklin
Poor quality, very dated, terrible special effects
The Time Machine, 1978, Hennig Schellerup Director
John Beck, Priscilla Barnes, Andrew Duggan
A remake for television
The Island of Dr. Moreau. 1977, Don Taylor Director
Burt Lancaster, Michael York, Nigel Davenport
The Shape of Things to Come, 1979, George McGowan Director
Jack Palance, Carol Lynley, Barry Morse
The Island of Dr. Moreau. 1996
Val Kilmer, Marlon Brando
The Time Machine, 2002, Simon Wells Director, Warner Bros.
Guy Pierce, Samantha Mumba, Orlando Jones, Jeremy Irons
A contemporary variation of Wells perennial story, directed by his great grandson

PART V

The Lure of Global Issues

21

A Solution to World Conflict

There is an oft repeated Chinese curse that can be expressed with the phrase, 'may you live in interesting times'. It condemns a man to face the trials of change without the benefit of consistent rules or reliable friends. It is doubtful that Wells was ever cursed by the Chinese, but there is little doubt that he lived in what may be the most interesting period of the last few hundred years. They were times of turmoil and times of promise. As one century moved into the next he saw the last major British Colonial conflict in the Boer War and he lived through the travesty and injustice of the First World War. He experienced the surge of industrialization in Europe and the heady times of the early twentieth century. Like many of his contemporaries he developed very specific ideas about how the world's problems could be solved, and he was not the least reticent in letting others know what he thought.

The notoriety Wells gained from his writing reinforced his personal conviction that he was an authority on many of Europe's emerging social issues. He wrote copious volumes on the importance of socialist philosophy, utopian ideals, and above all, the necessity of world government. To Wells, the concept of world government seemed to be an obvious and necessary requirement to the avoidance of continued global conflict. Although some of his contemporaries may have had trouble taking him seriously when he spouted his colorful ideas and socialist propaganda, he was truly a man in earnest. It would be interesting to know just how close to complete world government he believed man could actually come. As he neared the end of his writing career he made it clear in *The Fate of Homo Sapiens* and *The New World Order* that the human race could not survive without some form of universal management and control. As he usually did, Wells rewrote his political ideas several times and within the space of two years he published *The Common Sense of War and Peace, Guide to the New World*, and *The Outlook for Homo Sapiens*. In his later years Wells' writing began to reflect what seemed to be an increasing despondency. As the Second Great War came to a close he could see how few were actually listening to him. He was convinced that mankind was headed toward complete self-destruction and he had too little time left to make a difference.

Between the two World Wars Wells was actively engaged in a variety of public campaigns to promote his favorite causes. These causes varied from one year to the next but usually included some aspect of world government, the League of Nations, universal education or the International Bill of Human Rights. On some occasions his progress came to a halt or changed direction because he over estimated the enthusiasm of his supporters and the commitment of active political organizations. At the close of the Second World War he realized that any movement towards world government initiated by the League of Nations was irrevocably stalled, and without the mandate of the worlds most powerful governments there would never be an organization with the strength to impose a global system on the world. Without a global administration there would never be universal education for millions of illiterates, nor a judicial system that would respect the rights of individuals of all races and religions.

Wells was both a novelist and an idealist. This isn't an unusual combination and it may account for a few of his more esoteric and impractical ideas. But if he actually believed that world government could be achieved, then he was only remotely in contact with reality. As was often the case, Wells could design and write about what he thought were optimum social environments and utopias free of oppression, starvation and disease. He could write about social systems where everyone was well educated, with ample free time to discuss the subtleties of perfection. But Wells either omitted or quickly disposed of the difficult bits. Specifically, how do we get there, how long will it take and how much will it cost? His thinking was packaged in the same wrapper and elitist style that he despised in others. He believed that getting social agreement between European nations, Great Britain and North America would result in a world solution. He expends precious little ink on the thousands of tribes, sects and religious fanatics that had never heard of H.G. Wells and would never conform to his plans or agree with his social philosophy. The ideal socialist utopia was, and still is, a figment of the white European imagination. It would not be remotely considered by the Arab mind, Central African tribes or Mongolian nomads. Nor would it gain much ground with the diverse races and cultures of South East Asia that were based more on religion and tradition rather than political ideals. European socialist philosophy would not register, even remotely, with two thirds of the world's population.

These potential geopolitical issues were not worthy of any lengthy discussion in Wells' writing except perhaps in *What is Coming?* wherein he includes a chapter entitled *The White Man's Burthen.*[1] This essay considers the responsibility of Europeans in managing the widely scattered colonial empires collected in the latter half of the nineteenth century. It's written in a slightly condescending manner and deals with the lesser corners of the world in a few pages. Although he disagrees with the imperialism that created these far-flung assets, his answer to their inclusion in the global community simply becomes the white man's burthen. In spite of a few speaking tours in Europe, America and Australia his view of the world was usually very small and restricted to the English speaking social environment in which he grew up. The Zulu wars in South Africa, for example, were not an issue in his ultimate solution to world government.

Wells had several ideas that he considered minimum requirements in achieving uniform global government. These were concepts on which he wrote numerous volumes, often rehashing the same material a dozen times. One of these ideas was the necessity of a thorough and universal education. Much to his credit he believed that education could achieve almost any success. He had various schemes for providing uniform tutelage. He proposed a world encyclopedia wherein anyone could find the sum of the world's knowledge, or at least an index to the world's knowledge. He explains how a copy of the encyclopedia could be on the shelves of every home in Britain. In keeping with his local view of the world he omits the set of encyclopedias in the camp of the Mongolian nomads. The problem of language for his encyclopedia would easily be solved by using English (or by inventing a new language that nobody could read). Of course, we can be almost certain that the French would agree readily to this idea.

Wells took many of his beliefs seriously enough to turn them into action. His very first publication in 1893 was entitled *A Textbook of Biology*. It was intended specifically for tutelage in biology. His lifelong commitment to education provided the incentive for his later non-fiction trilogy *The Outline of History (1920)*, *The Science of Life (1930)*, and *The Work, Wealth and Happiness of Mankind (1931)*. These books were intended to provide a basic grounding in history, biology, economics and sociology for the literate public. In spite of the bias and limited scope of the books, they were indeed used in English speaking schools and public libraries for many years and through many editions.

Wells spent a large amount of time on other global political issues including the International Bill of Rights, and the League of Nations. It is unfair to downplay the significance of his work on these projects. He believed these issues to be a significant part of an ideal world government, a government of well educated, free thinking academics who would control the world and deal appropriately with dissenters. The fate of the dissenter is occasionally considered in his novels where the use of a firing squad, gas, or prison is considered. The fate of the ignorant and poverty stricken masses often remains undefined as if these were mere details in the utopian scheme. In spite of what often seemed to be noble means, Wells was driving toward an unrealistic end. At the time of his death he had no way of seeing that the world would never approach the goals he'd set. There was little question in 1945 that mankind was badly in need of new management so it wasn't unrealistic for him to believe that this new management might eventually be achieved, or even to believe that new management had to be achieved for the survival of mankind. Wells can never be accused of having a static mind. A century later he may have had a completely different approach to solving the world's problems. The next three chapters will look at some of his global projects and the environment in which they evolved.

22

The World Encyclopedia

There is no mistaking the fact that Wells' mind was seldom idle. He was perpetually writing, scribbling notes, correcting typescripts and drawing cartoons or 'picshuas', as he referred to them. When engrossed in thought or making plans for his next book he would often come up with ideas that might help push along his design of the ideal utopian world. Some of these ideas were constructive regardless of the social implications, and others were a bit foolish and poorly conceived. One of his worst and most impractical brain waves was published as *The Idea of a World Encyclopaedia*. Wells by nature was a satirist and often spoke and wrote with tongue-in-cheek. When a strange idea came bouncing from his pen readers were prepared to smile and give him credit for an amusing anecdote. But in the case of his world encyclopedia it seems that he was as serious as he could be, although it was probably one of his most inane ideas, poorly thought out, and impossible to implement.

On the twentieth of November in 1936 Wells made a presentation to the Royal Institution, an organization that possessed a large membership of academics and scientifically trained educators. Wells was forever passing himself off as a scientist and loved to deliver a speech designed to stir the imagination of those in his audience, especially this kind of audience. Although Wells was a poor speaker with a halting manner and a high-pitched voice, he was usually very proud of his speeches. After presentation, this particular speech was delivered in typescript to Leonard and Virginia Woolf for publication by their Hogarth Press. It appeared as a short pamphlet, about 8000 words, and No. 35 in their Day to Day Pamphlet series. The title was appropriately *The Idea of a World Encyclopaedia*.

This was not the first time Wells had brought up the encyclopedia idea. As far back as 1914 he had included a similar concept in *The World Set Free* and he repeats the thought a number of times in various tracts over the years. It's perhaps surprising to note that Wells would present such an idea without a shred of evidence as to its practicality and no research related to the demand for such material. Any criticism from others about his project he would brush off with a wave of his hand. Wells got away with this tactic often and was seldom brought to task. When he was questioned, he would react with irritation and fire off a dozen letters to friends and newspaper editors about the individuals or institutions that had dared to suggest alternatives. His world encyclopedia idea provided many opportunities for both humorous and satirical goading but there seems to be little evidence that anyone ever contested him on the practical issues, which in simple terms were completely illogical and unrealistic.

What Wells was proposing was an encyclopedia in its literal and physical sense. A massive set of books that would contain an index or summary of all the world's knowledge. This wasn't an educational concept, a method of teaching, or a scheme to record history. It was a set of books. Presumably it was a set of books that could be purchased by any educated or literate citizen with the necessary funds. In Wells' own view '…the World Encyclopaedia would be a row of volumes in his own home or in some neighboring house…'[1] Perhaps if Wells had assembled more background material of his own he might have realized that, even in 1936, this encyclopedia would fill the purchaser's house, his neighbor's house and possibly several other houses. If it was designed more as an index to knowledge rather than as a repository of the world's knowledge, then the Encyclopedia Britannica had already done that very thing and had provided regular updates for a century or more. But competing with Encyclopedia Britannica was the furthest thing from Wells' mind.

He believed that there was enough knowledge in the world to enable mankind to always make the best of decisions and plans, and if this knowledge were assembled in some easy-to-manage form it would avoid the incredible folly of poor decisions like those made in negotiating the Treaty of Versailles. He states the premise rather eloquently when he says that '…all the directive ideas needed to establish a wise and stable settlement of the world's affairs in 1919 existed in bits and fragments, here and there, but practically nothing had been assembled, practically nothing had been thought out, nothing practically has been done to draw that knowledge and these ideas together…'[2] Indeed it seems to have escaped him that even with all the facts and ideas at hand, politicians and military icons are capable of some of the worst and most bone-headed decisions known to history. Wells is using his practical and 'scientific' mind on a problem that will never be practical or scientific. Collecting knowledge in a set of books that can be stored in one's home will not remedy the issue of foolishness or bad judgment. At best they might help avoid a trip to the library, and only if they contain far more than a summary or index of man's knowledge.

As Wells began to reveal his plans for contents of the work he suggested that he did not want to see an encyclopedia tainted with propaganda and advertisement, but it '...should consist of selections, extracts, quotations, very carefully assembled with the approval of outstanding authorities...'[3] By the time Wells wrote this pamphlet he was an experienced propagandist and he makes it clear that no one else's propaganda should appear in his encyclopedia unless approved by '...outstanding authorities...'

A speech on this subject to the members of The Royal Institution would naturally have its detractors. Wells was prepared for them by anticipating what he assumed would be their two main objections. These are trivial objections that probably never entered the minds of the assumed detractors in the audience. The first objection might be that '...no two people think alike, quot homines, tot sententiae...'[4] and it will not be possible for theologians, economists and scientist to agree on a uniform encyclopedia. Wells response to this was simply that anyone who thinks in such a manner is guilty of mental laziness and is trying to avoid having their intimate convictions overturned and examined. The minor differences among contributors of different disciplines would appear only for the sake of argument and serve to bring man's knowledge into closer harmony. The second objection seems to be even less substantive. He suggests that detractors will accuse him of wanting to stereotype people and make them all think alike by collecting their knowledge from the same source. His response to this objection was that '...these elegant people who want the world picturesquely at sixes and sevens are hopeless cases...it does not enhance the natural variety and beauty of life to have all the clocks in a town keeping individual times of their own, no charts of the sea, no timetables...'[5]

In his speech Wells has developed his premise, made up a few trivial objections, and eagerly trampled them back to the ground. The speech then takes on some of the more practical issues of implementing the work and assembling his encyclopedia. And here his vision falls short again. He wants his encyclopedia to be a world encyclopedia. He dismisses all of the world's languages but English (or Esperanto) because it is more subtle and more widely used than others. The encyclopedia would eventually be translated into all other languages. Students would perform the work of compiling the material and they would be continually reissuing updated segments of the encyclopedia. This would become possible because college tutoring and normal lecturing work would no longer be required. The encyclopedia would eliminate the need for lecturers and tutors, and it would ensure that students could avoid corruption of their minds.

Maintaining the encyclopedia by continually reissuing it in new and updated sections is imaginative folly in itself and smacks of Orwellian rewriting of history. Any historical catalog or index should certainly have material constantly added to it, such as an index of technical journals or a bibliography of reference material, but the material is not rewritten. Perhaps this is where the propaganda comes in. The issue of translation serves to muddy the issue again. Anything rewritten or reissued by the working students will also have a thousand reinterpretations delivered by the hundreds of translators required to provide the universal scope.

Wells fully admits that his project will be immense, but he seems unable to grasp the magnitude of the knowledge that he wants to assemble. For example he can '…imagine something on the scale of ten or twenty thousand items…'[6] in the bibliography he would attach to the work. In 1936 when he prepared this speech, the Cambridge University Library, one of England's copyright libraries, could have easily eclipsed that number of relevant items. The bibliographies and catalogs of the rest of the world's research centers and universities might have doubled the list again, which of course must be a fundamental requirement of a world encyclopedia.

When it comes to paying for the project Wells tends toward the naïve again. He simply states that he sees '…no reason why the capital needed for these promotion activities should not be forthcoming…'[7] To ensure this capital he will grant the work a monopoly and will direct its distributors to collect taxes and revenues from its use. One can't help but wonder how Wells planned to include the literature, translate the catalogs, create the monopoly and collect the revenue from the Tutsi tribes of central Africa.

Finally he placed any potential detractors from outside the captive audience in their appropriate place, and he did it rather unsympathetically. If a man of science, or one of the intellectual elite objects, then he '…is apt to show himself a very Simple Simon indeed. And of course from the very start various opinionated cults and propagandas will be doing their best to capture us or buy us…'[8] Why capturing or buying an encyclopedia would become an obsession for '…opinionated cults…' is difficult to understand, but Wells was convinced they would be out there, ready to impede his progress towards a World Encyclopedia.

It's easy to look back fifty or one hundred years and pick at the folly of obsolete concepts, but this is an example of a mixture of ideas that didn't make much sense when first conceived and they make even less sense in the future they were intended to serve. In the information age of the twenty first century an entirely different solution has fallen into place through natural selection. The internet provides the world's population with access to government records, university libraries, international museums and archives, and of course, access to many of the world's dictionaries and encyclopedias, largely without cost or inconvenience. The significance of the comparison to twenty-first century solutions is two-fold. First Wells had little concept of the massive requirements of what he considered to be an encyclopedic repository of the world's knowledge. He conceded that it would take many volumes, and many years work, but he made the same classical mistakes over and over again. His concepts were based on a very narrow view of the world around him. Although he certainly did not have tunnel vision, he simply could not conceive the enormous size of the world that existed beyond his sight. This was true of his simplistic view of economics, his belief that a global government made up of the intellectual elite would resolve the world's conflicts, and his conviction that socialism would do more than any other form of government, even those that had evolved and survived through one hundred of years of trial and error.

Wells would never have believed anyone describing the future World Wide Web, much less the fact that it would evolve on its own over the next century. It's ironic that the so-called World Wide Web was conceived and implemented by an English physicist working in Switzerland for the purpose of getting his research results to colleagues scattered around the world.[9] It was not a social experiment, it did not change the way people talk to each other, it wasn't proposed or developed by any government and it avoids the massive expense that government would inevitably have required and could never have justified.

Was Wells prophetic? Perhaps some of his fans might think so, but his '…row of volumes…' was not even a remote solution to the problem of gathering information into a compact centralized location. It could not have been accomplished at any time in past centuries and is patently irrelevant in the foreseeable future.

23

The League of Nations

After the First Great War the victors divided the tarnished spoils and placed onerous sanctions on the defeated nations. The settlements were incorporated into
the Treaty of Versailles signed in 1918. Although this treaty achieved a temporary pacification across the new map of Europe, it also produced a deep resentment of the victors by the vanquished. All combatants had been bloodied by a
long and obscene war that produced widespread devastation previously unknown
to the world. It was important to establish an agreement that would settle territorial disputes and provide some assurance that such a conflict would never arise
again. The beaten Teutonic Empire resented the imposition made by the Treaty
of Versailles. Old boundaries had been moved, nations were divided, strict sanctions were imposed, and restitution was extracted. In spite of their humiliation
the subjected nations were anxious to find a way out of defeat and back into the
global community.

Diplomats from all corners of the world soon became aware of the failings of
the Versailles agreement and were eager to participate in an international group
that might provide the mechanism for more just and even-handed settlements in
the future, and equally important, a group that could establish pacts and agreements that might prevent the recurrence of war on the scale of the First World
War. By 1920 approximately forty nations had come to an agreement on a draft
constitution and the League of Nations was established in Geneva. In simple
terms its fundamental purpose was to promote world peace by establishing a
mutual aid pact. Any member nation invaded or attacked would be supported by
all members of the League. A mutual support pact of this nature made it difficult
and impractical for member nations to participate in military aggression against
other members because of the overwhelming force and onerous sanctions that
would result. In many respects its basic concepts were much the same as the classical NATO Alliance formed after the Second World War.

Although participants in the League of Nations were well aware of the potential for disagreement among the members, they were not prepared for the number of arguments and the magnitude of dissention that arose. The United States eventually refused to join the League in spite of the contributions and support made by Woodrow Wilson. This was a great disappointment to most of Europe because the United States was emerging as a global power and could provide the resources and diplomacy necessary to make the League work. However, few could see that the United States was rapidly retreating into a newly grown shell of isolationism. This was a mistake that would not be obvious to most Americans for another generation.

The edges of the League of Nations began to fray further as militant and often arrogant nations flexed their military muscle in geographical areas where empires of the past had left numerous colonial remnants. Italy invaded Ethiopia against the wishes of the League. In spite of obvious violations of the League's charter, the sanctions brought against Italy were soon lifted because of pressure from Great Britain and France who needed Italy as an ally against Germany. If history is not littered with enough false hope, Japan withdrew from the League because its members refused to recognize the Japanese conquest of Manchuria. To make matters worse, the Soviet Union was expelled for invading Finland. By the time the shadow of war was again upon Europe the League was totally ineffective and all trust between nations had been lost. At a time when its presence and influence might have delayed, if not prevented the Second Great War, the League fell apart and war blossomed again. In 1946, after more death and destruction, the alliance was dissolved and its remnants were turned over to the newly created United Nations.

Although heads of state among the nations signing the Treaty of Versailles gained most of the credit for designing and creating the League of Nations, there were many other diplomats and workers behind the scenes promoting the cause and laying out its constitution, infrastructure and financial requirements. These included politicians, civil servants and academics who saw the potential benefit of an international organization. H.G. Wells was unquestionably one of the League's earliest and most vocal proponents. As early as 1917 he was campaigning for a unified world governing council and was publicly using the title *League of Nations*. He wrote a series of articles for London newspapers on various topics related to World Government. In 1918 many of these articles were collected and republished by Chatto and Windus as a book entitled *In the Fourth Year*.[1] Wells participated in, and made presentations to a number of organizations on the subject of world government. In Britain the League of Nations Union was a typical representative of the organized proponents of an international body designed to administer economics, justice and military issues. This latter group published one of Wells articles in pamphlet form under the title *British Nationalism and the League of Nations.*[2]

In 1919, immediately after the Great War was settled, Wells and several of his colleagues contributed to another book published by the Oxford University Press entitled *The Idea of a League of Nations.*[3] This was revised in another small booklet, also published by the Oxford University Press, entitled *The Way to a League of Nations.*[4] As the title implies this second effort was a more practical treatise intended to promote a tangible mechanism for achieving a unified global League of Free Nations. Not only did Wells do a lot of writing on the subject, historical records also indicate that he spent a great deal of his time working with others on the concept of an international governing body.

In early 1918, before the armistice, Wells was invited to assume a position in a branch of the British Ministry of Information. He seemed eager to take up the opportunity and began his participation in the department of Enemy Propaganda. As might be expected he concentrated more on promotion of his social and political agenda that he did on government propaganda, and soon lost interest in the post and its original purpose. He resigned after a few months work. This entire episode was probably a great disappointment to Wells since he longed for a position in government or some other position of import that could provide a pulpit for his socialist solutions to the world's ailments. When he saw a potential opportunity, he charged ahead with his own brand of propaganda, never dreaming that the government may have had something else in mind. What was not evident until many years later was the fact that most of the public, including Wells and his colleagues, were completely unaware of the separate agenda being pursued by the Allied powers as the war neared its end. Lloyd George, Georges Clemenceau and Woodrow Wilson had their own issues in mind. They were already planning how they would carve up the pieces of the defeated aggressors when they ultimately met at Versailles. However, even their surreptitious plans did not mature entirely as expected. The United States refused to sign the treaty, largely because they couldn't get their own way in the war settlement, and the treaty that was finally ratified was subject to years of disagreement and revolt by the subjugated nations. Eventually, in 1939, the infamous Treaty of Versailles collapsed and was followed by the onset of the next great war.

The period between 1914 and 1918 was a terrifying time for all of Europe. It was also a major turning point in global history. Everything was changing. Warfare had lost its dignity and had descended to an obscene battle among the elite and privileged of Europe. Industrialization was a juggernaut that pushed war into a competition of machinery as much as a battle among men and their beliefs. Wars were no longer fought solely on a battlefield. The enemy was now chased and slaughtered throughout the world. Wells was convinced, as were many of his contemporaries, that things had to change. A revolution in government had to emerge from the war and a new system of global government had to be put in place to ensure that the death and destruction engendered by The Great War would never occur again. What better opportunity for a well respected author and avowed socialist to rise to the fore and tell the world how this goal could be achieved!

Contemporaneously the Russian revolution of 1917 was being viewed by Wells with an active interest. He was among the first from the West to congratulate Maxim Gorki for the overthrow of the Tsarists. Here he saw the beginnings of a major change in world politics. The resulting Soviet Republic had quickly achieved many of the things that Wells believed were necessary in imposing a fair and equitable government on the masses. The advantage of an armed revolution was a simple fact. The old guard could be thrown out instantly without the years or decades required by a Wellsian social revolution. However, to advocate anything more aggressive in Britain would brush very closely to sedition, especially in 1917. The opportunities presented by the Bolshevik revolution almost certainly excited Wells. Russia had become a socialist laboratory and deserved very close attention.

Wells was not blind to the atrocities and economic chaos in Russia generated by the revolution. Nor was he unaware of the corruption and the newly established class system created by the revolution. In 1919 he went to Russia with his oldest son G.P. Wells and visited Gorki, who naturally assured him that most of the terrible things the British had heard about the Bolsheviks were untrue. Wells followed his visit with a defense of the principles of Bolshevism that didn't sit well with many at home. Churchill was one of those who were especially offended by Wells remarks, and as noted in Chapter 2, he wrote with his usual sharp sarcasm that Wells ought to have no difficulty in becoming and expert on the internal conditions of Russia after a visit of only fourteen days.

Wells made another visit to Moscow in 1934 with a number of colleagues and managed to schedule a meeting with Stalin. On his return he arranged for the publication of a small book about the meeting entitled *The Stalin-Wells Talk*.

Naturally the visit, and the subsequent book, created a fuss among western politicians who had begun to see Stalin for the barbarian he really was. They believed, with some justification, that Wells could not see the forest for the trees, and that he was blinded by his insistence on the higher ideals of a socialist state. Stalin would quickly prove himself worse than any of the Russian Tsars and he was instrumental in creating a state that became more oppressive and decadent than any of the imperial empires of the nineteenth century had ever been.

But Wells was an eternal optimist and was convinced that he could do a much better job than the Bolsheviks in designing and staging a revolution. It would be a quiet revolution based on what he called 'the open conspiracy' He wrote and lectured regularly for many years after the war about the necessity of major change, a change that would constitute a quiet revolution. The disappointment that he and the rest of the world saw in the Bolshevik revolution, which was literally a case of barbarians at the gate, was something that could be fixed. In Wells words, '…the Englishman could design and build a better revolution…'

The period between the two world wars was an active time in Wells life. After the close of the First World War he expanded his group of friends, did some travelling and participated in many social and political organizations. He made a great deal of money from his books, newspaper articles and lectures. Wells had gained a powerful voice with a wide spectrum of followers. He was in the prime of life and fully intended to use his influence wherever he thought it could do the most good. Some of his critics were not very kind about his ability to jump from one burning issue to another. The issues were often not burning until Wells made them so, and when he tired of one issue he left its dying embers and went off in other directions. This was the case with The League of Nations. Its failings were becoming more numerous and its critics were becoming more vocal. Wells blamed the failings on bureaucratic foolishness and the inability of politicians to establish a world governing body firmly in control with the muscle and the police force necessary to ensure that the rules were obeyed and that the goals of the organization were maintained. In simple Wellsian terms, they had not listened to any of the advice he had offered, so they were naturally bound to fail.

It became more and more clear to Wells as the Second World War approached that his open revolution was not going to happen and the new world government would never exist. This was a contributing factor to the disappointment and depression he experienced in the last few years of his life. After devoting much of his time during the twenty years between the wars to idealism and a new world order, he had to face the fact that he had been largely ignored. It was a sobering blow to his ego and his pride. Had Wells not been quite so single minded in his approach to the League of Nations he might have seen that his dream of world government and the political goals of a mutual aid society were two entirely different things. The League of Nations was not a path to Wells utopian vision and world leaders would never provide it with any governing power. The only thing it would ever have in common with Wells goals was the prevention of war. It quickly failed in this mission for the same reason that Wells global utopian government would never work. Its participants had entirely different objectives and could never agree on a common cause.

24

An International Bill of Human Rights

In the late 1930's Wells became interested in the creation of an International Bill of Rights, or a policy declaration that might be acknowledged by other nations to help establish the basic concept of The Rights of Man. This was a prominent public topic on the eve of war in Europe when the English and many of their European colleagues were wondering why they should be fighting another war. Wells became part of a privately constituted committee formed to draft a Bill of Rights. The group included Lord Sankey who later chaired the committee. When the declaration was published in its final draft it became known as the Sankey Declaration even though Wells was often acknowledged as being the major contributor to the work.

In 1940, after the Second World War began to unfold, Wells republished this Bill of Rights along with several letters he wrote to *The London Times,* and a couple of essays on the history of the document's creation. It was released by Penguin Books Limited as number S50 in a series of Penguin Specials and entitled *The Rights of Man*. A Penguin Special was a book of topical interest that could be published in a short period of time. Since most of the topics in *The Rights of Man* were political or social issues and criticisms of wide interest they had to be published while they were current to gain any reasonable distribution. Penguin Books thus provided an appropriate fast and cheap vehicle for many prominent writers to get their social and political tracts exposed during the early part of the twentieth century.

There are a number of things that are interesting, if not remarkable, about the small book Penguin published for Wells. The first is the fact that Wells even considered an agreement with Penguin Books to publish his work since they were not a classical publishing house. The second is the amount of time and effort he put into the subject of Human Rights and his persistence in ensuring that the committee's work was published, and thirdly, some of the changes in his social philosophy were beginning to sound almost like contradictions of is earlier writings.

Penguin Books was to build a century long and highly distinguished publication history in Great Britain and the British Commonwealth, but when Wells completed an agreement with them, they were a small organization. First run novels were not part of their tradition. They leaned towards essays, educational and historical material, and reprints of classical works. Penguin was a young publishing firm in 1939 and was probably more interested in publishing Wells than Wells was in working with Penguin. But Penguin was one of the few organizations that could get Wells and his Bill of Rights colleagues the distribution they wanted. Thus the two came together in 1939 with *In Search of Hot Water.*[1] This was followed by *The Rights of Man or What Are We Fighting For?*[2] and *The Common Sense of War and Peace*[3] in 1940. Shortly thereafter Wells and Penguin parted ways. Penguin would return to Wells after his death to republish a number of his novels, but they never collaborated on more than these three small publications during his lifetime.

Throughout his career as a writer Wells had running arguments with his publishers. Some were trivial and some were long venomous disagreements. His notoriety produced good sales for most of his books, and he depended on this notoriety to help get his social and political message out. Regardless of his efforts some books were clunkers that were little read, and to this day appear only on the shelves of research libraries. His Penguin books were certainly widely distributed and read by a wide cross-section of the literate public in 1939, but today they probably fall into the research library category.

As Wells got older and his writings became more controversial, he had trouble earning the large sums he gained from earlier and more widely distributed books. He often demanded substantial advances and grumbled constantly about the size of the royalties he got from publishers. He questioned the methods they used to report total book sales and suggested how they could improve their advertising and distribution techniques for his books. This made him unpopular with many publishers. He was known to drop an agreement in a huff with one publisher and run across the street to make a deal with one of its competitors. The new publisher would acquiesce to Wells' demands and ultimately get burned by the disappointing sales of his latest books or by the demands he placed on his contracts. By the end of Wells life he was running out of publishers and had to return, hands clasped, to some of his old publication partners. Although Penguin Books Limited did not exist when Wells first began writing, they were certainly not the kind of publisher he would approach for a new contract. They probably could not afford him, nor did he always write the kind of thing they were interested in publishing. But time changes many things, including publishers and authors. Wells was constantly in need of money and in need of a vehicle to present his work to the public. Penguin Books, for a short period, was this vehicle. It was probably not the most profitable vehicle, but a reliable and distinguished one nonetheless.

Wells did not claim to be the originator or the proprietor of this new Declaration of the Rights of Man, although some give him credit for getting it started and ensuring that it was brought to public attention. In fact he cites the original French declaration made in 1789 by quoting *Les Droits de l'Homme, droits naturels, inalienables et sacres, ont ete inscrits dans la Declaration de 1789.*[4] The French parliament also passed a similar revised declaration in 1936. Clearly, in the case of the French, it was largely an academic exercise. In the light of history, the Sankey Declaration of Human Rights can probably be placed on the same academic shelf. But at the time of this latter publication, the entire issue of human rights had become a very current and controversial topic. Europe was again on the brink of war. The public throughout Europe was frustrated, frightened and annoyed. They began to think seriously about their rights. The old guard, based historically on monarchy and empire, had been dealt a fatal blow in the previous war, but only small segments of Europe had benefited. And now the broken nations at the center of the world were being forced to defend themselves again. For what? What rights remained to them? What rights will man gain from more war?

The concern about human rights was not new to H.G. Wells and he was delighted to jump into the fray expressing his wisdom and demonstrating his myriad talents. His voice could be heard through his many newspaper contacts, speaking engagements and publications. Wells spent a good part of the next four years working on draft revisions of the Declaration and trying to interest larger and larger groups in promoting the ideas to governments and international organizations around the world. Several drafts of the Declaration were published over this period. They contained numerous revisions and changes to suit special interests and influential organizations. Most of the changes are of little significance in themselves. A final draft was eventually published in 1943. It contained substantial revisions to the original draft and paid homage to the many groups who wanted to contribute to the promotion of a cause as noble as a Bill of Human Rights. For a while Wells even toyed with having the Declaration published in one of the simplified languages being promoted at the time, such as Esperanto.

He believed this would make the Declaration accessible to a wider range of the world's population where language differences might otherwise restrict it. He still didn't seem to understand, after half a century of political exposure, that the illiterate were simply illiterate, and publishing something in a compromised language, regardless of its simplicity, did not expand his readership or the readership of something as noble as human rights.

Translating a Declaration of Human Rights into a new and simplified language to make it more widely read is an indignity that needs to be explored. Wells shows a significant lack of vision and understanding. Half the world population cannot read or write. They speak hundreds of different languages and dialects and they belong to thousands of tribes, sects, religions, and political systems. Wells consistently ignores the issue of diversity when he designs his utopias and proposes new social systems for mankind. Occasionally he will pay lip service to the Black African or a remote sect in the Punjab, but in large part they do not figure into his *scientific methods*. Human rights need to be practiced now, not at some future time when everybody can speak Esperanto or English Basic.

The issue of human rights and the need to have these rights defined and respected throughout the world is very much a 'motherhood and apple pie' issue if we can use today's vernacular. It's one of those things that you just can't disparage and be respected as a person. However, there were several things that seemed to escape Wells as he worked towards a published version of human rights, and they are perhaps the reason why human rights are still such a prominent and virtually unattainable goal around the world. Indeed the manifestation of these rights will continue to be a major issue well into the next century. Importantly, human rights are not something that ought to be negotiable. But Wells, his committees, various special interest groups, and political parties certainly gathered around tables and made countless speeches on how they though a Bill of Human Rights ought to be worded and how it should be adopted. In many respects it's ludicrous to think that human rights will mean the same thing to everybody in the world. It is just as disconcerting to think that the rights you'll be permitted as a human being were compiled by a committee in some far off place. The issue drops to a new low when we consider that the Declaration will probably be adopted by those nations and political systems that already attribute a high level of respect to human rights, while those nations to whom it should be directed will completely ignore it. Certainly Hitler or Stalin would not have been deterred by a mere Bill of Human Rights. Indeed Hitler may well have happily signed the bill in 1939 and sent it back to Great Britain with Neville Chamberlain, along with his signed and sealed non-aggression pact.

Jump half a century ahead in time and up sprouts a new generation of despots to whom the issue of human rights should be directed. This includes the likes of Idi Amin, Mao Tse Tung, Duvalier, Pinochet, and perhaps a dozen others. By the middle of the twenty-first century two or three more generations of brutal dictators will have coursed through the Middle East, central Africa and South East Asia. In no case will the rest of the world be able to hold any of these barbarians to a Bill of Human Rights. Especially when other nations believe the Bill might only have been used as a form of justification for military aggression by western nations. Certainly this was the case in the British Empire as it moved into the twentieth century, as it is now the case with the United States as we move into the twenty-first century.

Wells was seventy-four years old when *The Rights of Man* was published. He was a long way from the Fabian exploits that produced *This Misery of Boots*. He was a much wiser and more experienced writer, and his age was beginning show. He repeatedly comes close to contradicting some of his tracts written around the turn of the century. However, Wells never suggested that his ideas had been revised, or that he had found a better way to achieve his goals, he simply put a different slant on his proposals. Often this was a slant that was appropriate to the issue at hand. The result might be a rewrite of a series of newspaper articles, letters, socialist tracts or segments of books that he had previously published. Publishers were getting more difficult to find as he repeated himself time and time again. His books were getting smaller and his readership had become much narrower and often restricted to a dedicated group of socialist reformers who hung on Wells every word.

Anyone reading the Declaration of Human Rights can see that it is as much a socialist manifesto as it is a list of fundamental human rights. In some respects it's puzzling that Wells spent so much time working on the Declaration. He promoted it at lectures, wrote about it in the London papers and discussed it with any dignitary that would listen. Wells would never have considered that Human Rights might be part of a paradox. He was too close and too devoted to the issue. However, there is little evidence that he ever stopped to consider how basic the issue of human rights should be. Why did Wells and dozens of prominent writers and politicians spend so much time discussing, revising, and updating something so fundamental and unchangeable?

Indeed Wells spent many hours revising the text and publishing revised versions of the Declaration. He considered issues of wording that are based entirely on his interpretation of meaning and understanding. 'We have replaced that word "roam" by two words, better words they are, from Magna Carta, "come and go," so that not only the spirit but some of the very words of that precursor live in this, its latest offspring.'[5] Here Wells seems to envision himself picking the fruit of the Magna Carta and presenting it to the world in a form that would be more appropriate to his contemporary circumstances. The paradox has other faces and colors. Why did Wells spend so much time on words and meanings and then propose that a new simplified language like Basic English or Esperanto be used to deliver the Declaration to the rest of humanity. Certainly the fine shades of meaning so laboriously worded and reworded would be lost in Esperanto, and if not, they would be lost in the teaching of new language skills and in the decades it would take for them to become established. Wells should have been perceptive enough to know that the meanings of words would change or disappear with time, and they would change with geography and culture. After all he was one of the originators of the concept of travel in time and space. Why then did he seem to forget himself when it appeared to be convenient?

The following version of Wells Declaration comes from *The Rights of Man* published in 1940. It is probably many revisions from what he eventually labeled as a final draft, but it is complete enough that he considered it worth publishing, and it certainly could be considered as part of the justification for the western world's involvement in another world war. In Wells many revisions of his version of the declaration he fairly stated that he used the masculine when meaning all men and women. Some detractors argued that he missed important issues of freedom entirely. Whether there ought to be more or fewer declarations in the Bill is not necessarily a significant issue. The manner in which the declarations are stated was such a significant issue that far more research and development time was spent on the abstract issue of semantics than was spent on ensuring that the very core of freedom was guaranteed to all, instead of the wealthy and privileged, a category in which Wells made certain he was included. The following notes are an attempt to illustrate how something as basic as human rights can be embellished to the point of irrelevance and how fundamental concepts of rights can be colored by a political agenda. The ten basic rights appear as they were published in *The Rights of Man* in the 1940 Penguin version referenced above.

'(1) That every man is joint heir to all the resources, powers, inventions and possibilities accumulated by our forerunners, and entitled without distinction of race, colour or professed belief or opinions, to the nourishment, covering, medical care and attention needed to realize his full possibilities of physical and mental development and to keep him in a state of health from birth to death.'

This first declaration might be condensed to 'all men shall inherit the resources of the state'. The reader must assume that the socialist state is the custodian of nourishment, shelter, medical care and attention. The first declaration thus immediately introduces the concept of entitlements and implies that the state will provide an inheritance rather than simply declaring that all men are born with a fundamental right to these resources.

'(2) That he is entitled to sufficient education to make him a useful and interested citizen, and further that special education should be so made available as to give him equality of opportunity for development of his distinctive gifts in the service of mankind, that he should have easy access to information upon all matters of common knowledge throughout his life and enjoy the utmost freedom of discussion, association and worship.'

Perhaps 'all men are entitled to an education' would convey the meaning of this declaration without requiring that man be made an interested citizen, or embellishing it with conditions on his access to information.

'(3) That he may engage freely in any lawful occupation, earning such pay as the need for his work and the increment it makes to the common welfare may justify. That he is entitled to paid employment and to a free choice whenever there is any variety of employment open to him. He may suggest employment for himself and have his claim publicly considered, accepted or dismissed.'

There can be little argument that 'every man is entitled to gainful employment' might be a valid right for all able bodied workers without adding how he is to be paid and that he may be accepted or dismissed by some undefined entity. The entity we must assume to be state management officials and the intellectual elite who are best qualified to sit in judgement on individual claims for employment and appropriate compensation.

'(4) That he shall have the right to buy or sell without any discriminatory restrictions anything which may be lawfully bought or sold, in such quantities and with such reservations as are compatible with the common welfare.'

Man's fundamental 'right to private property' is herein restricted to those things that are compatible with the common welfare. This is an interesting justification that Wells makes in his concept of the socialist state. Private property is acceptable. Without the right to private property the socialist state would lose most of his followers. But this right must have reservations. The declaration does not state who determines the 'reservations', or whether officials are elected to an office that determines what is compatible with the common welfare. It is assumed that they will be the same intellectuals that Wells sees running the utopian administration of *Men Like Gods.*

'(5) That he and his personal property lawfully acquired are entitled to police and legal protection from private violence, deprivation, compulsion and intimidation.'

This is perhaps as simple as Wells and his Human Rights colleagues become in stating and qualifying a fundamental right, but 'all men are entitled to protection under law' might avoid inappropriate qualifications like 'compulsion' and 'deprivation'.

'(6) That he may move freely about the world at his own expense. That his private house or apartment or reasonably limited garden enclosure is his castle, which may be entered only with his consent, but that he shall have the right to come and go over any kind of country, moorland, mountain, farm, great garden or what not, or upon the seas, lakes and rivers of the world where his presence will not be destructive of some special use, dangerous to himself nor seriously inconvenient to his fellow citizens.'

It is simple enough to state that 'man has the right to free movement under the law' without getting into moorlands, gardens, lakes or other things that might be inconvenient to his fellow citizen. With these qualifications Wells again introduces the requirement for the state, or its appointed adjudicators to determine what a '…reasonably limited garden…' ought to be, or what '…seriously inconvenient…' might mean. This is a good example of a declaration that has suffered grievously by tinkering to the point where it becomes meaningless. It's almost preposterous that the term '…what not…' should appear in an international declaration of human rights. Wells squandered no love on barristers or solicitors but he and his fellow advocates were simply creating a feast for the sharks of jurisprudence.

'(7) That a man unless he is declared by a competent authority to be a danger to himself and to others through a mental abnormality, a declaration which must be annually confirmed, shall not be imprisoned for a longer period than six days without being charged with a definite offence against the law, nor for more than three months without a public trial. At the end of the latter period, if he has not been tried and sentenced by due process of law, he shall be released. Nor shall he be conscripted for military or any other service to which he has a conscientious objection.'

'All men have the right to a speedy and fair trial' is a fundamental premise in the legal system of most countries in the western world. The addition of embellishments determining who is mentally abnormal or what is meant by a '...definite offense...' is entirely a matter of inserting opinion into a fundamental legal right. Appending relief from military conscription to the end of this declaration is entirely out of place, and it adds a further requirement that a judgement be made on the definition of conscientious objection. The fundamental declaration of human rights should not be subject to a multitude of interpretations left open by ambiguous statements about the law.

'(8) That although a man is subject to the free criticism of his fellows, he shall have adequate protection from any lying or misrepresentation that may distress or injure him. All administrative registration and records about a man shall be open to his personal and private inspection. There shall be no secret dossiers in any administrative department. All dossiers shall be accessible to the man concerned and subject to verification and correction at his challenge. A dossier is merely a memorandum; it cannot be used as evidence without proper confirmation in open court.'

'All men have the right to confront their accuser' may be one of the issues Wells and his colleagues are trying to address here. However, the meaning of this declaration is fogged substantially by the definition of a dossier, who has the right to see it, and whether or not it might distress or injure its subject. This is a good example of Wells habit of inserting irrelevant issues or terminology and then failing to attach any definition or bounds on the new issues. An appeal to the authors' perception and insight into human rights must be made in trying to decipher the meaning of this declaration.

'(9) That no man shall be subjected to any sort of mutilation or sterilization except with his own deliberate consent, freely given, nor to bodily assault, except in restraint of his own violence, nor to torture, beating or any other bodily punishment; he shall not be subjected to imprisonment with such an excess of silence, noise, light or darkness as to cause mental suffering, or to imprisonment in infected, verminous or otherwise insanitary quarters, or be put into the company of verminous or infectious people. He shall not be forcibly fed nor prevented from starving himself if he so desire. He shall not be forced to take drugs nor shall they be administered to him without his knowledge and consent. That the extreme punishments to which he may be subjected are rigorous imprisonment for a term not longer than fifteen years or death.'

'No man shall be subject to cruel and unusual punishment'. Many versions of the basic right to be free from torture or unusual punishment have been defined.

It's as important an issue as any other fundamental right and shouldn't be qualified by superfluous definitions of what might constitute torture. Issues like '...excess of silence...' and the '...company of verminous or infected people...' belong in the law books of nations, not in an international list of fundamental rights.

'(10) That the provisions and principals embodied in this Declaration shall be more fully defined in a code of fundamental human rights which shall be made easily accessible to everyone. This Declaration shall not be qualified or departed from upon any pretext whatever. It incorporates all previous Declarations of Human Rights. Henceforth for a new era it is the fundamental law for mankind throughout the whole world.'

This is almost a contradiction within itself. First Wells and his colleagues state that the declaration is to be more fully defined by future work, but shall not be qualified on any pretext. Further, if it is to be revised, and if it is required to incorporate all previous Declarations, then the correction of errors, changes in interpretation and new social circumstances can only be contradictions of past declarations. It's also unusual that Wells, who believed so much in his abilities as a prophet, did not anticipate that portions of his declaration would become obsolete or inapplicable in as little time as half a century.

The published Declaration of Human Rights appeared in several versions over several years. Some of this publication history is discussed by Smith in his biographical work, *Desperately Mortal* and Smith has reproduced a later version of the so-called Rights in the appendices of his book. It's worth noting that as the Rights were republished they ebbed and flowed with the changes in writers, and changes in political views. If Wells accomplished anything in his work on human rights, he may have made it clear to those who followed his writing that their fundamental rights were often entirely a matter of current opinion, or a function of current committee membership.

The issue of human rights was a global issue at the beginning of the Second World War and the Sankey committee was far from unique. Although the Sankey Declaration received a lot of press, it was only one of many groups that were professing the need to verbalize the issue of rights. Statesmen, labor unions, women's groups and political parties were all getting in on the act. As the isolationist shell around the United States began to crack, Roosevelt presented his own version of freedom to the US Congress in January of 1941.[6] His speech presented what became known as the Four Freedoms and included freedom of speech, freedom of worship, freedom from want, and freedom from fear. The

Four Freedoms slogan was used as part of a War Bond campaign. Even Norman Rockwell got in on the act with a series of paintings.

To Wells this would have been an oversimplification and an inappropriate popularization of something he thought was serious business. A quick review of the ten items in his declaration suggests that it is as much a socialist manifesto as it is a Declaration of Human Rights. This isn't a hasty conclusion. The left leaning political slant to Wells' privately constituted committee is only part of the reason for the Declaration's political color. In addition, fully half of the items in the declaration attempt to define freedom in terms of man's relationship with the state. The items are verbose and dance around the central issues making them open to a wide and potentially contentious interpretation. The adjective 'fundamental' is lost in these declarations. In this respect perhaps Roosevelt should earn the prize by stating something as simple and fundamental as 'freedom of speech'.

PART VI
Education and The Church

25

Wells, Belloc and History

Wells was involved in argument and controversy of one form or another through most of his literary career. He delighted in taking issue with the writings and opinions of others, and he often did it publicly, provoking a response that demanded further comment. His list of targets included politicians, writers, publishers, the church, industrialists and businessmen of all kinds. Especially those businessmen he could label as capitalists contributing to the corruption of the social fabric. No well known and controversial writer could appear regularly in the highly public atmosphere of the London tabloids without attracting the attention of other equally pugnacious and argumentative writers and politicians. George Bernard Shaw, G.K. Chesterton and Hillaire Belloc often responded to Wells' diatribe with venomous barbs and refined wit. One such contest between Wells and Belloc seemed to take on a life of its own.

The newspaper and periodical business in Britain during the 1920's provided an ideal medium for public debate and political controversy. There were literally dozens of daily and weekly publications that catered to everything from country living to religion and the arts. Some periodicals were more radical than others and their editors were always eager to publish replies to articles and letters submitted by well known personalities. Hillaire Belloc was a popular writer in London during this period. He was a devout Catholic and considered himself a well-qualified spokesman for the church and its beliefs. Belloc was not impressed with Wells' advocacy of birth control much less his references to eugenics, evolution, abortion, free love and other equally abrasive topics. These issues were considered to be inherently evil and they undermined the teachings of the Catholic Church.

When Wells began publication of *The Outline of History*[1] as a serial, Belloc quickly took issue with the treatment of the early development of mankind, the portrayal of the church, and what Belloc perceived as Wells rewriting or reinterpretation of history. *The Outline of History* originally appeared in twenty-four fortnightly parts. Belloc methodically wrote a biased reply to each part of the work. These replies were published regularly in *Universe*, the Catholic weekly news magazine, and in other Catholic periodicals. This was the type of attack that Wells could not ignore and he produced a set of six articles of his own which he submitted to the editors of *Universe*. As might be expected, the magazine refused to accept Wells' rebuttals. Wells answer to the dilemma was fast and simple. He published the articles himself in the form of a little book entitled *Mr. Belloc Objects*.[2]

This little book contains fifty-five pages with a foreword and five chapters. The title page is preceded by two caricatures from the cartoonist Walter Low, one of Belloc and one of Wells. Low was a good friend of Wells and the friendship shows in his portrayal of a firm countenance in the cartoon of Wells and an unflattering and glowering caricature of Belloc. The foreword briefly outlines Wells' position and points out how he had been forced to underwrite publication of the material on his own. He urges the publisher to advertise the book in Catholic journals so that he may be fairly heard. Wells' arguments in this tract are based largely on Belloc's objection to the inclusion of material on natural selection in a work of history. To Wells, the story of man and his evolution from a primitive creature to his present level was a fundamental part of history. Belloc didn't limit himself to Darwinian arguments. He searched for other bits of carelessness by Wells and used them to make both Wells and his work look foolish. It was generally accepted when *The Outline of History* was published that Wells had stretched some of his facts a bit and had chosen subjects that he agreed with while omitting those he didn't believe in. He also tended to write critically of opposing social ideas, especially those related to the church. This was ample fodder for Belloc's cannons. To his credit Wells did make an effort in later editions of the work to correct obvious errors, but these corrections did not include a reinterpretation of history.

Belloc was a short pompous overweight buffoon as far as Wells was concerned and he expressed his dislike of the man in as many words. But Belloc was well respected as a writer and in some circles was the heroic defender of justice and the church. Belloc couldn't resist a showy argument in the press any more than Wells could and he chose the *Outline* as an example of Wells' ability to change the facts to suit his own purposes. The truth or facts on which the arguments were based was never really the issue. The public issue was the manner in which two arrogant dilettantes went about their battle of words. Wells certainly took the time and space to rebut Belloc's arguments and he repeatedly pointed out that the Catholic Church was now, and would forever be, anchored in the Stone Age. History may ultimately have been on Wells' side, but at the time it was an argument that couldn't be won and it did little more than amuse the readers. Books have been written about public arguments between literary figures, and Wells often appears between such covers.

Belloc was not soon to be silenced or outdone. He produced another article entitled *Mr. Belloc Still Objects*. They managed to call each other as many names as they could muster without generating explicitly libelous material. The bantering went on for many months during 1926 and 1927 and never arrived at any specific conclusion, nor did it seem to create more than a prurient interest in the reading public.

Wells was left upset and concerned about the exchange of words. He was certainly not bothered about throwing mud at Belloc, but rather about damage to his own reputation brought on by others he considered to be rather stupid and ignorant. This was the point in time when he was trying desperately to pass himself off as a scientist. The Royal Society membership was something he coveted and his friend Dick Gregory was doing his best to help him gain the recognition he needed for membership. The public display of temper in his argument with Belloc did not help his case, nor did the implication that Wells was rewriting history. That is not the image a scientist wants to create. Further, Wells was still working on what he considered to be his masterful educational trilogy, *The Outline of History*, *The Science of Life* and *The Work, Wealth, and Happiness of Mankind* and he did not want controversy to spoil either his potential for sales or the reputation he believed his masterwork deserved. Nevertheless, Wells was made of arrogant stuff. As noted in a previous chapter he managed to create another tempest a few years later with Herbert Thring over the collaborative effort he established to write *The Science of Life*.

There can be little doubt that arguments, public or private, about the religious character of Wells writing increased his dislike of the church. Childhood memories of his mother's blind devotion planted the seeds of atheism in his mind. He abhorred the hold that religious belief took over its subjects. Discord with someone like Hillaire Belloc not only created a strong dislike for his literary antagonists, but it reinforced his loathing of the church in general and the Catholic Church in particular with its hypocritical doctrine. This resentment and loathing were to eventually overflow ten years later in the small tract he entitled *Crux Ansata: An Indictment of the Catholic Church*.[3] Here he vents his spleen, in public again, with statements that were sometimes out of place and sometimes poorly considered.

26

Indicting the Catholic Church

It's difficult to read the work of H.G. Wells without sensing his continually broiling animosity towards religion in general and the Roman Catholic Church in particular. This animosity came to a head during the Second World War and culminated in his book *Crux Ansata; An Indictment of the Roman Catholic Church* published by Penguin in 1943.[1] Wells was not happy with the British decision to avoid bombing raids on Rome and he agreed with the popular opinion that the Catholic Church was guilty of complicity with the fascist Italian government.

What is not immediately obvious is that Wells' dislike of religion and most of its institutions has its roots in his childhood. He was an impressionable youth and his early contact with the church produced little respect for the institution. His mother's blind faith in the teachings and litany of the Anglican Church left him puzzled and ultimately offended. As he grew up his resentment of authority and privilege grew with him and he placed the church in the same category as other institutions he disliked. He produced valid reasons for his objections in his autobiography and in many newspaper articles. At least they were valid reasons to Wells, but his readers can't help but consider other less obvious reasons for his antagonism. He simply hated authority of any kind and would not tolerate individuals or institutions that produced rules that he ought to follow or that suggested how he ought to conduct himself.

Wells' attitudes became more vitriolic and much more public as he became a successful writer. His journalism and novels were highly intolerant of the Catholic doctrine. During the war years he recommended that Roman Catholics be excluded from the British Foreign Office and the diplomatic service because of their loyalty to Rome. He also voiced his objections to mixed marriages and Catholic involvement in education and commercial publications. These are attitudes that would not be tolerated in the politically correct environment of the early twenty-first century. But Wells, and many of his vocal colleagues, were allowed to voice strong opinions in the twentieth century because of a substantially different political environment. Hate, racism, animosity and revenge were the motivation behind many decisions made between the two great wars and anyone who expressed opinions based on these vices was easily tolerated and often viewed as sympathetic to the war effort. But in the face of disagreement Wells had to understand that he might lose large numbers of readers and supporters every time he expressed opinions that were too controversial. Some might feel that he was losing his way, or his ability to think clearly. The loss of public support became less and less important to Wells as he began to age, and in some respects his age provided him with a new found freedom to be intolerant with less consequence.

By 1942 the war in Europe was at its worst. The allies had developed a policy of selective attacks against German and Italian targets on the continent. In particular this policy avoided bombing raids on Rome. The reasons were manifold, but Wells decided, perhaps with some justification, that the reasons were much more subtle and should be exposed to public scrutiny. Perhaps Catholicism was at the root of decisions in Great Britain regarding air attacks on Rome, not the need to protect antiquities or the innocent public. Thus Wells begins his indictment of the Catholic Church in *Crux Ansata* with a chapter entitled *Why Do We Not Bomb Rome?*

The first half of the ninety-six page tract is spent on the history of the Roman Catholic Church and the emergence of Protestantism in Great Britain. Wells does not hesitate to relegate Catholicism to the fiery depths of hypocrisy and idolatry. He offers a reserved credit to Anne Boleyn for the Anglican Church and suggests that the Vatican never quite reconciled the loss of the British in the Church of Rome. In its determination to recover these losses the Vatican has continuously waged a campaign to regain the favor of public and politicians alike. This campaign has produced unseen benefits that include the protection of Rome from the heavy damage that was directed towards Italy and Germany.

Very few people escape Wells wrath. He lambastes the poor Englishman for always wanting 'to play the game' and to avoid the 'bad form' that might be implied by counting ones change after a purchase. Most of his ammunition is, of course, reserved for the Pope Pius XII. He ends the tract by outlining his perception of the Pope's limitations with the statement 'It is necessary to insist upon his profound ignorance and mental inferiority.'[2]

Many of the past mistakes Wells has made in his criticisms are repeated in this little book. He again considers the world of biology to be the only field of science worth mentioning. As old and experienced as Wells has become, he still has a very narrow view of science and technology. When using it to flail the Pope he declares that anyone '…living on the dole and reading the abundant literature of an ordinary public library, can…acquire the knowledge of modern biology and modern thought…incomparably greater than the equipment of any Pope…'[3] The controversy surrounding the Vatican's apparent ignorance of the Nazi atrocities is a familiar refrain, even today. During the Second World War Pius XII held the Vatican throne and he did not escape criticism, during or after the war, by the millions who suffered from his apparent complicity with the Nazi oppression. The Pope was not only a highly visible target, but one that would evoke only small sympathy from a nation of Anglicans.

Wells verbal assault on the Pope was clearly a manifestation of his intense dislike of Catholicism and Catholic priests. 'Watch a priest in a public conveyance. He is fighting against disturbing suggestions. He must not look at women lest he think of sex. He must not look about him, for reality, that is to say the devil, waits to seduce him on every hand. You see him muttering his protective incantations, avoiding your eye. He is suppressing 'sinful' thoughts.'[4]

The nature and circumstances of this assault were not uncommon in an environment where newspapers and books were the main means of communication. Radio was popular, but still limited primarily to non-commercial government sponsored broadcasting. Television did not exist and international communication was limited. The war created extreme hardship and privation. This allowed strong opinions to float to the surface. But much of what Wells wrote in the last few years of his life went beyond strong opinion. It gradually became a diatribe that wouldn't be tolerated in a politically correct environment. In fact the logic with which he summarizes *Crux Ansata* approaches a childish tantrum that can easily be excused among friends, but has no place in print. In his defense, Wells was a man who had run out of time and what little remained he would not spend in delicate persuasion.

27

The Undying Fire

Wells was a firm believer in the value of education. He was ever mindful of his humble past and he bore few illusions about the role played by education in getting him out of the downstairs quarters in Bromley and into the upstairs apartments of Hanover Terrace. It is not surprising, therefore, that he placed substantial importance on the education of his two sons when they began to grow up. He was in a financial position to search about England for the institution and curriculum that most appealed to him.

In 1914 he found what he was looking for in the Oundle School. Its headmaster was F.W. Sanderson and Wells made a point of learning as much as he could about the man's history and academic qualifications. As the First World War was descending on Europe he sent his two sons Frank and Gip off to the Oundle Boarding School. From that point on the Oundle School became a major fixture in his life. Although little has been published about Wells involvement in his sons' schooling there can be no doubt that he was in constant contact with them and with the school's headmaster.

Many years later, in 1922, Wells was part of a presentation in which Sanderson was giving a lecture on public education. During the presentation Sanderson collapsed at the podium and died. This left Wells with a feeling of loss and guilt. He filled the emptiness by making an agreement with Sanderson's widow to assist in writing a memoir of Sanderson's life. True to Wells' form the memoir evolved into an argument with Mrs. Sanderson as to how the man should be presented. It is not clear how the issue was settled but after it was resolved Wells proceeded on his own with a biography of Sanderson that he titled *The Story of a Great Schoolmaster*.[1] Sanderson was not the only educator involved in his boys' schooling, but he had become a good friend and Wells believed he deserved a small place in history. Wells could provide that place with a biography that would be widely read under his pen.

Wells never dropped the issue of education during his long career. He tackled it from a number of directions, including his concept of a World Encyclopedia, public education, a good grounding in scientific studies and a thorough indoctrination in the prevailing socialist ideals. One of the methods he used to present his views on education, and many other subjects, was the so-called *discussion novel*. Wells didn't invent the format but he certainly was one of its primary advocates. He used the *discussion novel* to present lengthy arguments in support of whatever issue was in his current favor.

This type of novel is neither easy to write, nor easy to read. The writer has to present a plausible story within which the characters can fully argue the topic at hand. Protagonists present the author's thesis, and the antagonists rebut with some of the currently popular sentiments. If the reader is not interested in the argument, or not a believer in one or the other side of the issue being discussed then the book may well be returned to the shelf.

Wells usually did a good job of creating a *discussion novel* that appealed to his growing audience. Sometimes he would mix a conventional novel containing characters, plot and action, with one or more laborious discussions between the characters on topics such as the status of women, war in Europe or socialist ideals. Wells was a fine and practiced writer and could usually pull off another novel that pressed his current thinking on the reading public. However, occasionally his literary discussions were tedious, ill fitting and stilted. In some circumstances he would add an extra chapter to his novel to present a summary of his ideas on a related topic. *The World Set Free*[2] contains several examples of these compromises.

Perhaps one of Wells most successful *discussion novels* is *The Undying Fire*.[3] It's well written and the arguments were popular at the time it was written. It's an interesting tale based on the biblical story of Job. Wells' contemporary Job takes the form of a school teacher. There is little in the story to grip the reader, and most readers will certainly be able to predict the story's outcome, but it flows more smoothly than his other *discussion novels*. Wells was pleased with this novel and considered it one of his best. 'The Undying Fire is artistically conceived and rather brilliantly coloured; I have already expressed my satisfaction with it as the best of my Dialogue-Novels; and it crowns and ends my theology. It is the sunset of my divinity.'[4] More important to the contemporary reader is that it's a good example of how Wells manages two of his favorite subjects at the same time, religion and education.

The novel's hero is Job Huss. He is a school teacher who has suffered all the trials of the biblical Job and is on the eve of a surgical procedure that will kill him, or cure him. Further the school board has just appeared on his doorstep to terminate his tenure at their school. For another 200 pages he argues the necessity of a broad education with the schools directors and his doctor. He is adamant about the teaching of history and the importance of education in maintaining a nation and a social system. Although his arguments are not all sound or logical, they flow smoothly and the book is not difficult to read. The end of the story also fits admirably with the theme. Job undergoes surgery successfully, gets his teaching position back, finds his lost son and has his financial problems solved. In sympathy with the trials of the biblical Job, he kept his faith. Thus *The Undying Fire*. The story line and the arguments are a bit trite, but they were not intended to be original. Wells assumes the reader can get past the naiveté of the biblical parable and see the contemporary logic.

Although *The Undying Fire* does not mark a peak, or a pivotal point in Wells career, it does stand out as a hallmark of the writing that he could produce. Over the remaining twenty years of his career he seemed to produce fewer riveting romantic adventures and his *discussion novels* became repetitive, disjointed and difficult to follow from one thought to another. What is perhaps most discouraging to the Wells enthusiast is the fact that, as time moves further into the twenty-first century, fewer and fewer people have heard of H.G. Wells, and those who have, remember only his *fantastic romances*. This is frustrating to the academics who believe that the work of H.G. Wells should stand beside the greatest literature in the English language.

Most English speaking people schooled in the 1940's and 1950's after Wells had died, were well aware of his presence in the school room. Students read his history books, studied his ideas, and were thrilled with his novels. Nearly all scientists and engineers who grew up in the period immediately after the Second World War read the classical works *The Time Machine* and *The War of the Worlds*. As Wells literary fire disappears into the past, these *fantastic romances* are the shining beacons that show his continued presence in the halls of literature. His legacy is not in his *discussion novels*, not his pamphlets, nor his attempts to foretell the future. It lies in his few imaginative adventures published in the nineteenth century.

PART VII

Forecasting The Future

28

Early Anticipations

In 1901 Wells published a book entitled *Anticipations of the Reaction of Mechanical and Scientific Progress upon Human Life and Thought*. To avoid Wells' often wordy titles it's now simply referred to as *Anticipations*. This was his first effort at publishing a non-fiction book about his vision of the future. Wells was very pleased with the book when it was published and he remained pleased with it throughout his career. Indeed it can be considered a turning point in his writing as he moved from fiction set in the future to non-fiction prophesy of things to come. Most of *Anticipations* was written in the first year of the new century. The heady celebrations of the fin de siecle were over and, as happened when the 21st century rolled in, book shelves were filled with predictions of the scientific and social evolution of the next 100 years. Wells had a number of successes with his novels and this provided him with the resources and the confidence to launch a new book containing his ideas of the future. When he introduced the work for *The Atlantic Edition* in 1923 he included a note about his reasons for writing the book. 'After producing the rather scattered suggestiveness of "The Sleeper Awakes" and its associated short story, and stimulated perhaps by the fact that every one about him was summing up the events of the past 100 years, the writer set himself, with such equipment as he possessed, to work out the probabilities of contemporary tendencies as thoroughly as possible, and instead of a story make a genuine forecast.'[1]

Wells had no hesitation in covering a wide spectrum of human progress from transportation systems to the social revolution he believed was necessary for the survival of mankind. He also devoted a chapter of the book to the issue of approaching war, although at the time it didn't take much foresight to see the impending conflict. *Anticipations* was republished a number of times and in the 1914 edition Wells added an introduction in which he indicated his satisfaction with the book and with the accuracy of his predictions. 'It is a better book than I have been in the habit of thinking it was, and whatever the values of both of them [the original and the revised edition] to the world at large may be, the H.G. Wells of thirty-three has little to be ashamed of in presenting his book to the criticisms of the H.G. Wells of forty-eight.'[2]

There can be little doubt that *Anticipations* was a change of pace for Wells and that he enjoyed putting many of his ideas for the future of mankind into a real world perspective. However, his predictions should be carefully qualified. Wells admits himself to '…moments of leaping ignorance…' but in all fairness keeping score of his prophetic hits and misses is the wrong way to view this work. Wells accuracy as a prophet in 1901 certainly didn't affect the book's public reception. How well he did in predicting the future should be based on an assessment of the tools he had at hand, and how he used those tools, not on an assessment of his accuracy based on one hundred years of hindsight.

Writers who claim an ability to foretell the future or who simply lay out the probable course of history usually deal in generalizations and provide conclusions that are obvious to most of the population. For example, it isn't too difficult to predict that the City of London will grow substantially over the next 100 years. It's a bit more difficult to suggest that London's population will increase by 5.3 million people in 87 years. The more specific predictions become or the further they are pushed into the future, the less reliable they likely to be. By far the greatest portion of *Anticipations* contains predictions of the former general type. In other words the book contains many short term generalizations. When Wells made very specific predictions he was usually wrong, and this may account for the moments of leaping ignorance to which he confesses.

Anticipations opens with a chapter entitled *Locomotion in the Twentieth Century*. The issue of transportation has always been one of the most prominent issues in the development of civilization and a revolution in the development of rail systems was underway at the end of the nineteenth century. Wells' studies in the biological sciences certainly don't deter him from launching into the issue of steam engines or highway construction with all the confidence of a professional engineer or industrial scientist. With few examples, little evidence, and no scientific logic he predicts that man will posses moving underground sidewalks, and that trains will never exceed 50 miles per hour in speed or 4 feet 8 inches in width (a dimension long established by the width of a horse cart). He was a bit more reasonable when he forecast that the internal combustion engine would soon be in popular use in automobiles and that roadways would be especially prepared to support the motor car. The fact that development was already in progress to accomplish these ends suggests this prediction didn't require much of a leap. Wells tries to convince us that development of equipment and machinery will not be determined by the law of supply and demand, which is '...the most egregiously wrong and misleading phrases that ever dropped from the lips of man...' On the contrary, he suggests that man will develop a supply of technological advances before a demand will develop.

Wells discussion of the future of transportation does not include many dramatic speculations or recommendations. Rather, it's a shallow discussion of the current transportation system in England and how it is likely to grow to meet the demands of an obviously expanding industrialized nation. If Wells deserves any credit perhaps it's for recognizing that transportation is a critical component in the development of the human social system.

The chapter entitled *Probable Diffusion of Great Cities* is a compelling topic for a writer looking into the future. Large cities are a logical consequence of our social system and as centers of commerce and services they will change continuously to meet the evolving needs of the population and the changing character of mankind from one century to another. Wells begins his arguments to support the changes in large cities with an understanding of the importance of transportation and communication. There is little doubt of the influence of these issues on cities of the past. Demographic data are available on the development of major population centers as far back as the Roman Empire. In spite of this Wells begins his analysis of cities with a grossly false assumption in the first lines of this essay. Then he proceeds to ignore his own statements through the rest of the chapter. He states 'Now the velocity at which a man and his belongings may pass about the earth is in itself a very trivial matter indeed...'[3]

Wells knew that velocity is simply time divided by distance. He based much of his argument about the ultimate size of cities on the fact that size could not exceed that which allows tradesmen to enter the city, sell their wares or farm produce, and return to their homes within the period of daylight. He reasoned that this must be about two hours distance, or about four miles. The efficiency of trains might increase this to eight miles. The size of a city, he reasons, must therefore be based on the velocity of a man and his belongings. The fact that tradesmen and farmers may eventually have no need to enter a city, or that customers may travel out to the suburbs to make their purchases was never part of Wells' equation.

Most of Wells argument on the size of cities was based on the issue of transportation. 'The determining factor in the appearance of great cities of the past, and, indeed, up to the present day, has been the meeting of two or more transit lines, the confluence of two or more streams of trade, and easy communication.'[4]

This is a fact of life dating back to prehistoric times and does little to substantiate Wells' prediction of the future growth of large cities. He fails to consider some of the obvious changes that were occurring around him as Britain moved into the twentieth century. The important and often controlling factor in the growth of cities had moved well beyond markets and transportation. But Wells largely ignores the issues of water systems, sewage disposal, housing development, schools and hospitals, banking facilities and many of the other social issues that he continually throws at his readers in other tracts. Large cities were not growing just because the rail system had improved, but because the entire complexion of cities was changing. Now, tall and safe buildings were being constructed for mass housing, underground water systems could deliver large volumes of fresh and uncontaminated water to all parts of the city. Sewage was being removed and efficiently treated rather than being dumped into the street. Private enterprise flourished within the city center creating a host of services to support a population that was no longer dependent on the farmer or tradesman coming into the city every day to sell his goods.

By 1901 London was the center of international trade and commerce. Huge steel and shipping industries were controlling the migration of workers. The manufacture and remanufacture of trade goods being delivered to the far corners of the earth created cities that had no other reason for their existence than the commerce on which they thrived. In spite of Wells efforts to design a socialist state that would own the property and assets on which great cities were based, he seems to have completely failed to carry his philosophy of state ownership into predictions of the future of large cities.

Another major social failure in Wells' vision of the growth of large cities exists in his concept of human activity. In fact he demonstrates a distinct lack of insight into anything that does not exist outside his own sphere of influence. He routinely uses London as his example of a great city and illustrates how it will grow into the future. The instruments of expansion would be enhanced communication offered by the telephone, and the addition of services like theatres, hackney cabs and libraries. It's difficult to understand how cities like Bombay or Jakarta fit into his concept since, by the turn of the century, they had grown to millions without the benefit subways, telephones, theatres or libraries.

Wells inexorably moves from the physical aspects of the future to the social aspects. At the turn of the century many of his political ideas were just beginning to form and he had not refined his ideas to the point where they could be easily accepted by anyone other than the radical left. As he began to outline what he envisioned as a new and just society he stepped through most of his prejudices, one by one. Any reader of Wells should find it difficult to miss his dislike of the British aristocracy and the wealthy ruling classes. There is little doubt that most of this animosity results from his humble background. However, he becomes decidedly two-faced in his solution to the ills of the monarchy. Rather than building an equitable and just social system, Wells is more inclined to strive for what he considers to be the perfect world or the basis for utopia. In doing so he creates a new elite social class or ruling class, in which he logically includes himself, his friends, and people he thinks have the same beliefs.

Much like the Bolsheviks, Wells' socialists will create their New Republic on the backs of the working and downtrodden masses, then quickly turn on them and eliminate the less desirable. As in most socialist philosophies the decisions about whom and what is less desirable are not made by consensus but by the new elite. Wells sees slums and lower class citizens as a part of the expanding global system for another century. 'All over the world, as the railway network has spread, in Chicago and New York as vividly as London or Paris, the commencement of the new movement has been marked at once by the appearance of this bulky irremovable excretion, the appearance of these gall stones of vicious, helpless, and pauper masses. There seems every reason to suppose that this phenomenon of unemployed citizens, who are, in fact, unemployable, will remain present as a class, perishing individually and individually renewed, so long as civilization remains progressive and experimental along its present lines.'[5] His comments about the class system in South Africa and the Southern United States are exactly the type of thing that the politically correct twenty-first century almost prohibits us from quoting. Wells' will take a number of years before he fully develops his solution to the problems created by the great masses of dreary and uneducated people

Wells does not often get into the detail that he presents in the first half of *Anticipations*. His chapter on *Certain Social Reactions* is a speculation on the daily life and activities of a middle class family around the year 2000. Thus, he presents his beliefs about the makeup of life a full 100 years in the future. Some of this speculation is amusing (such as his instruction on the best way to clean a window) and some of it is surprisingly accurate. He points out that much of the drudgery of maintaining a household will disappear. There will be little for servants to do with all the labor saving devices and tedious tasks like window cleaning will be simplified by automatic cleaning devices. Houses will be smaller, they will be heated by central heating to eliminate the fires, and private bathrooms will become common. A bit of research indicates that many of these improvements and social conveniences were being tried at the end of the 19th century, so Wells was not inventing anything new, but he was presenting adventurous ideas to a reading public that probably were seldom exposed to speculation about the future.

He postulates that changes in the makeup and purpose of the family will be significant. Marriage and divorce laws will be relaxed and more of the care of children will be passed to the hands of educational institutions. Education in itself will become a critical part of the new social system as the role of the ignorant tradesman and laborer disappear. Those communities that refuse to advance or contribute to new forms of education will lose the trade and industry of the future and possess a disproportionate number of dependent and uneducated people, or what Wells refers to as 'an exceptionally large contingent for the abyss.'

Wells is uncomfortable with the lower classes and he has many ways of demonstrating his loathing of the upper crust that existed in England at the turn of the century. He points out that 'These people of the governing class do not understand there is such a thing as special knowledge or an inexorable fact in the world; they have been educated at schools conducted by amateur schoolmasters, whose real aim in life—if such people can be described as having a real aim in life—is the episcopal bench, and they have learnt little or nothing but the extraordinary power of appearances in these democratic times.'[6] How this upper crust differs from the rich and famous of today is left to our imagination. Perhaps he felt that by ensuring the ignorance of wealthy and powerful entertainers and sports stars of the future would keep them out of the upper crust and guarantee their participation in the great middle class. He was certainly correct about their ignorance and mind numbing incompetence, but he badly misjudged their power and influence. If anything, we are faced with a 'governing class' with even more 'extraordinary power' and much less 'special knowledge' than ever before. Regardless of what he implies in other tracts or discussions, Wells wants to build a great utopian middle class to support his ideal socialist state.

Even though he admits to differences between tradesmen and engineers, he still assumes that they will play an equal role in his future society. The harder he works at this artificial equality, the more people begin to look, think and act alike. Into this formula Wells must place a governing class of educated elite. Naturally he must find a way to deal with this dichotomy in his new democratic system. He calls these two groups the Power and the Work and spends a great deal of effort in explaining how they must work together to develop a just society.

Wells considered himself to be an expert in modern warfare. He never clearly explained the qualifications and experience behind this expertise, but throughout the war years of the early 20th century he did not hesitate to offer his advice to generals and governments on how the wars should be fought. He also claimed a great deal of credit (and bashfully denied his contributions) for various developments or inventions like the tank, aerial warfare and the atomic bomb. Occasionally Wells was especially perceptive, if not original. In *Anticipations* he discusses at length the causes and vulgarities of War. In his opinion nationalism is a major contributor to a warlike mentality and nationalism is the product of patriots. 'Now patriotism is not something that flourishes in the void,—one needs a foreigner.'[7] This was written before 1905 and one would not notice its century old origins on the killing fields of 2005. The foreigner is today, more than ever before, the source of our patriotic flag waving and most of our fears, both real and imagined.

An entire chapter in *Anticipations* is devoted to Wells vision of the materiel and tactics of future warfare. He writes with the authority of a military historian, and nowhere apologizes for his amateur standing in military experience. However, he generally stays on safe ground by not going too far afield or too far into the future. He covers military ground from weaponry to tactics and correctly predicts the use of repeating machine guns, ironclad vehicles or tanks, the use of the aeroplane in combat, and specialized naval vessels. These were all part of the mechanized warfare that became a reality ten years later in the First World War. When Wells moves into the use of the newly developed machinery he tends to stray a bit from popular thought. He suggests mounting machine guns on bicycles, using tanks to sweep rifle brigades out of the way, and is convinced that airmen will have to fire out of the rear of 'aeroplanes' to avoid problems from rifle recoil. How much thought Wells put into his suggested use of war machinery is lost to history, but regardless of how well his prophesy was thought out he produced as many misses as hits. It's usually only the successes that are picked out of prophesy and presented to the public as a sign of prescient genius. In Wells case he was sometimes credited with being the actual inventor, not just the predictor, of things like tanks and atomic bombs. In the case of the armored tank Wells came to believe himself to be the inventor of the tank and defended his position in later writing.

In fact most of Wells ideas on warfare were probably gleaned from military publications and periodicals of the time. The weapons and machinery he discussed were already being developed and were in practical use by the time the participants in the First World War began to flex their military muscles. Accurate predictions were thus stretches of less than ten years. A few successful visions not-withstanding, he made some colossal blunders that are not commonly acknowledged by his advocates when they speak of prophesy. For example, in 1870 Jules Verne wrote his well received novel *20,000 Leagues Under the Sea*. The novel provides an extensive description of a large submarine used for extensive sea travel and adventure. By the time Verne published his novel several attempts at building rather crude under water vessels had already been made, including practical designs developed during the American civil war. Wells would certainly have been aware of these developments, but Verne was not one of his contemporaries and it was unlikely that Wells would try to capitalize on something that Verne had already popularized and Wells clearly had not invented. His response to submarines therefore was rather short and pointed. 'I must confess that my imagination, in spite even of spurring, refuses to see any sort of submarine doing anything but suffocate its crew and founder at sea.'[8]

Wells closes *Anticipations* with a chapter on future government. Idealized socialist and utopian governments would become a favorite topic in Wells writing over the next two decades. In 1901, when *Anticipations* was published, Wells was speculating more on the things he would like to see in a future government than predicting the type of government we might expect in the next hundred years. The last chapter is entitled *The New Republic* and it presents the germ of his ideas on race, eugenics, education, the governing elite, control of private property and the basic structure of his developing world state. Wells had just turned forty years of age and was off on a new social and literary tack.

29

What is Coming

In 1916, about midway through the First World War Wells published a book entitled *What is Coming? A Forecast of Things after the War*. It was a collection of twelve essays or articles in which he discussed various changes in the political and economic character of the world after the war. About fifteen years earlier the publication of *Anticipations* had met with considerable success. Its enthusiastic reception had established Wells as something of a prophet, although his qualifications and abilities were no more significant than those of any other writer dabbling in the business of prophesy. It would be a century after publication before Wells accuracy and vision could be assessed. In the meantime his proponents would look for those prognostications that fit contemporary circumstance, and his detractors would search for those statements that were farthest from the truth of history.

Wells success with *Anticipations* and the encouraging reception of his newspaper articles in both Britain and the United States boosted his confidence. It was easy for Wells and his readers to take the success of his books as a sign of success as a prophet. He thus boldly opened *What is Coming?*, a new book of prophesy and forecast, by invoking his modest scientific training again as one of the most important factors in his reliability as a prophet. 'But for some of us moderns, who have been touched with the spirit of science, prophesying is almost a habit of mind. Science is very largely analysis aimed at forecasting. The test of any scientific law is our verification of its anticipations. The scientific training develops the idea that whatever is going to happen is really here now—if only one could see it.'[1] This statement is followed by an outline of the successful forecasts he had included in *Anticipations*, and indeed he generously points out that he missed the mark on a number of dates and assumptions. However, his new book takes an entirely different approach to prophesy and is shaped by events that did not exist in 1900 when he wrote *Anticipations*.

The war was the driving force behind Wells new predictions, as it was for many other writers and journalists who were speculating on the end of the war. He recalled a small collection of articles he published in 1914 entitled *The War That Will End War*[2] in which he optimistically hopes that this global war would sort out the last of the differences between the Imperial powers of Europe and leave the world at peace for all time. This title became an oft repeated mantra in both Britain and the United States. Even in the present day, nearly one hundred years later, the First World War is commonly referred to as 'the war to end all war', a slightly corrupted quotation regularly repeated but seldom credited to Wells. Regretfully, as the conflict drew to a close it became more obvious that a final solution would never be the result.

Early in the war the German Empire, whipped into a state of nationalistic frenzy by their Kaiser, were looking forward to about a year of warfare. The war was to end with their triumphant March into Brussels, Paris, Istanbul and perhaps even London. Early in the conflict it became obvious that the classical military tactics of the nineteenth century were hopelessly inadequate and that combatants were being forced into more mechanized and scientific methods of killing troops and destroying military and civilian resources. 'The war of the great attack will have given place to the war of the military deadlock...'[3] The English in their well protected island nation were nervously speculating about the course of the war. Even if an invasion never occurred, Britain was nevertheless deeply involved in the defense of her allies in Europe. Wells was a major contributor to speculation about the direction of the war and he wrote weekly opinion pieces for English and American newspapers.

By 1915 even the Germans were beginning to see the certainty of triumphant victories gradually slipping from their grasp. The Great War was becoming a war of attrition and it would end when all parties reached a state of exhaustion. An armistice would result from a negotiated settlement. The unquestioned British naval superiority made it difficult for the Germans to feed their war machine, and maintaining supply routes by land was expensive and time consuming. It was beginning to appear that the Germans would run out of resources before the Allied powers, leaving the way clear to an armistice. Wells correctly saw the war coming to a halt in 1918 or 1919 followed by a land grab on the part of the Allies, and protracted negotiations to reach a settlement on reparations.

Wells often delves into the complexities of global economics with questionable results. He will certainly have read John Maynard Keynes but in 1915 little of the Keynes wisdom we know today had been published. Wells was not too sympathetic towards the capitalist system that controlled the major economies of

Europe. Thus, when he ventures opinions on the causes and solutions to bankruptcy in Europe, both during and after the war, his methods and motives tend to move him in a direction slightly to the left of the facts. But he correctly assumes that when the war is settled the note and bond holders of Europe will begin to reap the profits of reconstruction. Most of the currencies of Europe were thoroughly debased and little value remained in the hands of those without tangible assets. Britain on the other hand maintained the integrity of the Bank of England and the pound note continued to be exchangeable for the gold sovereign. If any nation retained a stable economic system throughout the war, it was Great Britain, buoyed by her massive overseas investments and a global food supply.

The Great War did eventually come to an end and an onerous treaty was signed at Versailles in 1919. The western allies were not in a charitable mood and the German Empire was dismembered, stripped of its government, and its borders redrawn to suit the victors. Over eight million troops had been destroyed and twenty million were wounded. Damage to cities and infrastructure was incalculable in any financial terms. Few prophets missed the mark on one of the blackest periods in human history. As the clouds began to clear, the shape of Europe over the next generation was an open question and speculation was rife. This was an obvious opening for Wells to propose a future for Europe much closer to his ideal socialist state, than the old imperial system. As did many other idealists, he made the mistake of neglecting the difference between what he believed ought to happen, and what was most likely to happen in Europe.

Wells believed that the lessons of the war would result in governments shedding their nationalist images and moving away from individualism. He deemed nationalism to be a selfish and destructive human trait that would inevitably create dissention among sects, cultures and nations. Capitalism must also be curbed since it was based on greed and resulted in uncontrolled growth and a wide separation between classes of people. Wells was certain the nations of the world were beginning to see these problems and that solutions would be gradually forthcoming. Indeed, wasn't the League of Nations taking the first steps toward uniting the world in common sense and uniform justice?

Wells dislike of property owning capitalists knew no bounds. In particular he trod dangerously close to slandering the large ship owners who had profited from the war (and lost half of their ships in the bargain). 'I do not think one can count on any limit to their selfishness and treason.'[4] By association he believed the British people would no longer stand for the private ownership of such a large sector of the nation and '...the end of the war will see, not only transit, but shipping, collieries, and large portions of the machinery of food and drink production and distribution no longer under the administration of private ownership, but under a sort of provisional public administration.'[5] Wells believed that not only would Britain come to its senses with expropriation of private enterprise, but within twenty or thirty years the rest of the world would fall into step. '...the Allies will be forced also to link their various State firms together into a great allied trust, trading with a common interest and a common plan with Germany and America and the rest of the world...'[6]

As if to assure us that the future world will be specifically directed by Wells himself, he points his old stick at lawyers again. Wells loathed lawyers and constantly tells others about their 'sucker-fish' determination to gain control of business, government and the press. His solution to these ills is not quite so dramatic as others, probably because he can't reasonably envision the complete eradication of the legal profession or the complete whitewashing of the press. He thus guesses that Britain and Europe will see '...a legal profession with a quickened conscience...' and a press which operates as '...an estate of the realm, as something implicitly under oath to serve the State.'[7] It seems inevitable that socialists designing a new utopia for the good of all mankind must take control of the press and all communications. Wells, like most socialists was aware that without a controlled press and legal system the new global republic might quickly get away from its autocrats. Unfortunately neither Britain nor the rest of Europe ever produced a legal profession with a quickened conscience and it's their great good fortune that they have not been subject to a government controlled press. Wells also rolls in the added benefit of major revisions in the educational system. To conform to his plan, the great schools of Oxford and Cambridge must certainly be required produce more scientists and academics and fewer lawyers and industrialists.

As Wells ventures further into the future, and further abroad, to discuss the eventual state of colonial nations he becomes less specific and admits to the impracticality of imposing too much on the future. In truth he provides very little in the way of vision beyond Britain and Central Europe. He rambles through countless topics from the significance of women to the importance of the British flag in India. His brief summaries and prophesies are usually nothing more than current public opinion dressed up in Wells own biases and prejudices. This is not one of Wells better books. It is however, a good example of the type of writing he was doing between 1910 and 1920. Journalism was becoming his mainstay and a very profitable one at that. American newspapers would buy a whole series of articles under contract to keep their readers informed on the progress of the war from an English writers' perspective. After the war Wells agent arranged a number of speaking engagements in the United States, Canada and Australia. It was a successful and profitable time and he now resided almost completely in the realm of journalism. *What Is Coming?* is thus a journalists forecast of the world after the war and not a particularly insightful effort at prophesy.

30

Where We're Going

Analysis of Europe's reconstruction and political direction after the Great War was a common topic in English language newspapers throughout the world. As noted in the previous chapter, Wells was a routine contributor to these columns. Most of his work consisted of opinion pieces and proposals for solutions to social problems. During the decade after the war his writing for periodicals began to shift to topics on the future of the world. He retained copyright privileges to these articles and produced several books that consisted entirely of previously published newspaper columns. In 1924 he published *A Year of Prophesying* which consisted of fifty-five newspaper articles published between September 1923 and September 1924. He followed this in 1928 with a similar book entitled *The Way the World Is Going; Guesses and Forecasts of the Years Ahead*. This latter publication contained twenty-six articles written in 1927 on a wide range of topics, and a lecture he delivered at the Sorbonne in Paris in 1927. It's a good example of Wells' thinking during the 1920's and is highly representative of the type of journalism he produced at the height of his career. Although journalism had become major part of his work and a substantial source of income, he still found time to produce one or two novels every year. It would be unthinkable to limit a prolific writer like Wells to a few dozen newspaper articles per annum.

The Way the World Is Going is typical of the literary style Wells had developed after several years experience in the newspaper business. This style is perhaps one of the principle reasons why his life's work is not filled with outstanding literary masterpieces. After 30 years of writing, Wells was consistently sharp and witty, and he continued to provide colorful opinions for his readers. At the same time his journalistic style was carried over to his novels and resulted in pedantic, authoritarian and often tiresome narratives. The pen of a novelist and the pen of a journalist are not always compatible bedfellows.

Wells wrote a short introduction to the collection of articles included in *The Way the World Is Going*. He used the introduction to explain the scope of the material and the background from which the articles were drawn. Some of these articles were originally prepared under contract for American newspapers in addition to his usual batch of essays written for the London papers. He wrote topical material for American readers including slanted comments on the Sacco-Vanzetti trial. His American publisher paid for all of the articles but refused to print the latter since they considered his comments inappropriate. Wells also uses his new introduction to *The Way the World Is Going* to complain about the 'mutilation' that his work had suffered at the hands of various American editors. In this volume he claims to have restored his work to its original condition. Knowing Wells' habit of continually revising and republishing, the work's original condition was probably what he thought it ought to be at the time this collection was published.

Not all of the material sticks to the theme of prophesy. Chapter XXIII is entitled *Some Plain Words for Americans*. It was obviously prepared for American newspapers and is a pithy response to criticism directed at Wells by other journalists, and a few politicians, who were upset by the editorial interference of this English upstart in American affairs. In particular Wells made additional comments about what he considered to be the injustice of the Sacco-Vanzetti affair. In an era of growing isolationism Americans were particularly sensitive about anything that appeared to be outside interference. Wells was also undiplomatic enough to have made a number of unflattering remarks about the City of Boston and the Commonwealth of Massachusetts. It was not unexpected therefore, that most of the antagonistic comments came from Massachusetts where his columns could be read in regional newspapers. The inflammatory articles were written at the peak of his career, and at a time when his audience was very large and international in scope. This provided Wells with the backing and courage he needed to pounce on almost any provocation from any direction. He opens by pointing out '…the right of British and European people generally to have and to express opinions about American affairs. The converse right has never been questioned, and is exercised freely by Americans…'[1] Before getting into the basic issues of the disagreement he also affirms his personal position, '…I maintain my right as a free-born Englishman to think freely about the affairs of the United States, and to say what I think to be true and right and proper about all or any of these affairs. I refuse to regard the people of the United States as in any way a Holy People. It is not blasphemous to deny them perfection.'[2] Wells devotes several pages to a wordy defense of his position and explains that he has always exhibited a fondness for Americans and has taken an even-handed approach to international affairs. Thus he would like to continue to sail into New York harbor under the invitation of an aspiring eagle. 'I do not want to have that vision replaced by the butt view of a proud but isolated ostrich…'[3] Fortunately for Wells, his friends on both sides of the Atlantic were usually unaffected by his literary outbursts and continued to help him arrange lecture tours and newspaper contracts in the United States from which he earned large quantities of money.

In 1926 Britain was forced to suffer the trauma of a nationwide labor dispute now known as The General Strike of 1926. The source of the dispute was a need for improvement in wages and working conditions for the thousands of coal miners that provided the coal to fire growing industries and to heat the homes of thousand of Britons. Coal was the fuel of the nation. It had fueled the nation's growth through the nineteenth century, and while the United States was learning to use oil and petrochemicals, Britain was still burning coal in the twentieth century. The use of coal as a primary source of energy was becoming a controversial topic. It was mined amid continuous labor problems; it was dirty; it was expensive to transport; and it produced endless clouds of black smoke. What better subject for Wells to tackle with his pen. Unfortunately he missed the significance of his subject when wrote the article entitled *Fuel-Getting in the Modern World*. Little did he know how significant the issue of energy would become over the next one hundred years. Neither Wells nor any of his socialist colleagues could ever have imagined that the bulk of the nation's future energy supply would not come from coal but from oil and gas buried deep below the North Sea. What better example of how predictions of the future are usually just projections of present day resources and biases.

Wells predicted that the coal industry in Britain would have to change or the supply of coal would be continuously interrupted. He was right in his assessment of the problem, but entirely wrong in his picture of the future. Wells believed the problems in the coal industry were largely created by greedy capitalists who squeezed the workers and pocketed government subsidies while selling Britain's energy assets abroad. His solution to the entire problem was to ensure that Britain '…must prepare to subsidise and then nationalise her coal supply, or she must face the clear prospect of retrocession from her position of leadership in the world.'[4] Certainly Britain was about to lose her position of leadership, but it was not because the coal industry avoided nationalization, it was because Britannia had just regained her industrial footing when she was crippled with another gigantic war.

Wells could not resist telling his readers what he believed the future held for various new developments, inventions, products or services. He was not content to express his likes or dislikes; he went beyond the simple concept of opinion and explained to his readers how some developments would quietly disappear while others would make a major impact on the world. This collection of '…guesses and forecasts…' were not as well thought out as those in *Anticipations*. They lack continuity and his predictions were usually wrong more often that right. His novels often produced more realistic visions of the future than any of his journalism. Perhaps this was as much a result of prejudice as carefully considered fact. When he disliked something he quickly became certain that it would not be around for long, or that it would have an entirely deleterious impact on the world. His vision of scientific advancement was entirely a biological one and attempts to impress his audience with judgments on nuclear fission, aircraft development, mechanized warfare and countless other little pontifications were often received with amusement during his lifetime. Half a century after his death they are simply passed over as opinions of one who knew little more than hearsay about his subject.

Wells became familiar with the world of radio broadcasting in the 1920's and he prepared some material with the BBC in London. During this period radio broadcasts were becoming very popular, but they had little practical value beyond short term entertainment. Wells didn't believe that anyone would listen to news or political issues on the radio since it was much more practical to read about issues in a newspaper or magazine where one could see the text and consider the facts. The entertainment that was available on radio, Wells believed, would be heard only by those who were semi-literate and they would eventually tire of sitting in front of the radio listening to the noise of radio static, fading voices and dull programming. In a newspaper article entitled *The Remarkable Vogue of Broadcasting* he was not enthusiastic when he said '…the future of broadcasting is like the future of crossword puzzles and Oxford trousers, a very trivial future indeed.'[5] He goes on to say with regret that 'There could be one very fine use made of broadcasting, though I cannot imagine how it could be put upon a commercially paying footing.'[6] As for the people that listen to radio 'There are in the world a sad minority of lonely people, isolated people, endangered helpless people, sleepless people, suffering people who must lie on their backs, and who cannot handle books—and there are the blind.'[7]

As noted in an earlier chapter Wells thought a bit more kindly about the movie industry but he did not hesitate to become a movie critic when the need arose. In 1927 a German movie maker produced a film at Ufa studios entitled *Metropolis*. It's a story set one hundred years in the future and presents a visual image of man and his robots. In contemporary terms the film is considered a landmark production and is on the list of required viewing for most students of film and theatre. However, Wells was not impressed, and he produced another newspaper column entitled *The Silliest Film*. His dislike of the film and the people who produced it was largely the result of his belief that they had plagiarized his novel *The Sleeper Awakes* written about thirty years earlier. Further, the film was a satirical account of mankind's future in a highly controlled and mechanized society. This did not sit well with Wells. He considered any attack on the sanctity of his socialist system to be an attack on himself and he often reacted with a venomous pen. He thus pointed out to his English readers that the German producers had '…set to work in their huge studio to produce furlong after furlong of this ignorant, old-fashioned balderdash, and ruin the market for any better film along these lines.'[8]

During the 1920's Wells wrote about many subjects that were topical and controversial. His columns were short, pointed and attracted large numbers of readers from both sides of the Atlantic. He covered topics on Fascism, Communism, Democracy and the Labor Movement. He ventured his opinions on marriage, vivisection, séances, dreams and common delusions. He was quick to inform his readers about the progress of science and industry and to explain how things could have been done better, or how industrialists were corrupting the system and choking off the progress that so many working souls had sacrificed to produce. To read the work of H.G. Wells requires the reading of one or more of his collections of journalism, and *The Way the World is Going* is a classic of this period.

31

Wells' Inventions

Wells is often credited as the being the originator of a number of physical devices and ideas. Several biographers have attributed him with surprising creations and provide examples of how he had to defend himself against those who attempted to discredit him. Other writers have suggested that Wells didn't invent much of anything and they produce quotations indicating that he didn't always claim credit for himself as some writers have assumed. In fact some of his so-called inventions were almost forced on him by generous and well meaning fans. The issue of originality or credit for ideas has thus been surrounded by criticism and skepticism.

Without a doubt Wells supporters and detractors hold strong opinions on both sides of the argument and there still exists some confusion in the minds of a few of his contemporary readers. A bit of research into some of the ideas Wells is credited with suggests that much of the credit was generated long after he had died and that part of the many arguments he became involved in during his latter years included defense of his historical political and social positions. When this defense required reminding people of his prophesies or inventions, he often did so without hesitation.

One of the interesting inventions credited to Wells is the military tank. In 1903 he wrote a short story for *The Strand Magazine* entitled *The Land Ironclads*. It is a tale of soldiers in the field being attacked by a mobile machine bristling with guns, cannons and covered by heavy steel armor. Wells indicates in the introduction he later wrote for the Atlantic edition that he wrote the story to develop an idea that he had presented in *Anticipations*, which was published in 1901. 'It develops an idea already thrown out two years before in "Anticipations," an idea which, with the help of Mr. Churchill at the Admiralty, actually fought its way at last into the British military mind in 1916. The military mind is much the same the whole world over: no other army, luckily for the British, had even that much alertness.'[1]

This is a very telling quotation in that it shows that Wells made no direct claim to the invention of the tank but he clearly establishes that he had documented the idea of its use as early as 1901. Secondly he lauds Mr. Churchill for his efforts in promoting the use of the tank. Much later he would be upset with Mr. Churchill for refusing his offers of advice and assistance in conducting the war effort. Thirdly he takes a shot at the military for being so stupid in their reluctance to accept the idea of an ironclad vehicle on the battlefield.

It doesn't take much research into military history to understand that Wells had grossly oversimplified the time and effort required to design and test military machinery, something very new to an army in which His Majesty's Light Horse Brigade was still an active unit. Further, it probably never entered Wells mind that Churchill's efforts to promote the use of armored vehicles came from his experience with naval battleships and probably had little to do with Wells prophesies, short stories, or public pontifications. Although anyone who read and wrote as voraciously as Churchill would certainly be aware of Wells work and his position on the war. In 1903 when Wells wrote *The Land Ironclads*, the invention of an armored vehicle was a non-issue. However, after the war it became a public issue when Wells took one of the military's finest to task. An officer had the audacity to suggest that he was responsible for introducing the tank to the army after seeing armored carts being used in the field to carry supplies. Little did the officer know that he had lit Wells fuse and there was no escape from the power of his pen. This disagreement exposes the significant difference between coming up with an idea, and inventing something. Wells was full of new and reworked ideas, and he read as avidly as he wrote. Undoubtedly he could glean ideas from a wide range of publications and reuse them without a hint of plagiarism. But this process of reusing ideas is a long way from designing, developing and testing a new piece of machinery. Wells was not an engineer and he had very little training beyond his work in biology. To attribute him with the invention of the tank, or any other piece of military machinery including aircraft, bombs or communication equipment, is a stretch of the facts and it ignores the work of dozens of scientists and engineers and hundreds of hours of testing and retesting by troops and support staff in the field. Wells acknowledges in passing, with statements like 'Leonardo da Vinci notwithstanding', that there were others before him who introduced the idea of armored vehicles in warfare. Perhaps their only deficiency was the absence of an internal combustion engine to justify the term 'Tank'.

Wells was often chided for his outlandish opinions and his poorly conceived newspaper attacks on others. He did make a trip to the continent during the war and he toured the front, as best as it could be toured at the time. On his return to

England he had many ideas on how the war could be won and didn't hesitate in telling the military how foolish their tactics were and that he had conceived brilliant plans for transporting supplies and using aircraft for surveillance. It is unlikely that Wells was able to conceive, in two weeks, something that an entire military establishment in the thick of war for the last two years had never been able to develop.

Wells quickly became an expert, in his own mind at least, in most of what he touched. Military matters were no exception. He considered himself a scientist and placed few bounds on the capabilities of a scientist. The issue of ironclad vehicles makes it clear that Wells had little understanding of the difference between science and engineering. Like most people who are convinced of the superiority of their own ideas Wells wrote that it was 'absurd that my imagination was not mobilized in scheming the structure and use of these contrivances.'[2]

Little wonder that some would chuckle when he charged forth with another earth shattering claim of invention or a new solution to the social ills that created the war. Wells certainly did not invent the tank, and he never claimed he did. However he was probably the first to write extensively about its use and he was quick to defend his early efforts, especially when preempted by a military officer who may have been in grade school when Wells was writing about modern warfare.

The entire concept of warfare was changing in the first few years of the 20th century and the capabilities of machinery fascinated Wells. He has been credited with the *invention* of the atomic bomb and the tactics of aerial warfare. Fortunately this brings us into a domain where most people can see the difference between writing about something and spending thousands of hours in development, or the difference between science and engineering. Wells could no more have invented the atomic bomb that he could have flown to the moon. However he was a master at writing about both. In his novel *The World Set Free* he has his characters throwing atom bombs over the side of their biplane and watching them create a mass of flaming ruin.

Military tactics and the use of tanks in warfare were never far from his mind. When he completed work on *The Outline of History* in 1920 he included a chapter that outlined the progress of the First World War. This chapter, like much of the history written by H.G. Wells, was colored by his opinions, which were in turn colored by his current political and social activities. A quotation on the use of ironclad vehicles in warfare again convinces us of his lack of professionalism as a scientist, engineer or military tactician. 'Military science is never up to date under modern conditions, because military men are as a class unimaginative, there are always at any date undeveloped inventions capable of disturbing current tactical and strategic practice which the military intelligence has declined. The German plan had been made for some years; it was a stale plan; it could probably have been foiled at the outset by a proper use of entrenchments and barbed wire and machine guns, but the French were by no means as advanced in their military science as the Germans, and they trusted to methods of open warfare that were at least fourteen years behind the times.'3

Outline of History continues like an editorial opinion piece. In case the reader missed his point the first time, he would repeat it with further emphasis in typical Wellsian fashion. On the same page as the above quotation he continues with a single laborious sentence that might have won the war on its own. 'At that time the essential problem of trench warfare had already been solved; there existed in England, for instance, the model of a tank, which would have given the allies a swift and easy victory before 1916; but the professional military mind is by necessity an inferior and unimaginative mind; no man of high intellectual quality would willingly imprison his gifts in such a calling; nearly all supremely great soldiers have been either inexperienced fresh-minded young men like Alexander, Napoleon, and Hoche, politicians turned soldiers like Julius Caesar, nomads like the Hun and Mongol captains, or amateurs like Cromwell and Washington; whereas this war after fifty years of militarism was a hopelessly professional war; from first to last it was impossible to get it out of the hands of the regular generals, and neither the German nor allied headquarters was disposed to regard an invention with toleration that would destroy their traditional methods.'4

Clearly Wells was upset by the fact that no one paid much attention to him when he offered advice about the war, or any other technical or social issue. Like the rest of the world, he was blessed with 20/20 hindsight and able to place his criticism more accurately than he did when producing his prophesies at the turn of the century. Wells was about 50 years old by the middle of the First World War and near the peak of his career. However he was losing ground among many of his regular readers because of foolish claims and rash statements about others. When his opinions and offers of professional help were rebuffed he would often launch a vitriolic defense that simply made more enemies. As his credibility among social and political leaders deteriorated, he simply became more frustrated and irritable.

The issue of H.G. Wells and inventions covers a wide spectrum of ideas, equipment and machinery. He was an imaginative science fiction writer and a prolific self-described prophet. There is little doubt that some of his ideas would be on the mark and that he might receive credit for having described some contrivance before anyone else did. His ideas go far beyond military issues and include moving sidewalks, window cleaners, anti-gravity devices, time machines, exercise equipment, moon rockets, and many other fanciful concepts. The argument about whether or not he deserves credit for any of these so-called inventions is the same as the previous one, i.e., he wrote about them but he certainly didn't invent them.

PART VIII
Closing The Book

32

At the End of His Tether

During the last two years of his life Wells published three small books of essays, opinions and collected newspaper articles. The first of these three is entitled *'42 to '44: A Contemporary Memoir upon Human Behaviour During the Crisis of World Revolution*, published by Secker and Warburg in March of 1944. Much of this book is a rehash of older ideas and revisions of previously published material. Wells also includes his 1942 doctoral thesis in the appendices. He was proud of his thesis, written very late in his career, but not so late that he couldn't use it to lend scientific justification to his ideas about human evolution and behavior. The second of these three books is entitled *The Happy Turning: A Dream of Life*, published by Heinemann in 1945. It can perhaps be correctly called a short story and is definitely a change of pace from the previous book. It depicts the author entering a dream state in which he uses conversation and description to justify many of his old ideas about religion. The third in this series, and the last book Wells produced, is entitled *Mind at the End of Its Tether* published by Heinemann in 1945. This last book is the smallest of the three and in some respects the most controversial. Certainly as the last entry in a prolific writing career it has been judged, misjudged, dissected, analyzed and reinterpreted as often as any of the books published in the latter part of his life.

These three books taken together represent the final milestone in his literary career and are perhaps the culmination of his efforts to convince the human race that they are headed for extinction unless major social and political changes are made. Although they represent a significant phase in his thinking, and are a good example of his evolving literary style, none of these three books made much of a contribution to his body of work and none were literary landmarks with wide distribution. Today only academics and Wells enthusiasts have ever heard of these titles.

'42 to '44 is a collection of 35 essays in two parts. The first part is on *The Heritage of the Past*, and the second part on *How We Face the Future*. Wells explains

in the preface how he collected and rewrote most of the material and he points out the advantage of hindsight when assessing the Second World War and its participants. Wells viewed himself as an active participant in the war, although not everyone saw him in the same light. In essence he was an accomplished, well known, and wealthy writer sitting, in his own words, at his 'base behind the battlefront'. Some of the senior military establishment, for whom Wells had very little respect, often accused him of meddling in things he new nothing about.

Wells makes it clear that '42 to '44 is a collection of essays and ideas was not intended for wide distribution to the general public. In fact a small press run of about 2000 copies was released. 'I have issued it therefore deliberately as an expensive library book, and I intend it to remain an expensive library book. There will be no cheaper edition issued at any time and I doubt if second hand copies will ever become abundant.'[1] Wells later confesses that he had rushed to print with this material because he was told by his doctors that 'he could not last for another year'. As it turns out he lived for another two years and had a chance to address some of the issues he believed he missed as he rushed this material to print.

In many respects this requirement for urgent thinking by Wells has been a great benefit to literary history. The bulk of the material in '42 to '44 is lucid, to the point, well thought out, and is a good historical account of the war effort as of March 1944. This is largely because the work was addressed to the general public when it was first written for newspaper distribution. By the time it appeared in this collected form it was designed more to build what Wells thought would be his legacy, than to address the general reader.

In 1945 Wells published *The Happy Turning*. It was an interesting break in his stride and has led a number of biographers and critics to assume that he had changed his mind about many of his social and religious convictions. In truth, he may have been ready to take himself a little less seriously, but he certainly had not changed his mind on most issues. *The Happy Turning* is a short story written in the first person with the author, passing through a dream meeting people in unusual circumstances. Wells opens the story by pointing out that 'Some time ago I dreamt a dream that recurs with variations again and again...'[2] It would be out of character if Wells didn't launch himself into religious, political and social arguments. The difference in this small book is that he uses the stories' characters and circumstances to justify his ideas. Much more logic and gentle reason pervades this story than is normally expected from Wells. This is perhaps why some biographers consider the book to be a change in his thinking. Of his last three books, this one is probably the least significant.

By 1946 Wells admitted to becoming tired and frustrated. He lived in London at 13 Hanover Terrace near Regents Park and had remained in residence throughout the war years like many other writers, entertainers and businessmen who refused to let the bombs drive them out of their homes. In 1946 the war was over and Wells was approaching his 80th birthday. He had become thoroughly convinced that mankind was in a downward spiral that would end in decimation, if not elimination, of the human species. Two violent and terrifying wars in less than 40 years provided Wells with ample proof of his thesis.

His last book certainly expressed some of this frustration. It was a small book of only thirty-four pages entitled *Mind at the End of Its Tether*. It was published in 1945 and Wells considered it a final summary of the ideas he'd published earlier in *'42 to '44* and in other essays and pamphlets. His frustration at the lack of impact his ideas had made on his audience is expressed in the preface to the book. 'So far as fundamentals go, he [the author] has nothing more to say. The greater bulk of that research material may now go down the laboratory sink. It is either superseded or dismissed. It will go out of print and be heard of no more.'3

Wells did not have the time or the energy to beat around the bush. Critics have suggested that he had given up on the world and was completely despondent over the lack of progress he'd made in impressing politicians and the general public with the necessity of change in our social system. Others take the opposite view and insist that he was determined and obstinate to the end. His son George Phillip Wells is included in the latter category. When *Mind of the End of Its Tether* was reprinted by the H.G. Wells Society in 1968, G.P. Wells wrote in his introduction to the new edition, 'Old and tired, yes. Broken in health, yes. And spirit, no.'4 Probably G. P. Wells had the better insight. Certainly H.G. Wells displayed all of his arrogance, pomposity, and a propensity for errors in judgement, all within the first few sentences of the little book. The second paragraph encapsulates the pages that would follow and certainly confirms that Wells had not lost the use of his pen.

Continuing to write in the third person Wells states 'If his thinking has been sound, then this world is at the end of its tether. The end of everything we call life is close at hand and cannot be evaded. He is telling you the conclusions to which reality has driven his own mind, and he thinks you may be interested enough to consider them, but he is not attempting to impose them upon you. He will do his best to indicate why he has succumbed to so stupendous a proposition. His exposition will have to be done bit by bit, and it demands close reading.

He is not attempting to win acquiescence in what he has to say. He writes under the urgency of a scientific training, which obliged him to clarify his mind and his world to the utmost limit of his capacity.'[5]

Clearly the 'Mind' in the title is mankind itself and Wells was convinced that mankind was fast approaching its demise and in order to understand why, the reader must have to pay close attention to what the writer has to say. Then, falling back for the last time on his *scientific* training, which has gone unused for over half a century, Wells proceeds to tell us why he's convinced that the world is coming to an end. Close reading of this work is indeed prerequisite to its understanding. Something he calls the Antagonist appears to become responsible for the coming disaster. The first chapter takes up half of the little book. It is difficult to follow and it contains little logic or *scientific* postulation. In the latter part of the first chapter Wells points out that the basis for some of his conclusions is 'The searching scepticism of the writer's philosophical analysis...'[6] At this point some readers may not be too sure where the writer's conclusions come from or whether they bear the weight and significance he suggests.

The last chapters of the book are difficult to tie to the first but they seem to be part of the justification that Wells needs to complete his thesis. By throwing in a bit of *scientific* logic Wells believes he has increased the credibility of his proposition. These final chapters appeal to geologic records and recent archeological discoveries to justify his evolutionary concepts. Other writers suggest that these chapters were written as a new conclusion to *A Short History of the World* first published in 1922. Regardless of their origin or original purpose Wells uses them to illustrate the rise of mankind from a primitive state, and perhaps the rise of another more sophisticated creature, after the certain destruction of Homo Sapiens. Wells was an avid reader and he certainly kept abreast of new ideas and new developments in science and technology. However, as he often does, he collects a set of loose facts in his head, throws in a few technical terms, and draws some rather strained, and occasionally comical, conclusions. He points out to the reader, for example, the reason why there are so few fossilized remains of early man, or the Hominidae. 'Since they are open air animals with sufficient wits to avoid frequent drowning, the fossil traces of their appearance are few and far between.'[7]

To Wells' contemporaries and to his present day followers, *Mind at the End of Its Tether* makes perfect sense. It is the crown on Wells' philosophy of mankind, his steady progress towards certain destruction and the evolution of a new species. Perhaps it is an appropriate cap to his last few years of work, but to others, a devastating war was over, the economy was returning to normal and cities needed to be rebuilt. Nobody was going to sit around and contemplate their end after just surviving a terrifying holocaust. Wells died on Thursday, August 13th, 1946 at 4:15pm in his home at 13 Hanover Terrace. He wrote no more for the London papers. He published no more books and few people looked back to read his later writing. He quickly began to disappear from the minds of the post-war generation. School children continued to use his *History* and *Science of Life* in the classroom but it soon became clear that the work was dated and full of Wells' personal biases and political sentiments.

One can't help but wonder what Wells present day image might be if he'd devoted the last two or three years of his life to the creation of another *fantastic romance*. Although he had long since abandoned the imaginative and adventurous novels and short stories, some biographers have pointed out that they weren't forgotten by his old friends. He was, for example, approached by Alexander Korda to consider an updated post-war version of the movie *Things to Come*. It is truly unfortunate that he didn't have time to see this proposal through. It's also unfortunate that Wells left this world at a time when science fiction began to blossom and gain some well deserved respectability. Had he remained with us for another ten years he may have found a second childhood.

33

Where Is H.G. Wells Now?

The century between 1850 and 1950 produced some of the finest writers the English language has ever known. Whether or not H.G. Wells fits into this category is a matter of opinion. His advocates vehemently insist that he represents a milestone in literature and that he changed the face of the world through his work. His detractors believe that, with the exception of a few stories early in his career, his impact was minimal and he was more a repetitive journalist than a writer. Perhaps the truth lies somewhere in between. The previous chapters are intended to illustrate that much of his notoriety comes from his controversial personality and his political ideas rather than his writing. Regardless of his fame or his staying power he is a good example of a personality that fits Churchill's 'riddle wrapped inside an enigma rolled up in mystery.'

Journalism was a part of Wells life throughout his career. When he was a young man in London he supported himself and his first wife, Isabel, by writing book reviews and newspaper articles. His success in selling humorous anecdotes and short stories encouraged him to write more and to explore the rapidly growing writer's market in London. For a period of about six years between about 1895 and 1901 his imagination flourished and the public devoured his work. The chronological list of his novels and short stories, in Appendices One and Two respectively, make it clear that everything the casual reader knows about H.G. Wells is based on his work in this short period. He wrote over sixty of his approximately seventy short stories, and he wrote nearly all of the novels that are in popular sale over a century later. What happened during the remaining forty years of his career?

If Wells had continued writing his *fantastic romances* and had honed his witty style to the polish shown by some of his contemporaries he might have produced work that would carry him into the *finest writer* category. But he didn't. His desire to write imaginative stories disappeared very quickly after the turn of the century. He took up a number of social and political issues, not all of them popular, and he wrote voluminously and repetitively to support and promote whatever his current cause might be. These causes ranged from The League of Nations, socialist and utopian governments, the conduct of whatever war was in progress, labor movements and dozens of minor perceived inequities that would enflame his conscience for a few weeks. He was a vocal opponent of government action in both World Wars and he publicly derided politicians and businessmen whom he believed were detrimental to the welfare of the nation. He did not falter in producing a continuous flow of publications. He produced well over one hundred books after the turn of the century, but there were no more books like *The Time Machine* or *The War of the Worlds*. As a novelist Wells rested his laurels early in his career without ever realizing he was trading his success as a novelist for notoriety as a journalist. His reputation as a story teller gradually diminished and he became known as a socialist and a promoter of world government. As his wealth and popularity grew he assumed a more arrogant attitude, became argumentative and gained enemies as quickly as he made friends. More than one biographer has suggested that many of Wells readers kept up with his work as much out of amusement as out of interest in his work.

It became evident to Wells later in his career that much of his work to modify political thinking, and to encourage new forms of government that might reduce or eliminate the folly of war, was wasted effort. This generated a level of frustration that didn't improve the quality of his writing. His ideas were not being as carefully thought out as they had been during his younger and less certain years and were often based on prejudices and slanted perceptions. Wells could alienate people quickly and he often upset his staunchest supporters. His visions of utopian government were based on good intentions and an honest desire to eliminate the evils of the world, but he had few practical answers to the achievement of his goals. In fact some of his proposals were of a highly questionable nature resulting in a readership that would not always take him seriously. His utopian ideals required keeping people in line with stringent government regulation and a forceful discipline. This included marriage and birth regulations, state education and the elimination of the dull and base members of the population. Little wonder than his friend Aldous Huxley produced *Brave New World* in 1932 with a satirical attack on a social system that included test tube babies, brain washing and government control of all human endeavors.

After producing something as practical as *Anticipations* in 1901 with its many recommendations for social and industrial improvement, it's puzzling why his vision of utopia was not followed by a detailed plan for the creation of such a state. Wells was an avid proponent of an ideal socialist state but very little of his work ever dealt with building and managing the infrastructure or the practical operation of the system once the state is achieved. He convinced a large number of people that his socialist system was the best thing for the future of mankind but a bit more introspection might have made it clear that his vision of a socialist state was a practical impossibility. Had he spent more time and newspaper columns trying to add social programs to the existing democratic system he might have produced a lasting impact. He did attempt to gain a seat in parliament as a Labour party representative but polled dead last. Certainly his constituency was not interested in him or his party. Wells blamed this on the myopic vision of the University District Electors rather than on his appeal as a candidate.

There have been many past writers who have had strange and sometimes impractical ideas, but few were as controversial as Wells and few ever published the volume of work he produced or attempted to cover the wide range of subject material. Wells often pushed himself on the reading public and made it clear that alternatives to his ideas were usually not acceptable. This tends to alienate people. The popularity of a leader of men and a noble prophet will always outlast the memory of someone who might occasionally be branded a crackpot and possess the moral character of a guttersnipe. Wells commonly slid into the latter category and it had a substantial effect on the thinking of those who bought, read, and recommended his work to others.

Wells grew up with a healthy dislike of the British class system. He was the product of a lower class family and grew up in the London suburbs. His mother was a devout Anglican and his father a bit wayward and more interested in cricket than gainful employment. Wells never admitted that the system he despised was the system that educated him and provided him with opportunities unavailable fifty years earlier. He quickly gained considerable wealth and notoriety and slid smoothly into the upper classes that he damned a few years earlier. Even with his successes and wide acceptance he was still quick to criticize those above him as parasites on the system. He was also bitter about his lack of acceptance by the Royal Society, even though his membership would have been a joke, and he blamed most of his social failures on the evils of the capitalist system and the greedy industrialists who controlled it. In effect, Wells had become one of the wealthy intellectual elite that he despised. Even though he wrote himself into many of his novels and prophetic essays, he could never really see himself for what he'd become.

Those who've read widely from Wells dozens of books often consider him to be one of the century's greatest prophets. Indeed, he even considered himself to be an accomplished prophet. Although he readily admitted to a few failures, he eagerly and confidently pointed out that his record of accurate prophesy, especially on the subject of war, needed to be more carefully assessed by politicians and military specialists. Forecasting was a common procedure at the dawn of the twentieth century. Wells was not alone or especially original in the business of prophesy, but he had built a large and dedicated audience and his reputation had expanded well beyond Great Britain. Neither was Wells any better than any of the other prophets, he simply spoke with a louder voice and he spoke to an audience that was eager to hear about the new century.

With a few exceptions, Wells produced very little that was new at any time in his career. His claims at invention usually had nothing to do with invention, he simply put something in print before his colleagues or competitors could make the front page, and would vehemently defend his originality when the issue of credit arose at a later date. In some circumstances the logic of his claim to originality was difficult to fathom. He would preface an idea by explaining that he had read about it on previous occasions, then he would proceed to expand the concept and explain how useful it might be to the rest of society. If the idea was developed by others at some future time he would not hesitate to claim credit for the proposal and explain how he had introduced it to the world.

The promotion of socialism was a lifetime endeavor for Wells. His ideas on socialism were not especially original and he certainly was not the first to put these ideas into a novel or to speculate on how they might be received in the future. When Wells came up with an idea that he was certain would solve some of England's existing social problems he would repeat himself over and over again, in newspapers, pamphlets, books, and even from the podium. He was an avid proponent of free education and believed in making books and libraries easily accessible to the public. He wrote about history, biology and economics and published material in text book form at prices affordable to most of the working class. In spite of this basic practicality he still came up with ideas on the fringe of reason, such as *The World Encyclopedia*, the promotion and teaching of Esperanto, or military suggestions that included machine guns mounted on bicycles.

So where is H.G. Wells in the twenty first century? It's fair to assume that few writers have ever produced the volume of material that Wells published. However, this massive volume of material didn't necessarily include similar quantities of literary merit. Wells' contemporary acceptance is based on his work in the nineteenth century, not on his political tracts, or newspaper columns written after the turn of the century. Only serious students are even aware of most of this latter material. When his work is compared to other English writers of the same period he is usually viewed as a story teller rather than a writer. Even his ability to create a story does not compare well with the work of Rudyard Kipling, J.R.R. Tolkien, Conan Doyle or C.S. Lewis, most of whom Wells would have known or read during his lifetime. Why then was Wells such a popular success? The answer to this question is probably because he made as much an impact on the public through his controversial newspaper articles, his public appearances, and movie screenplays as he did through his novels. By contrast, someone like Tolkien gained notoriety entirely through his writing and he rarely appeared outside his Oxford University confines.

Wells loss of audience as a literary artist began very early in his career. His success as a novelist is based only on the work he produced during his brief and *finest hour*. By the time the First World War was over the educational system in Britain had produced a whole new generation of literate and well educated Britons. Their reading habits were different from their parents and they were more likely to ignore H.G. Wells. In fact the new generation's familiarity with Wells was to be gained from his appearance in the local newspaper as a news maker rather than through his columns on the editorial page. It's not surprising to find, three generations after his death, that Wells is all but forgotten and if it were not for *The Time Machine* or *The War of the Worlds* reappearing at regular intervals in movie theatres, very few of the current generation would ever have heard of him. Little wonder that he expressed frustration as he watched the Second Great War come to a close in 1945. Mankind had learned nothing from his lifetime of campaigning for social reform and it seemed that the world's leaders had paid precious little attention to his warnings of war and an inevitable collapse of the political system. By August of 1946 he was gone. H.G. Wells had come to the end of his literary tether.

References

Chapter 2

(1) Frank Wells' correspondence to William Baxter in the Bromley Public Library.

(2) A letter to Grant Richards of Phil May's Annual dated Nov 6th, 1895. As published in *The Early H.G. Wells*, Bernard Bergonzi, Manchester University Press, 1961, Page 23.

(3) *The Time Traveler*, Norman and Jeanne Mackenzie, Weidenfeld and Nicolson, London, 1973, Page 117.

(4) *Experiment in Autobiography*, H.G. Wells, Victor Gollancz Ltd, London, 1934, Volume II, Page 666.

(5) Ibidem, Page 666.

(6) *The Time Traveler*, Norman and Jeanne Mackenzie, Weidenfeld and Nicolson, London, 1973, Page 228.

(7) *H.G. Wells and His Family*, M.M. Meyers, International Publishing Co., Edinburgh, 1956.

(8) London Daily Express, December 1920.

(9) *The Time Traveler*, Norman and Jeanne Mackenzie, Weidenfeld and Nicolson, London, 1973, Page 379.

Chapter 3

(1) *Experiment in Autobiography*, H.G. Wells, The Cressett Press Ltd, London 1934, Chapter 8, Page 506.

(2) Ibidem, Chapter 8, Page 541.

(3) Ibidem, Chapter 8, Page 598.

(4) Ibidem, Chapter 8, Page 639.

(5) *The Early H.G. Wells*, Bernard Bergonzi, Manchester University Press, Manchester, 1961, Page 20.

(6) Ibidem, Page 22.

Chapter 4

(1) *The Early H.G. Wells*, Bernard Bergonzi, Manchester University Press, Manchester, 1961, page 3.
(2) *The Atlantic Edition*, H.G. Wells, Charles Scribner's Sons, New York, 1924, Volume IV, Preface to Volume IV, page ix.

Chapter 5

(1) *Mankind in the Making*, H.G. Wells, Chapman & Hall, London, 1903, Preface, page v.
(2) Ibidem, Preface, page vi.
(3) Ibidem, Preface, page vi.
(4) Ibidem, The New Republic, page 26.
(5) Ibidem, Thought in the Modern State, page 373

Chapter 6

(1) *The Time Traveller, The Life of H.G. Wells*, Norman and Jeanne Mackenzie, Weidenfeld and Nicolson, London, 1973. Chapter 12, page 184.
(2) Ibidem, Chapter 12, page 185.
(3) Wells Archives, personal correspondence between G.B. Shaw and H.G. Wells
(4) *The Time Traveller, The Life of H.G. Wells*, Norman and Jeanne Mackenzie, Weidenfeld and Nicolson, London, 1973. Chapter 12, page 190.
(5) Ibidem, Chapter 12, page 190.
(6) Ibidem, Chapter 12, page 193.
(7) Wells Archives, personal correspondence between H.G. Wells and L.H. Guest
(8) The Fabian Society website, 2004

Chapter 7

(1) Cat. No.33, *The Collector's Bibliography of the Works of H.G. Wells*, Gordon D. Feir, Southern Maple Publications, 1992. This edition is rare since it was printed in limited numbers.
(2) *This Misery of Boots*, H.G. Wells, The Fabian Society, London, 1907, Page 40.
(3) Ibidem, Page 27.
(4) Ibidem, Page 37.
(5) Ibidem, Page 23.
(6) Ibidem, Page 25.

(7) Ibidem, Page 15.
(8) Ibidem, Page 41.
(9) Uppark, The National Trust Guide Book, 1985. The former Fetherston-haugh Estate, one of Wells' temporary homes while his mother was employed by the estate's owners.

Chapter 8

(1) *The World Set Free*, H.G. Wells, E.P. Dutton & Co., New York, 1914, (First American Edition), Page 83.
(2) *The Interpretation of Radium and the Structure of the Atom*, Frederick Soddy, G.P. Putnam's Sons, New York, 1909.
(3) *The World Set Free*, H.G. Wells, E.P. Dutton & Co., New York, 1914, (First American Edition), Page 115.
(4) Ibidem, Page 92
(5) Ibidem, Page 125
(6) Ibidem, Page 151
(7) Ibidem, Page 163
(8) Ibidem, Page 169
(9) Ibidem, Page 170
(10) Ibidem, Page 249
(11) Ibidem, Page 271

Chapter 9

(1) *Socialism and the Scientific Motive*, H.G. Wells, Cooperative Printing Society, London, 1923
(2) *The Time Traveller, The Life of H.G. Wells*, Norman and Jeanne Mackenzie, Weidenfeld and Nicolson, London, 1973. Chapter 18, page 287.

Chapter 10

(1) *Things to Come: A Film Story Based on the Material Contained in His History of the Future 'The Shape of Things to Come'*, H.G. Wells, The Cresset Press, London, 1934, Page 11:
(2) *The Prophetic Soul: A Reading of H.G. Wells' Things to Come*, Professor Leon Stover, McFarland, 1987.
(3) *Things to Come: A Film Story Based on the Material Contained in His History of the Future 'The Shape of Things to Come'*, H.G. Wells, The Cresset Press, London, 1934, Page 83.

(4) Ibidem, Page 104.
(5) Ibidem, Page 67.
(6) Ibidem, Page 109.
(7) Ibidem, Page 125.
(8) Ibidem, Page 135.

Chapter 12

(1) *The Problem of the Birth Supply*, H.G. Wells, The Atlantic Edition, 1924, vol. 4, page 309
(2) Ibidem, vol. 4, page 319
(3) Ibidem, vol. 4, page 319
(4) Ibidem, vol. 4, page 325
(5) Ibidem, vol. 4, page 321
(6) Ibidem, vol. 4, page 334

Chapter 13

(1) *News From Nowhere,* William Morris, 1890, London, A novel by the overt socialist writer William Morris that speculates on the character of a Marxist society three decades before it emerges in the post-Bolshevik era.
(2) *A Modern Utopia*, H.G. Wells, Atlantic Edition, Volume IX, page 33
(3) Ibidem, page 40
(4) Ibidem, page 61
(5) Ibidem, page 75
(6) Ibidem, page 127
(7) Ibidem, page 138
(8) Ibidem, page 138
(9) Ibidem, page 167
(10) Ibidem, page 174
(11) Ibidem, page 182
(12) Ibidem, page 301
(13) Ibidem, page 299
(14) Ibidem, page 247
(15) Ibidem, page 253

Chapter 14

(1) *Men Like Gods*, H.G. Wells, Cassell and Company Ltd., London, 1923, page 58

(2) Ibidem, page 73
(3) Ibidem, page 87
(4) Ibidem, page 111
(5) Ibidem, page 117
(6) Ibidem, page 160

Chapter 15

(1) *The New World Order*, H.G. Wells, Alfred A Knopf, New York, Second Printing, April 1940, page 6
(2) Ibidem, page 77
(3) Ibidem, page 52
(4) Ibidem, page 58
(5) Ibidem, page 89
(6) Ibidem, page 126

Chapter 16

(1) *Aldous Huxley: A Biography*, Sybille Bedford, Alfred A. Knopf Harper & Row, New York, 1974
(2) *George Orwell: A Life*, Bernard Crick, Secker & Warburg, London, 1980

Chapter 18

(1) *The Time Traveller*, Norman and Jeanne MacKenzie, Weidenfeld and Nicolson, London, 1973, Page 133, Wells argument with Heinemann over his early publications.
(2) Ibidem, Page 361, Wells argument with Thring over breach of contract.

Chapter 19

(1) *A Thesis on the Quality of Illusion in the Continuity of the Individual Life in the Higher Metazoa, With Particular Reference to the Species Homo Sapiens*, 1942, H.G. Wells Thesis presented to the University of London for the Doctorate of Science Degree, Section II, paragraph 27.
(2) Ibidem, Section VI, paragraph 77.

Chapter 21

(1) *What Is Coming?*, Cassell and Company, London, 1916, page 240

Chapter 22

(1) *The Idea of a World Encyclopaedia*, Hogarth Press, London, 1936, page 18
(2) Ibidem, page 8
(3) Ibidem, page 19
(4) Ibidem, page 21
(5) Ibidem, page 22
(6) Ibidem, page 26
(7) Ibidem, page 27
(8) Ibidem, page 29
(9) Timothy Berners-Lee designed and developed the concept of the World Wide Web while working in Geneva at the CERN high energy physics lab explicitly to enable immediate distribution of experimental data to colleagues around the world.

Chapter 23

(1) *In The Fourth Year: Anticipations of a World Peace*, H.G. Wells, Chatto & Windus, London, 1918
(2) *British Nationalism and the League of Nations*, H.G. Wells, The League of Nations Union, London 1918
(3) *The Idea of a League of Nations*, H.G. Wells, Oxford University Press, London, 1919
(4) *The Way to a League of Nations*, H.G. Wells, Oxford University Press, London, 1919

Chapter 24

(1) *In Search of Hot Water*, H.G. Wells, Penguin Books Ltd., Harmondsworth, 1939
(2) *The Rights of Man or What Are We Fighting For?*, H.G. Wells, Penguin Books Ltd., Harmondsworth, 1940
(3) *The Common Sense of War and Peace*, H.G. Wells, Penguin Books Ltd., Harmondsworth, 1940
(4) *The Rights of Man or What Are We Fighting For?*, H.G. Wells, Penguin Books Ltd., Harmondsworth, 1940, Chapter 10 'A French Parallel', page 85
(5) Ibidem, 'Free Trade and Profiteering', page 76
(6) *State of the Union Address,* the 77th Congress of the United States, Franklin D. Roosevelt, January 6th, 1941.

Chapter 25

(1) *The Outline of History*, H.G. Wells, Cassell and Company, London, 1920, first bound edition.
(2) *Mr. Belloc Objects to the Outline of History*, H.G. Wells, Watts & Co., London, 1926, No.3 in The Forum Series.
(3) *Crux Ansata. An Indictment of the Roman Catholic Church*, H.G. Wells, A Penguin Special, 1943, Penguin Books Limited, Harmondsworth, Middlesex, England

Chapter 26

(1) *Crux Ansata. An Indictment of the Roman Catholic Church*, H.G. Wells, A Penguin Special, 1943, Penguin Books Limited, Harmondsworth, Middlesex, England
(2) Ibidem, Page 94
(3) Ibidem, Page 95
(4) Ibidem, Page 95

Chapter 27

(1) *The Story of a Great Schoolmaster*, H.G. Wells, Chatto & Windus, London, 1924
(2) *The World Set Free: A Story of Mankind*, H.G. Wells, Macmillan and Company, London 1914
(3) *The Undying Fire*, H.G. Wells, Cassell & Co., London, 1919
(4) *Experiment in Autobiography*, H.G. Wells, The Cressett Press Ltd, London 1934, Chapter nine, page 675.

Chapter 28

(1) *The Atlantic Edition*, The Work of H.G. Wells, Charles Scribner's Sons, 1924, Volume IV, Preface to Volume IV, page ix
(2) Ibidem, An Introduction to the 1914 Edition of Anticipations, page 276.
(3) Ibidem, *Anticipations,* The Probable Diffusion of Great Cities, page 30.
(4) Ibidem, *Anticipations,* The Probable Diffusion of Great Cities, page 36.
(5) Ibidem, *Anticipations,* Developing Social Elements, page 71.
(6) Ibidem, *Anticipations,* The Life-History of Democracy, page 137.
(7) Ibidem, *Anticipations,* The Life-History of Democracy, page 148.
(8) Ibidem, *Anticipations,* War, page 175

Chapter 29

(1) *What Is Coming?*, H.G. Wells, Cassell and Company, London, 1916, page 1
(2) *The War That Will End War*, H.G. Wells, Frank and Cecil Palmer, London, 1914
(3) *What Is Coming?*, H.G. Wells, Cassell and Company, London, 1916, page 48
(4) Ibidem, page 111
(5) Ibidem, page 112
(6) Ibidem, page 120
(7) Ibidem, page 146

Chapter 30

(1) *The Way the World is Going*, H.G. Wells, Ernest Benn, London, 1928, Chapter XXIII, Some Plain Words to Americans, page 252
(2) Ibidem, Chapter XXIII, Some Plain Words to Americans, page 252
(3) Ibidem, Chapter XXIII, Some Plain Words to Americans, page 262
(4) Ibidem, Chapter XXIV, Fuel Getting in the Modern World, page 270
(5) Ibidem, Chapter XV, The Man of Science and the Expressive Man, page 177
(6) Ibidem, Chapter XV, The Man of Science and the Expressive Man, page 177
(7) Ibidem, Chapter XV, The Man of Science and the Expressive Man, page 177
(8) Ibidem, Chapter XV, The Man of Science and the Expressive Man, page 189

Chapter 31

(1) Preface to Volume XX of *The Atlantic Edition of The Works of H.G. Wells*
(2) *The Time Traveller*, Weidenfeld and Nicholson, London 1973, Norman and Jeanne MacKenzie, The War That Will End War, Page 310.
(3) *The Outline of History*, Cassell and Company, London, 1920, (First Single Volume Binding), The Catastrophe of 1914, page 568.
(4) Ibidem, The Catastrophe of 1914, page 568.

Chapter 32

(1) *'42 to '44: A Contemporary Memoir Upon Human Behaviour During the Crisis of World Revolution*, H.G. Wells, Secker and Warburg, London, 1944, Preface, page 8.
(2) *The Happy Turning*, H.G. Wells, Heinemann, London, 1945, Chapter 1, page 1.
(3) *Mind at the End of Its Tether*, H.G. Wells, William Heinemann Ltd, London, 1945, Preface, page v

(4) *The Last Books of H.G. Wells*, H.G. Wells Society, London, 1968, the last line of the introduction by G.P. Wells.

(5) *Mind at the End of Its Tether*, H.G. Wells, William Heinemann Ltd, London, 1945, Chapter I, page 1.

(6) Ibidem, Chapter I, page 13.

(7) Ibidem, Chapter VIII, page 31.

APPENDIX A

The Books of H.G. Wells

When it comes to the work of H.G. Wells, the definition of a book becomes a difficult issue since he published everything from four page folded pamphlets to heavy fourteen hundred page books in two or three volumes. For the purpose of the following list a book is loosely considered to be a volume bound in hardcover usually with more than fifty pages of material. This includes some of his short stories, but only when they first appeared in a bound volume. Wells published approximately eighty books during his lifetime plus numerous rewritten and edited collections that push the total closer to one hundred and twenty. Those few for which he is generally remembered in the twenty-first century are in bold-face type.

Textbook of Biology	W.B. Clive, London	1893
Honours Physiography	Joseph Hughes & Co., London	1893
Select Conversations With an Uncle	John Lane, London	1895
The Time Machine	**W. Heinemann, London**	**1895**
The Wonderful Visit	J.M. Dent & Co., London	1895
The Island of Dr. Moreau	**W. Heinemann, London**	**1896**
The Wheels of Chance	J.M. Dent & Co., London	1896
The Invisible Man	**C. Arthur Pearson, London**	**1897**
Certain Personal Matters	Lawrence & Bullen, London	1897
The War of the Worlds	**W. Heinemann, London**	**1898**
When the Sleeper Wakes	Harper, London	1899
Love and Mr. Lewisham	Harper & Bros., London	1900
The First Men in the Moon	**G. Newnes, London**	**1901**

Anticipations	Chapman & Hall, London	1901
The Discovery of the Future	T. Fisher Unwin, London	1902
The Sea Lady	Methuen & CO., London	1902
Mankind in the Making	Chapman & Hall, London	1903
The Food of the Gods	Macmillan & Co., London	1904
A Modern Utopia	Chapman & Hall, London	1905
Kipps: The Story of a Simple Soul	Macmillan & Co., London	1905
In the Days of the Comet	Macmillan & Co., London	1906
The Future in America	Chapman & Hall, London	1906
New Worlds for Old	Archibald Constable & Co., London	1908
The War in the Air	George Bell & Sons, London	1908
First and Last Things	Archibald Constable & Co., London	1908
Tono Bungay	Macmillan & Co., London	1909
Ann Veronica	T. Fisher Unwin, London	1909
The History of Mr. Polly	Thomas Nelson & Sons, London	1910
The New Machialvelli	John Lane, London	1911
Marriage	Macmillan & Co., London	1912
The Passionate Friends	Macmillan & Co., London	1913
An Englishman Looks at the World	Macmillan & Co., London	1914
The Wife of Sir Isaac Harman	Macmillan & Co., London	1914
Boon	T. Fisher Unwin, London	1915
Bealby: A Holiday	Methuen & Co.	1915
The Research Magnificent	Macmillan & Co.	1915
What is Coming	Cassell & Co., London	1916
Mr. Britling Sees it Through	Cassell & Co., London	1916
The Elements of Reconstruction	Nisbet, London	1916
War and the Future	Cassell & Co., London	1917
God The Invisible King	Cassell & Co., London	1917

The Soul of a Bishop	Cassell & Co., London	1917
In the Fourth Year	Chatto & Windus, London	1918
Joan and Peter	Cassell & Co., London	1918
The Undying Fire	Cassell & Co., London	1919
The Outline of History	George Newnes, London	1920
Russia in the Shadows	Hodder & Stoughton	1920
The Salvaging of Civilization	Cassell & Co., London	1921
The Secret Places of the Heart	Cassell & Co., London	1922
A Short History of the World	Cassell & Co., London	1922
Men Like Gods	Cassell & Co., London	1923
The Story of a Great Schoolmaster	Chatto & Windus, London	1924
The Dream: A Novel	Jonathan Cape, London	1924
A Year of Prophesying	T. Fisher Unwin, London	1924
Christina Alberta's Father	Jonathan Cape, London	1925
The World of William Clissold	Ernest Benn, London	1926
Meanwhile	Ernest Benn, London	1927
The Way the World is Going	Ernest Benn, London	1928
The Open Conspiracy	Victor Gollancz, London	1928
Mr. Blettsworthy on Rampole Island	Ernest Benn, London	1928
The King Who Was a King	Ernest Benn, London	1929
The Autocracy of Mr. Parham	Heinemann, London	1930
The Science of Life	Amalgamatred Press, London	1930
What Are We to do With Our Lives	Heinemann, London	1931
Work Wealth and Happiness	Doubleday, Doran, New York	1931
The Bulpington of Blup	Hutchinson & Co., London	1932
The Shape of Things to Come	Hutchinson & Co., London	1933
Experiment in Autobiography	Victor Gollancz, London	1934
Things to Come	The Cresset Press, London	1935

The Anatomy of Frustration	The Cresset Press, London	1936
The Croquet Player	Chatto & Windus, London	1936
Man Who Could work Miracles	The Cresset Press, London	1936
Star Begotten	Chatto & Windus, London	1937
Brynhild	Methuen & Co., London	1937
The Camford Visitation	Methuen & Co., London	1937
The Brothers	Chatto & Windus	1938
World Brain	Methuen & Co., London	1938
Apropos of Dolores	Jonathan Cape, London	1938
The Holy Terror	Michael Joseph, London	1939
In Search of Hot Water	Penguin Books, London	1939
The Fate of Homo Sapiens	Secker & Warburg, London	1939
The New World Order	Secker & Warburg, London	1939
The Rights of Man	Penguin Books, London	1940
Babes in the Darkling wood	Secker & Warburg, London	1940
Common Sense of War and Peace	Penguin Books, London	1940
All Aboard for Ararat	Secker & Warburg, London	1940
Guide to the New world	Victor Gollancz, London	1941
You Can't Be Too Careful	Secker & Warburg, London	1941
The Outlook for Homo Sapiens	Secker & Warburg, London	1942
Phoenix	Secker & Warburg, London	1942
Crux Ansata	Penguin Books, London	1943
'42 to '44: A Contemporary Memoir	Secker & Warburg, London	1944
The Happy Turning	William Heinemann, London	1945
Mind at the End of Its Tether	William Heinemann, London	1945

APPENDIX B

The Short Stories of H.G. Wells

Wells original recognition came from short stories which he published at regular intervals in London's booming literary market created by dozens of newspapers and periodicals. Even some of his books were initially published in serial form by weekly periodicals. This list of about seventy short stories illustrates clearly that fifty of them were published before the turn of the century, and that with the exception of a few later stories, Wells had quit this type of writing by the time he turned forty years of age. He had given up on a literary genre at which was truly a master.

The Flying Man	The Pall Mall Gazette	1893
A Slip Under the Microscope	Yellow Book	1893
The Diamond Maker	The Pall Mall Budget	1894
Aepyornis Island	The Pall Mall Budget	1894
The Stolen Bacillus	The Pall Mall Budget	1894
Flowering of the Strange Orchid	The Pall Mall Budget	1894
In the Avu Observatory	The Pall Mall Budget	1894
The Triumphs of a Taxidermist	The Pall Mall Gazette	1894
A Deal in Ostriches	The Pall Mall Budget	1894
Through a Window	Black and White	1894
The Lord of the Dynamos	The Pall Mall Budget	1894
The Hammerpond Park Burglary	The Pall Mall Budget	1894
The Moth	The Pall Mall Gazette	1894
The Treasure in the Forest	The Pall Mall Budget	1894
In the Modern Vein	Truth	1894

The Temptation of Harringay	St. James Gazette	1895
The Case of Davidson's Eyes	The Pall Mall Budget	1895
The Argonauts of the Air	Phil May's Annual	1895
The Cone	Unicorn	1895
Pollock and the Porroh Man	New Budget	1895
A Catastrophe	The New Budget	1895
Sad Story of a Dramatic Critic	The New Budget	1895
The Reconciliation	Sun Literary Supplement	1895
The Misunderstood Artist	Select Conversations	1895
The Man With a Nose	Select Conversations	1895
The Plattner Story	New Review	1896
Story of the Late Mr. Elvisham	Idler	1896
In the Abyss	Pearson's Magazine	1896
The Apple	Idler	1896
Under the Knife	New Review	1896
The Sea Raiders	Sun Literary Supplement	1896
The Red room	Idler	1896
The Purple Pileus	Black and White	1896
Man Who Could Work Miracles	Illustrated London News	1896
The Jilting of Jane	Plattner Story and Others	1897
The Lost Inheritance	Plattner Story and Others	1897
The Crystal Egg	New Review	1897
The Star	Graphic	1897
A Story of the Stone Age	Idler	1897
A Story of the Days to Come	Pall Mall Magazine	1897
The Presence by the Fire	Penny Illustrated Paper	1897
The Rajah's Treasure	Thirty Strange Stories	1897
Le Mari Terrible	Thirty Strange Stories	1897

Mr. Marshall's Doppelganger	Gentlewoman	1897
Jimmy Goggles the God	Graphic	1898
Mr. Ledbetter's Vacation	The Strand Magazine	1898
The Stolen Body	The Strand Magazine	1898
Miss Winchelsea's Heart	Queen	1898
A Vision of Judgement	Butterfly	1899
Mr. Brisher's Treasure	The Strand Magazine	1899
The New Accelerator	The Strand Magazine	1901
A Dream of Armageddon	Black and White	1901
Filmer	Graphic	1901
Mr. Skelmersdale in Fairyland	The Strand Magazine	1901
The Inexperienced Ghost	The Strand Magazine	1902
The Loyalty of Esau Common	Contemporary Review	1902
The Magic Shop	The Strand Magazine	1903
The Valley of Spiders	Pearson's Magazine	1903
The Truth About Pyecraft	The Strand Magazine	1903
The Land Ironclads	The Strand Magazine	1903
The Country of the Blind	The Strand Magazine	1904
The Empire of the Ants	The Strand Magazine	1905
The Door in the Wall	Daily Chronicle	1906
The Beautiful Suit	Colliers Weekly	1909
My First Aeroplane	The Strand Magazine	1910
Little Mother Up the Morderberg	The Strand Magazine	1910
The Story of the Last Trump	Boon	1915
The Grisly Folk	Storyteller Magazine	1921
The Pearl of Love	Atlantic Edition	1924
The Queer Story of Brownlow's Newspaper		1931

APPENDIX C

Biographical and Critical References

Although the library of literary criticism on H.G. Wells is not as large as that of some of his contemporaries it does include several dozen books of biographical and critical material, most of it very useful. The following list is not intended to be comprehensive, but it represents material used in background research for this work, including the publications from which quotations are drawn.

The Outline of H.G. Wells, Sidney Dark, Leonard Parsons, London, 1922

H.G. Wells, Ivor Brown, Nisbet and Company, Ltd., (Writers of the Day Series), London, 1923

H.G. Wells, Geoffrey West, W.W. Norton & Company, Inc., New York, 1930

H.G. Wells, Prophet of Our Day, Antonina Valentin, John Day Company, New York, 1950

H.G. Wells, Norman Nicholson, Arthur Baker Ltd. (English Novelists Series), London, 1950

H.G. Wells, A Biography, Vincent Brome, Longmans Green and Co., London, 1951

H.G. Wells, Montgomery Belgion, Longmans Green and Company, London, 1953

H.G. Wells and His Family, M.M. Meyer, International Publishing Company, Edinburgh, 1955

Six Studies in Quarrelling, Vincent Brome, Cresset Press, London, 1958

Arnold Bennett and H.G. Wells, Harris Wilson, University of Illinois Press, Urbana, 1960

George Gissing and H.G. Wells, Royal A. Gettmann, University of Illinois Press, Urbana, 1961

The Early H.G. Wells, Bernard Bergonzi, Manchester University Press, Manchester, 1961 (reprinted 1969)

H.G. Wells, A Comprehensive Bibliography, The H.G. Wells Society, London, 1966

H.G. Wells, Richard Hauer Costa, Twayne Publishers, Inc., New York, 1967

H.G. Wells, His Turbulent Life and Times, Lovat Dickson, MacMillan and Company, London, 1969

The Time Traveller, Norman and Jeanne MacKenzie, Weidenfeld and Nicolson, London, 1973

The H.G. Wells Collection in the Bromley Public Library, A.H. Watkins (editor), London Borough of Bromley, Bromley, 1974

H.G. Wells and Rebecca West, Gordon N. Ray, Yale University Press, New Haven, 1974

The Fabians, Norman and Jeanne MacKenzie, Simon and Schuster, New York, 1977

H.G. Wells: A Pictorial Biography, Frank Wells, Jupiter Books, London, 1977

H.G. Wells and the Culminating Ape, Peter Kemp, The MacMillan Press Ltd., London, 1982

The Logic of Fantasy, John Huntington, Columbia University Press, New York, 1982

H.G. Wells in Love, G.P. Wells (Editor), Little, Brown and Company, Boston, 1984

H.G. Wells, Aspects of a Life, Hutchinson, London, 1984

H.G. Wells, John Batchelor, Cambridge University Press, Cambridge, 1985

H.G. Wells, Desperately Mortal, David C. Smith, Yale University Press, New Haven, 1986

H.G. Wells: Reality and Beyond, The Champaign Public Library (collected papers), Champaign, Illinois, 1986

The Collector's Bibliography of the Work of H.G. Wells, Gordon D. Feir, Southern Maple Publications, Houston, 1992

978-0-595-35019-3
0-595-35019-4